Search for the Breed

Also by Fred Grove
In Thorndike Large Print

PHANTOM WARRIOR
MATCH RACE

Search for the Breed

FRED GROVE

Thorndike Press • Thorndike, Maine

Library of Congress Cataloging in Publication Data:

Grove, Fred.
  Search for the breed.
  1. Large type books. I. Title.
  [PS3557.R7S4 1987]   813'.54   87-18140
  ISBN 0-89621-113-4 (lg. print: alk. paper)

Large Print edition available in North America by arrangement
with Doubleday & Company, Inc.

Cover design by James B. Murray.

For H.K., who saw what I did not.

Contents

CHAPTER 1

Last Respects

As Dude McQuinn and Coyote Walking saddled into Painted Rock that afternoon, Dude
could feel his anticipation building, as well as
an uncertainty, both emotions likewise keen in his
Comanche partner's high-boned face. Coming
to the town square, they drew rein as if of the
same thought and looked hopefully across at
the town's hotel, the Drovers' House. An old
man with a bib-like white beard and hair as
long as a buffalo hunter's sat rocking on the
broad porch. A couple in a buggy drove by and
waved, and the old man nodded, no more.

"There Grandfather Billy is," said Coyote
excitedly.

"Remember how he used to talk?" Dude
recalled. "How he was gonna buy him a hotel?
Gonna sit on the front porch and watch folks
go by? Gonna have his place by the f'ar when

9

the northers hit? That was his dream. Now he's got it. I just hope he's happy." Dude paused, looking again. "But judgin' from the way he just nodded at those folks, a bare nod at that, instead of wavin' . . . that's not like the Uncle Billy we knew. And look how hunched over he sits."

Just then the old man pushed up from his rocker, with difficulty it appeared, reached for a cane, and shuffled to the end of the porch to look down the street, where a rider on a smooth-looking chestnut saddler was passing.

"Oh, Lordy," Dude moaned, "he has to use a cane! Look how stooped he is! Coyote, I'm plumb worried."

Coyote stared hard. "Grandfather Billy poorly is. Maybe so devil in belly got? Bad — bad."

"I knew he'd just wither away once he took to his rocker and quit match racin'. Well, let's get over there. This looks worse than I ever thought possible."

They rode around the square and tied up in front of the hotel, apparently unnoticed by the old man shuffling back to the rocker. They went up the steps and walked quietly along the porch toward him.

"Uncle," Dude called, "how are you?"

Not till then did the old man take notice of

them and peer through silver-rimmed spectacles. "Who . . . ?"

"Damn it, Uncle. Don't you know us? It's Dude and Coyote." *Spectacles,* Dude thought. *Uncle's finally got him some spectacles.*

Unsteadily, the old man raised himself up, tottering, seemed to lose his balance. He would have dropped back had not Dude pulled him to his feet and started hugging him and slapping him on the back, Coyote doing the same.

The old man clutched them hard. Tears came to his clear blue eyes. "I can't believe it," he said, voice cracking. Dude felt actual pain, saddened. A voice so different from the old days: once sardonic, bold, persuasive, cool, and absolutely unflinching when the little outfit was threatened; often kindly, filled with laughter, often cantankerous as well when his arthritic joints ached; but never like this, the voice a mere whisper of the remarkable old codger Dude and Coyote used to know. In less than a year's time their onetime partner and mentor, William Tecumseh Lockhart, whom Dude always referred to as "Dr. Lockhart" when matching races with gullible country yokels, had become a shadow of his former canny and sometimes mysterious self.

"Didn't recognize Coyote . . . dressed like a cowboy," Billy stammered. He straightened,

11

struggling to regain his composure. "Now what are you two tumbleweeds up to?"

"Why, we came to see you," Dude said.

"Yes, Grandfather," Coyote said, smiling.

"Still calling me Grandfather, I see. Never could break you of that, and you an honor graduate of Carlisle School." All at once the rebuking expression faded and the old man smiled, and when he did, it was like a light across his pinched features, and the years seemed to fall away. "I'm mighty glad to see you boys. I've missed you and the horses. Truth is, I'm mighty poorly. Don't see how I'll get through the winter."

"Has something happened to Nancy Ann?" Dude asked, concerned.

"No, she's fine, thank the Lord. A man couldn't be blessed with a better wife. I'm just poorly. Like an old wore-out stud horse. About all I can do now is come in for my morning and evening feed."

"You takin' any medicine?"

"Just my toddies now and then."

Dude laughed. "And they don't help?"

"I wouldn't say they don't help, but you know that a doctor is his own worst patient."

"Well, there's more in your medicine chest than Kentucky sour mash."

The old man smiled thinly. "I can cure the

12

heaves and the colic, the blind staggers and bone spavin, what have you, a damned sight quicker than my feeling poorly." A note of old-time gruffness deepened his voice. He looked straight at Dude, then Coyote. "You still haven't told me your main reason for coming to Painted Rock."

Dude and Coyote exchanged glances and Dude commenced. "Our main reason is to see you. Don't say that's not good enough reason after all we've been through together. However, there is one matter that does concern us."

The old man tensed, his eyes showing a trace of alarm. "Mean after all I've schooled you two about how to doctor a running horse, you've let Judge Blair get down?"

Dude held up both hands in mock defense. "The Judge is in his prime, runnin' like the heel flies are after him, and Texas Jack is as good as ever. Only . . . we're havin' trouble matchin' the Judge in Texas. He's too well known."

"Are you using the switch?"

"Like always, Uncle. Just like you schooled us. We match Texas Jack. Get him beat as usual. Match him again after a little wait, get two-to-one odds, maybe three, then switch to the Judge. . . . Coyote is handy with the paint brush. Native Comanche skill, you know. A regular artist, I tell you. He can make the Judge look just like Texas Jack, and vice versa, like you used to. . . . We've pulled the old workhorse wrinkle, rubbed peroxide on the Judge's shoulders and neck and hindquarters to look like harness marks, and draped that oversize collar on him before we drive into town, and we've trailed him behind the wagon like an ol' packhorse. We've matched him under more aliases than a Texas outlaw. That is, till here lately. . . . By now word has got around. It's gettin' harder and harder to match him. Who wants to run against the fastest quarter horse in the Southwest? . . . They're on to Coyote too, him bein' the only Comanche jockey in Texas. When they see him, they connect him with the Judge. The two go together like beans and biscuits. I've even said he's an Egyptian camel driver, sent over here by the King of Egypt to learn about short horses. But, somehow, that didn't go over."

"I can see where that would even strain the credulity of an Alamo Texan," the old man responded, amused. For a moment Dude thought he was going to refer to the War Between the States as the Great Rebellion, one of his tetchy points. Instead, he looked up and said, his tone reminiscing, "My, how I do remember the many good horses the Judge has dusted. Like the time he took Pepper Boy in East Texas at three hundred yards, even though the local starter gave Pepper Boy the break. . . . Time that put-in stud slammed into the Judge at the break – almost knocked him down, and the Judge, because he's a balanced horse, changed leads and settled himself and ran down that sorrel called Daylight. . . . Time he beat Night Owl, that fast *grulla* at Flat Rock, after old Colonel Bushrod almost got the advantage and fixed the Judge by puttin' sponges up his nose, which we didn't find out till minutes before the race, and how we had to tear on outa town because it started to rain and the paint was runnin'." He began to rock back and forth, chuckling, while tears coursed down his thin cheeks. "But, like always, not till we'd collected the bets. Not that the colonel was a good loser."

"Not to forget," Dude chimed in, "when the Judge daylighted the mighty Hondo at Three Springs and the local folks won enough money to build a new schoolhouse." Dude slapped his leg. "And you pulled the double switch on Wolf Garrity, who thought he'd switched our slow horse for the fast horse before the race – only it was the Judge he'd brought in instead – and after the race in the rain, when the other side cried ringer and rushed into the barn,

15

you'd switched the horses again." He had to stop, chortling all the harder for the old man's enjoyment.

In the appreciative lull that followed, Coyote spoke, sounding almost like a Latin translation in his overly formal Carlisle-School English. "Forget I cannot Sugar Kyle and his fast horse Rattler at Lost Creek. How that mean white man tried to feed the Judge sugar cubes loaded with laudanum before the race, and that failing and the Judge running like buffalo runner he is, the gambler's man started to jump out on track and make the Judge break stride, and white father Dude grabbed that mean white man before he could and threw him down he did."

Dude nodded. "You really rode a race that day, Coyote."

"Coyote never rode a smarter race than he did that time at Wagon Mound," Uncle Billy broke in, his eyes glowing, "when we went up against that gray scorpion Sir James, who held the Pimlico record at four furlongs. I was concerned about that jockey Philo. Been suspended time and again back East for rough riding. I remember the Judge took the break by a length and held the lead through the first quarter. Then Philo got the gray under way. Gradually, took the lead. Then Coyote whooped and the

Judge came at 'em. That damned Philo whipped the Judge across the face. The Judge checked, as any game horse would. When the horses passed the three-furlong stake, the Judge trailed by a length and I was worried." The old man's eyes glittered memorably. "I heard Coyote whoop again and saw the Judge begin another charge. I saw Philo raise his whip. But this time, all of a sudden, Coyote took his horse outside and Philo missed his swing." Billy jabbed with his right fist. "We win it by half a length," he said as he looked at the Comanche. "That was when your experience won the race, Coyote, pardner," he added and sat back tiredly.

"Thank you, Grandfather."

The old man frowned at the name, but said no more, and Dude, hoping to arouse his enthusiasm still further, said, "That time we ran at Cherokee Gap was not only the most complicated mess we ever got ourselves into, but the slickest moves were pulled on us to get the advantage." He was thinking of good-looking Kate Taggart, the widow of Big Jim, who had been shot down years earlier after robbing the local bank. Dude had often wondered whether she and Billy had been sweethearts before she married Big Jim. Why? Because she knew about the switch.

"You mean," the old man said airily, "the way

Kate had her boys steal Texas Jack the night before we raced her unbeaten stud, Jackpot?"

"Thinkin'," Dude added, "they had taken our fast horse, not knowin' you had painted Texas Jack the evening before to look like the Judge and staked him out in the pasture near our camp, handy for the takin'?"

"I believe I remember that," the old man said, with mock modesty.

Dude continued. "That was clever, the way Kate had her son Monte rob the bank when about everybody in town was at the track. Only problem was that Monte, instead of bein' on a lightning-fast getaway horse, was on a slow horse and was caught within minutes and we got Texas Jack back. If Monte had made his escape, we'd have faced collusion charges because Monte rode our horse." He broke off, letting his mind reach deeper into that episode, and after a moment asked, "Uncle, mind tellin' us just how well you knew Kate before she married Big Jim? Were you sweethearts?"

"Don't recall I ever said one way or the other," the old man replied, looking innocent, his saintly face cherubic, and suddenly all three laughed together. That's our Uncle Billy, Dude thought, still guarding his mysterious past.

"We've had some luck, too," Dude said. "Such as the time we went up against Gideon

Lightfoot's unbeaten Thoroughbred."

"Luck!" the old man snorted. "We beat that stud fair and square at his best distance, five and a half furlongs."

"I mean when they used that damsel-in-distress wrinkle the night before the race to draw us out to the road, and give the doper time to sneak up to the horses, and they doped Texas Jack by mistake. Lucky you hadn't switched the markin's yet, or the doper'd got to the Judge. Lucky too, that Amos gave the alarm before the doper could do more damage, in case he figured we carried a look-alike horse. Do you still have Amos?"

The old man was indignant. "Think I'd get rid of my drivin' horse, even if he is blind? But I'll remind you boys of this. The race that made Judge Blair a name over the whole Southwest was when he beat Yolanda, the great Mexican speed mare, at Juarez. Tore that quarter mile apart in twenty-one and a fifth on a heavy track. Ran straight as an arrow from a bow. Beat that outstanding mare by a neck. That's the main reason you can't match him anymore." His animation stemming from the past faded and in moments, Dude noticed, he seemed to withdraw into the shell of himself. "Poorly as I am, there's nothing I can do to help you boys."

"But there is," Dude pleaded, and Coyote nodded vigorously. "You can come with us. We'll head back East this time, on the lookout for slick horsemen with fresh money. It'll be just like old times, Uncle. You callin' the shots behind the matches. Sizin' up the horses for us, whether to match 'em short or long, you entertainin' the yokels with your lectures and horse cures, so they'll hang around until the owner of the local favorite makes himself known, figurin' all the time he can daylight our ol' packhorse. If the crowd gets bored and starts to drift away, you demonstrate Professor Gleason's Eureka Bridle, 'guaranteed to hold any animal under any circumstances — so long as you tie it right.' Remember? . . . Coyote in the saddle, whoopin' the Judge on to the next finish line. Me the front man, sometimes too long on gab, you careful that I don't get hemmed in and the other side gets the advantage. We need you, Uncle. It's just not the same without you, pardner."

"I'd be about as much good to the outfit as a one-legged man at a butt-kickin' contest," said the old man, feebly. "Too poorly. I'm like an old buffalo bull run out of the herd that's gone up the draw to finish out his days. I'd be a burden to you, turn you two into no more than nursemaids. No, boys, my day is past. It's close to sundown for me."

How given-up Uncle looked! Dude could only stare at him, too dejected to say more at the moment, unable to recall other reminders of the exciting past that might be more convincing.

Coyote spoke rapidly, running his words together. "Grandfather, if come with us you will, I the cooking will do."

"You? All that fried bread and jerky?"

"And beans, Grandfather."

The old man shot him a suspicious glare. "What's wrong with Dude's cookin'?"

Coyote grimaced. "Too many cigaret butts in white father's biscuits."

A grin spread over the wan face. "I can believe that. Now I see what's behind all this soapy buildup. You two want me along to do the cookin'. That's all."

"Even though you make the best biscuits a man ever had melt in his mouth, you know that's not the reason," Dude swore. "We just want you to be with us like it used to be. You can take it easy. Just mosey along in your cushion-seated buggy behind Amos. Come camp time, I and Coyote will make the f'ars and wait on you and do all the cookin'. You can just sit by the f'ar while we bring your toddy and your plate. We can leave tomorrow. We're camped out south of town. Now what do you say?" Dude's voice broke. "Come with us, Uncle."

It seemed like such a long time to Dude that his old mentor sat there, an evident struggle going on within him, an alternate longing and denying. Dude's hopes sank as William Tecumseh Lockhart reached for his cane. "Those are powerful arguments coming from my old pardners. However, you must remember what I told you the wise man said: that the only constant in this world is change. I'm too old to do anything but sit on the porch and watch folks go by. Like I said, I'd be a burden to you and I refuse to be that. . . . Now, I have to go in. Time for my nap." He strained to his feet, his breath coming short, and leaning on the cane tottered to the door of the hotel. There he looked back. "Good luck," he said. "Take care of yourselves and the horses." His eyes moved from them to the horses. "I see the Judge is carrying too much fat. Work that off of him." Then he left them.

They rode in silence out to their camp, unsaddled and fed the horses, and built the supper fire, not one word yet spoken, each man sunk in depressed thought. Dude had the coffeepot on when a one-horse buggy drew up and a slender woman stepped down.

"Howdy, boys," she said cheerfully. "Remember me? Nancy Ann Hathaway, now Lockhart?"

Indeed, they remembered. They swept off their hats and smiled and bowed. She shook hands warmly. A trim, comely ranch woman in her fifties, she had large hazel eyes set in a well-molded face tanned a deep brown. She wore a narrow-brimmed western hat, a denim jacket, a man's gray shirt open at the neck, a dark blue skirt, and cowboy work boots.

"Mighty pleased to see you two," she said. "Billy said you were camped out here."

"We're mighty glad to see you, ma'am," Dude said. "You're just in time for supper."

"Yes, we are, Mrs. Billy," Coyote seconded, so formally that she smiled at him.

"I'm obliged. But I just came in from the ranch and I'd better get back to the hotel to see about Billy." The cordial liveliness vanished from her face. She hesitated, openly worried. "As you no doubt noticed, he's not well. He's lost interest. Just sits in that rocker day after day, staring. Oh, he'll come out to the ranch if a horse needs doctoring. He would never neglect a horse, nor any animal."

"Has he been to a doctor?" Dude asked.

"Once. The doctor prescribed a tonic. Billy took one dose and threw it away. Said he wouldn't give it to a sick mule. I talked privately with the doctor, who told me there's nothing he can do. That it's up to Billy to find himself again. If this goes on much longer . . ." She looked down.

Dude said, "We asked him — pleaded with him — to head East with us and match some races, but he said he's too poorly."

"That's exactly what I came to see you about. I've been desperate to write you, to tell you to come see him. But I didn't know where you were. Texas, Arizona, Indian Territory?"

"Mostly Texas," Dude said. "Judge Blair is so well known we can't match him anymore. That's why we're goin' East."

"Well, I want you and Coyote to take him with you. You must do it, somehow."

Dude was surprised. "We figured maybe you didn't want him to go."

"I want what's best for Billy. It means life or death for him. Not that he would ever admit it. He also feels he should stay here with me. Little by little, he's wasting away, off his feed, and has let himself get down. He misses the give-and-take of match racing, the jousting with slick horsemen trying to get the advantage. He won't admit that either." She made a gesture of rejection. "The worst mistake he ever made was to buy that hotel and sit down."

"It's no use," Dude said. "We talked and

24

talked. He won't go. Says he'd only be a burden."

"Are you pulling out tomorrow?"

"No hurry now."

"Will you please talk with him again, say tomorrow?"

"Yes, ma'am. We can try."

"Please do. If this keeps up, he won't be with us much longer. He's just pining away day by day." She shook hands again, forcing herself to be cheerful. "You are family, you know."

"There," Dude said as she drove off, "goes a real lady."

"White father," Coyote said solemnly, "strong, new medicine we must make before with Grandfather we powwow."

They rode into town, Dude on Texas Jack, Coyote on Judge Blair and dressed as if for a big race: only breechcloth, long-fringed, beaded moccasins, and a single eagle father in his blue-black hair. Three eagle feathers fluttered in the Judge's black mane. As before, they drew rein and looked across the square and there as before sat the old man in his high-backed rocker.

This time they loped around the square, so fast they raised dust, and idlers on the street quit chatting to gawk at the hurrying horsemen. As they dismounted and tied up in front of the hotel, Dude saw Billy take alert notice and snap out of his rocker and stand. He took a couple of steps before he reached for his cane.

"See that?" Dude said aside to Coyote. "Started off without his cane. Forgot it. Had to remember. Proves he don't need it. It's all in his mind."

Tapping with the cane, the old man shuffled along the porch and eased down the steps. Ignoring his former partners, he went straight to Judge Blair and stroked the distinctive blaze that came to a point between the wide nostrils, all the while murmuring nonsense to the horse, then stepped back, his eyes beginning to fill, his bearded mouth squeezed, his Adam's apple bobbing. He started to speak, choked up, almost overcome, and after a moment found his voice. "Just look at him. Has the eye of an eagle and the step of a deer. The true signs of a runner. A shame he was ever altered. A crime. Some fool did it, not knowing his breeding."

Dude said nothing, hoping sight of the two horses would sway him.

Uncle Billy hobbled slowly around the bay gelding, searching, gauging, inspecting, and seemed to lose himself in the appraisal, Dude noticed, to the extent that now the cane hardly touched the ground. The clear blue eyes became critical. "Like I said, the Judge is carrying too much weight. Looks as soft and fat as an alderman's town horse."

"He has picked up a little," Dude admitted. "That's because he's out of trainin'. Hasn't run lately."

"Cut back on his grain, add a pint of bran every day, and give him a light work every three days, in addition to riding him daily on the road," Billy said, using the same advisory tone he might on a total stranger, and ranged his eyes over Texas Jack, a dark bay like the Judge, the spitting image of his stablemate except he had no blaze, hence the need for artistry when making the switch, the Judge made to look like Texas Jack, the latter to become the Judge.

The old man circled Texas Jack, sizing him up, nodding to himself, and he said, "Texas Jack is almost as smooth-looking as the Judge. A tolerable racehorse the first hundred yards or so, and could run farther if he wanted to. That big difference is what makes a racehorse. His heart's not in it." He looked at Dude. "Guess you're ready to pull out?"

"There's no big hurry. We thought you'd like to see the horses and Coyote in his Comanche jockey outfit before we left."

That brought a dry grin. "Figured you'd induce me to change my mind, didn't you two?

No, boys, William Tecumseh Lockhart has come to the end of the trail," he said, his self-pity so sickening that Dude was disgusted. "Well," the old man continued, casting lingering glances at the horses, "you might as well visit a spell before you break camp. I need to rest awhile now on the porch."

Coyote took an Indian blanket off his saddle and he and Dude followed Billy to the rocker and took chairs. *We've lost the first round*, Dude thought, *but there are two more to go.*

They sat awhile in uncomfortable silence, the old man staring at the empty street, Dude wondering how to begin, dreading the outcome if they failed, until Coyote slanted an eye at him, meaning, *Now, white father*, and Dude led off, taking on a mysterious air. "Sure didn't want to pull out before I and Coyote told you what we stumbled onto down in San Antone." He let that sink in.

The old man jerked. "Onto what?"

"Remember when we first met and I told you how I came to own the Judge?"

"It was pretty vague. Guess I'm not too poorly to listen to another roundabout story."

"I won him in an all-night poker game in San Antone, remember? Won him off a Texas cowman who had won him off an Arizona cowman the night before, remember?"

"Well?"

"The Texas cowman told me the Judge was sired by the *great* Buck Shiloh, a son of the legendary Shiloh, and was out of the *great* Mexican sprint queen, Lolita. Well, the next day when I found myself with this racehorse, I bird-dogged around and learned there was no Buck Shiloh and no Lolita. None that veteran horsemen thereabouts knew. I had a mystery horse on my hands. And after the Judge won by daylight in record time, I knew I owned a once-in-a-lifetime runner."

"So?"

"Well, not long ago, when I and Coyote made San Antone, hopin' to match the Judge, only to get more turndowns than a snaggle-toothed country boy at a city dance, I happened to run into the very cowman I'd won the Judge off of." He let that simmer.

"Suppose you ran into him in a saloon?"

"The Lone Star, in fact. I'd stopped by for a little bedtime toddy."

"Uh-huh."

"Seems this cowman spends more time in town than he does on his ranch. Still fancies himself as a poker player, which is why he's still broke." Dude delayed, pretending to recollect.

"Is it gonna take you all day to tell it?" the old man barked.

"I bought him a drink," Dude drawled, "and one led to two and two led on till I lost count. The talk got heavy and naturally turned to horses. The cowman said he'd kicked himself ever since for losin' the Judge. You see, he didn't know the Judge could run. Hadn't had time to find out. That was when he gave me the clue."

"Clue?" Billy sat up straighter.

"We've always wondered about the Judge's breedin', remember?"

"*Remember?* Of course I remember. Could I forget? Now get on with the story."

Dude smiled to himself. Uncle was beginning to show some of his old-timey tetchiness, an encouraging sign. Maybe there was yet hope he would trail along with the outfit.

"Well," drawled Dude, even slower, "it came about like this. I mentioned how tough it was to match the Judge anymore and that he had to come down the ladder from quality folks, fast as he runs, and the cowman, he said, 'Guess you know where he came from, don't you?' and I said, 'How would I know? I just won him in a poker game. However, I did find out there's no such connection to any hot-air Buck Shiloh and any speed queen Lolita like you claimed.'"

30

Dude gazed off and rubbed his chin ruminatively. "Then the cowman grinned a little and said, 'That was hot air, sure. So was the name, Judge Blair. I wanted him to sound like a sure-enough high-class hoss worth a pile of money. Like Judge Thomas and Judge Welch, them scorpion Traveler colts. But I can tell you where he came from into Texas.'" Dude put off again, scowling in simulated concentration.

The old man squirmed and flashed Dude his impatience. "Either tell it or not. If you's reading the Bible aloud at an arbor prayer meeting, everybody'd be in hell before you finished the first chapter of Genesis. What did he say?"

Still, Dude ruminated.

Coyote nodded, meaning: *Good. Keep Grandfather interested, white father. Heap good, you are doing.*

After another pause, Dude said, "The cowman said the Judge had been shipped into Texas in a carload of work stock to a road contractor," and paused again.

"From where?" the old man demanded, peevish about it. "Didn't you know enough to ask?"

"From Illinois," Dude answered. "And he had collar marks on his shoulders and trace-chain marks on his side. The Judge had been worked."

"Dude," the old man fumed, "if I sent you to the well for a bucket of water, I'd have to pin directions on you so you could locate the well and for you to know what to do when you got there. Now, where in Illinois?"

Dude, pretending to have difficulty recalling, scratched his head and pursed his mouth and said at last, "Petersburg. . . . Yes, that was it — Petersburg, Illinois."

Billy fairly pounced on the words. "Petersburg? That section of Illinois used to be the fountainhead of quarter racing. The home of such scorpions as Dan Tucker and Peter McCue, Bob Wade, Hi Henry, Buck Thomas, Butt Cut, Nettie S, and Carrie Nation, to name a few. I could go on and on."

"That's not all," Dude said and looked off.

"What else might you recall?" jabbed the sarcastic voice.

"A name. The cowman gave me the name of a man to look up back there. That is, if I can just recollect it."

"Dude, I'm gonna send you back to the first grade, which you've already been through three times."

"The name," said Dude, not to be hurried, "is Si Eckert."

"Eckert — Eckert," Billy repeated, a going back surfacing in the clear blue eyes. "Can't say it rings a bell."

Dude had often theorized about what the old gent might have been before he became an essential member of the outfit. Was Lockhart an alias? Or had he been a law officer? Maybe so, maybe not. But in a showdown, when trouble had threatened after a race, Dude saw a six-gun blink in his mentor's hand quicker than a crooked gambler could flip a hidden ace. Yet, he had never been forced to fire a shot, the threat being enough to cool the tense situation and allow the outfit to collect the bets after the Judge had outrun the local favorite, generally by plenty of daylight, and ease out of town peacefully. Of one profession, Dude was positive. The old codger was definitely a skilled veterinarian. Besides being a raconteur and a worldly gentleman of the old school when donning dark frock coat, white shirt, string tie, and dove-gray, flat-topped hat and bench-made boots, he possessed an uncanny understanding of horses and their many puzzling ailments, particularly running horses, and from the cryptic contents of his odorous "medicine chest" — which was off bounds to both Dude and Coyote, unless he had directed one of them to get him a certain colored bottle — Uncle mixed remarkable "potions," as he called them, some of short duration, but nevertheless "good to trade on," as the saying went. There he also kept medical books, which he called "tomes," and a jug of Kentucky sour mash whiskey for "a little toddy" now and then, the *now* more frequent than the *then*.

Whatever Uncle Billy had been, he had always guarded his past with evasion or bluntness. Thus, Dude, now sensing an opening, asked, "Happens maybe, Uncle, you used to know some folks in Petersburg?" whereupon the old man snapped, "Now, did I say that?" which did not surprise Dude and which he interpreted as another encouraging omen. Yet for all the old man's eccentricities and crotchetiness, often perverse (though when feeling well he could be as benevolent as his saintly features promised: the blue eyes kindly, the cherry-red mouth jocular, the trimmed white whiskers framing a roundish little face, the distinguished bib beard and the mane of long white hair remindful of an Old Testament patriarch), Dude and Coyote held deep affection and respect for him, feelings which they dared not speak of to him for fear of being met with derision.

"Oh, just wondered," Dude went on cheerfully. "With that clue, I and Coyote hoped you might trail along with us to Petersburg, besides matchin' some races along the way. Maybe together we can track down the Judge's true breeding. You used to say you'd sure like to know, remember?"

For an instant Dude thought the old man was going to say yes, because the wish stood alive in his eyes. In a moment it died, and Uncle Billy was saying, "Yes, I'd like to know, but I'm too poorly to make that long trip." He took a ragged breath, a self-pitying breath that made Dude hurt. "I'll have to go in now for my nap."

Dude had one last shot left. "Hold on, Uncle. There's one more piece of information I haven't told you. It slipped my mind."

"That's not unusual for an Alamo Texan," Billy growled. "What is it?"

"The cowman gave me a sayin' for when we find Si Eckert. Guess you'd call it a password."

"Why would you need a password? Sounds like some secret organization."

"He didn't say. Just gave it to me. Said to recite it to Si Eckert."

"What is it?"

Dude had to hang his head. "There's one drawback. I wrote it down on a brown cigaret paper there in the saloon and stuck it somewhere. Now I can't find it."

35

"You can't remember it?"

"All I remember is it had the word 'horse' in it."

"That would be a big help. What if you find Si Eckert and don't know the password?"

"If we find Eckert, I'll see that he talks, password or not."

"Probably just whiskey talk," Billy said, making a gesture of dismissal. "I'll have to go in now, boys."

Dude bit his lower lip. End of round two. It was up to Coyote now. Loudly, Dude said, "Well, Coyote, 'pears there's nothing more we can do."

Billy was leaning forward to rise from the rocker, when Coyote quickly but gently held him there and tucked the Indian blanket around the old man's thin shoulders and began addressing him in a high and quavering voice. "Grandfather, sick you are. Devil in belly, maybe. Pray for you, I will." Lifting both hands high and wailing — a piercing wailing it was — he faced one way, then another. The wailing rose higher, and then turned into a sing-song chant, while he continued to turn.

"What in thunderation?" the old man shouted.

"He thinks you're gonna die," Dude told him, his tone deliberately mournful. "He's prayin' to the Four Great Directions. You know how Plains Indians are, Uncle? They can tell when a man's comin' to the end of the trail." He shook his head sorrowfully.

A man Dude took to be the desk clerk ran out of the hotel, calling, "What's going on out here?" and stopped, mouth agape at the chanting, half-naked Comanche.

Dude rubbed his eyes. "We're old friends, here to pay our last respects to Uncle Billy, who's gettin' ready to go out on that long trail from where no horseman ever rides back. Mr. Coyote Walking, here, who used to ride for Uncle, is chanting the final prayers before Uncle leaves us for that faraway place the Comanches say is beyond the sun where it sets in the West. It's called the Happy Place."

A roar of denial erupted. "Happy Place — hell!" The old man sprang from the rocker and threw off the blanket. "I'll show you two tumbleweeds I can still hit the trail."

Coyote suddenly ceased praying.

"But you're too poorly," Dude said flatly, to needle him. "You'd never make it. We wouldn't want to bury you beside the trail, far from home."

"Poorly, I may be. But William Tecumseh Lockhart can still train a racehorse." He wheeled on the clerk. "Matt, send a man out to the ranch. Tell Nancy Ann I'm pullin' out tomorrow with the boys for back East."

The clerk hesitated.

"Step to it!"

CHAPTER 2

Honest Abe

They left Painted Rock the next morning, the old man at the reins of his fast-striding blind trotter, Amos, hitched to the cushion-seated buggy. Dude was astride Blue Grass, his leggy Kentucky saddler, and Coyote, now back in white man's garb except for beaded moccasins, drove the matched sorrel team that pulled the camp wagon loaded with chuck, horse feed, and Billy's indispensable medicine chest. Judge Blair and Texas Jack trailed the wagon on halter ropes.

As the miles fell behind, Dude learned that Uncle, although still weak from lack of activity, hadn't lost his old-time tetchiness. When they stopped at noon and Dude brought him a dipper of water from the barrel lashed to the wagon's side, the old man said curtly, "Now, Dude, poorly as I am I believe I'm still able to go to water." Disdaining the offer and leaning on his cane, he shuffled over to the barrel, found a cup and helped himself, and shuffled back.

Dude met Coyote's eyes and they nodded: *Good. Heap good. Progress.* Still, Dude didn't like the cane. When Uncle put it aside, that would be real progress. They would have to be patient in the days ahead.

That evening at supper Dude brought out a cane-bottomed chair for Billy, who snapped, "Don't recall you ever had to do that before," and when Dude served him a plate of beans, jerky and biscuits, and a tin cup of coffee, the old man growled, "When I need a nursemaid, I'll let you know." He began to eat, sampling the beans first, warmed over from the day before, nodding to himself. Next, he took a tentative bite of biscuit, swallowed, had another bite, chewed slowly, experimentally, tasting, swallowed, blinked suddenly, yet said nothing. After a sip of coffee, he sawed off a chunk of jerky with his pocketknife and chewed at length before swallowing. He then said, "Generally, I'm not one to complain about the cookin', but Dude, pardner, there's enough baking soda in these biscuits to raise a bunkhouse off the ground."

"Guess my hand did get a little heavy," Dude

admitted sheepishly. "I'm always afraid my biscuits won't rise."

"And Coyote, pardner," Billy said, "when you're serving jerky, it's a good idea to throw it in a pot of water first and boil it awhile. Makes it tender. Also throw in some dried corn. Makes good soup. Too, if the jerky was dried on a barbed-wire fence and stock rubbed up against it, it's a good idea to brush it off a little."

"Yes, Grandfather. Tomorrow fried bread I will fix and dried prunes for you."

"Guess there's no big hurry," the old man put him off, and showing a rare tolerance said, "I'm poorly and have no appetite. Otherwise, I wouldn't have noticed. Whatever happened to that little wooden keg we used to keep the sourdough in?"

"We's crossin' a rocky draw one day and the wagon tipped against a boulder and busted it," Dude said.

"I see. Well, I understand kegs are still sold west of the Mississippi." And then he smiled in that secretive way he had. "You two may not think so, but I'd planned to go with you all along."

"Expect us to believe that?" Dude laughed.

"I hadn't had my nap. Coyote just hurried me a little. You see, I was afraid somebody would take advantage of you. Farther east you go, slicker the horsemen. When you get back to Illinois, you're up against some of the game's cagiest horsemen."

"Don't see how they could be any cagier than what we've run up against in the Southwest, and I'll throw in Kansas and Missouri."

"In addition," Billy said, falling into his familiar lecturing tone of old, "you have to remember they've crossed a lot of Thoroughbred sires on quarter mares. So some quarter horses carry greater speed at longer distances than we usually see out here."

"You mean more like the Judge, that can run short or long?"

"Exactly. We may have to lengthen the Judge out. Too, back there you'll find horses registered as both Thoroughbreds and quarter horses under different names."

Dude was outraged. "Sounds to me like the whole country back there is infested with crooks."

"Not crooks — *horsemen*," Billy corrected, a politic smile shaping the corners of his mouth. "All's fair in love and war and horse racin'. Same as in the Southwest, where we are known to use the switch, while at the same time the other side is trying to outslick us to get the advantage. Point is, back there if you happen to have a quarter horse that can go a distance of ground, and you want to run on recognized tracks, you give him a second name, add some phony breeding lines, and register him as a Thoroughbred." He sniffed, an exaggerated aloofness filling his tilted face. "We Thoroughbred people wouldn't dare lose to an unregistered *Equus caballus*. Think of the comedown, suh? The disgrace, suh? Think of what it would do to the breed, suh?"

"I don't cotton to uppity folks," Dude said.

"Nor I," Coyote declared and slapped his chest. "Among Comanches everybody the same."

"Except the chief?" Billy questioned.

"The chief feeds many relatives," Coyote said proudly. "Come they do, long they stay. Why I send money to my father. Feed them he would not, face he would lose. Comanches who have much, give it away. Comanches who have little, share the much. Comes out even. Everybody the same. Proud I am of my father, who generous is."

"No offense meant, Coyote. You know that. Your folks did a good job bringing you up. In all fairness, you can't criticize horsemen devoted to improving breeding and racing, and that's what the Thoroughbred people are doing, breeding the best to the best — and hoping for a dry track and an honest jock." He gave a tired grin. "Now, when we come to the next town, let's get a little wooden keg to start the sourdough in. Hope you don't mind if I take over the cookin' as soon as I get back on my feet?" Rising, leaving his supper unfinished, he grasped his cane, shuffled across to his bedroll under the wagon, and retired.

"He's still off his feed," said Dude worriedly. "But we can't nursemaid him too much, crotchety as he is."

"Grandfather medicine needs," Coyote said.

"Medicine? He's had his toddy."

"Medicine for spirit. Match race against tricky white man with fast horse." Coyote held his right hand to the corner of his mouth, index and second fingers separated, other fingers and thumb closed.

"Never had any trouble findin' one yet, have we? Right you are, Coyote. He needs a challenge. It will take a race to perk him up, to bring him back, out of that 'I'm poorly' self-pity. Meanwhile, we'll take it slow and easy with Uncle and look for a horseman who speaks with forked tongue."

From there they traveled leisurely through pleasant, rolling country, past well-tilled fields and tidy farmhouses and sturdy barns, past broad pastures of grazing cattle and the low shapes of distant ranch quarters. Late the third

44

afternoon, they came on a field beside the road bulging with corn, near a creek where the native buffalo grass stood thick and ungrazed. Finding no farmer's house in sight, Dude camped the outfit.

After unsaddling and helping Coyote with the unharnessing, he took two gunny sacks from the wagon and slipped across the road into the waving forest of stalks higher than his head, the smell of corn warm and tantalizing on the breeze. The sacks were soon filled. Glancing up and down the road, he hustled the sacks to the wagon, shucked some ears for the horses, and dropped others into the pot of water under which Coyote had started a fire.

Within ten minutes, a horseman came westward along the road and giving the outfit a sizing up, rode to the wagon and nodded. "Evening, folks. Guess you've come far?" He was a firm-jawed man, thick through the neck and shoulders, a man of menacing physical proportions offset by genial eyes and an obliging, hopeful manner. He wore a straw hat, blue shirt, and patched overalls. As he spoke, the roan workhorse he rode nosed the ears of corn that had spilled out of the sack by the wagon and Dude went a little weak. He could think of nothing more mortifying for a horseman, a Texan at that, than being charged with stealing a sack of corn.

"Quite a piece," Dude said, as friendly as could be. Caught in a fix like this, he knew there was only one course left: no beating around the bush. Admit you took it. "Didn't see a farmhouse as we came in from the west, so helped ourselves to your cornfield, if that is your field? And I reckon it is. Figured to pay in the mornin' at the first house we passed. If there's one thing I can't stand is some scrounger helpin' himself to a man's feed without the courtesy of payin' for it."

"Oh, that's all right," the man replied genially. "There's plenty. You're welcome to what you picked. I'm looking for a stray cow and happened to notice your string of horses. Guess you're a road trader?"

"Carryin' a racehorse right now," Dude said, relieved. "Sometimes we trade."

The farmer looked around. "Would one of you happen to be a vet?"

"There he is, right over there," Dude said, indicating Uncle Billy in the cane-bottomed chair. "If I do say so, he's one of the best. Dr. William Tecumseh Lockhart."

"What can I do for you, sir?" Billy asked, erasing from his features the last of his amusement over Dude's deliverance.

"Well, sir, I bought a horse not long ago

that's acting mighty peculiar. Never saw it before. Would you mind taking a gander at him in the morning when you pass by? Sure would appreciate it. My name's Homer Overman."

"Be glad to, Mr. Overman, though I won't promise any miracle cures." Uncle was being very professional, Dude saw.

"It may take a miracle. I'll be looking for you. Much obliged."

The following morning, after Dude had loaded three sacks of corn, the old man said, "Don't recall that Homer Overman said to help ourselves a second time," and Dude, with a possum grin, said, "Don't recall that he didn't." They broke camp, trailed eastward along the road, and soon came to a field fenced with bois d'arc. Beyond that, at the end of a lane, sat a gabled white house, a fat red barn, and a clutter of outer sheds and pens. In the corral by the barn stood a gaunt gray horse. Head down, spraddle-legged, ribs like staves, he looked all skin and bones. A scarecrow of a horse. A pathetic sight.

Overman joined them as they drew up by the corral. "I gave thirty-five dollars for this gelding," he exclaimed, "figuring he'd make a matched team with my gray mare. When I got him, he looked filled out and seemed active, kicked up his heels. Before long he turned into what you see now, gaunted up, a bag of bones."

"When did you buy him?" Billy asked.

"Ten days ago."

"I'll need to examine him," the old man said and stepped down from the buggy. The obliging Overman opened the gate and Billy went inside and strolled slowly around the poor animal, eyes scanning, up and down, across, inch by inch, it seemed to Dude. Billy turned to Overman. "You said he was fleshed up when you bought him?"

"In good flesh, almost fat. Now he won't eat and can't work."

Billy moved to the gray's head and sighted into the eyes. A moment. A long moment. Then, "His eyes, which are the mirrors of his inner self, look dull and glassy. I don't like that." Drawing his watch, he felt under the horse's lower jaw for his pulse, located it, timed it, and said, "The pulse of a rested, healthy horse beats from thirty-six to forty-six times a minute. Our old and faithful friend here has a pulse of seventy-five, which indicates a fever. His pulse is also fluttering a little."

"No wonder he's quit eating," the farmer said, dejected.

Next, Billy opened the gray's mouth and peered at great length, now and then adjusting his spectacles for closer inspection. "This

48

horse," he said after a thoughtful pause, "has no cups on his teeth and his gums have greatly receded. He's a worn-out horse. I regret to tell you, Mr. Overman, that he's twenty-five years old."

"Twenty-five!" Overman echoed, slapping a hand to his forehead. "Abe Tolliver swore he wasn't more than fifteen."

"The cups," the old man continued, "which are black rings in the center of the grinding surface of the teeth, disappear in the ninth year and the animal is known as smooth-mouthed. By the twenty-fifth year the nippers of the lower jaw are twice as thick as they are broad."

Overman groaned and shook his head. "I can't get over how filled out he was when I bought him."

"You mean he looked filled out." Billy moved to the gelding's side and pressed with a forefinger, which left a depression. "Mr. Overman, I regret to inform you further that I believe your horse has been treated with arsenic."

"Arsenic! That's deadly — that's poison."

"Depends on how much you use. Dab a little on a horse's tongue each day and his eyes will take on a youthful shine. He'll appear to pick up weight, which is only bloat as I just demonstrated, and will move around like a sound animal. It's an old trick, yet not widely used.

Otherwise, you would have caught it. This Abe Tolliver. He a road trader passin' through?"

"A barn trader in Blue Springs. Runs the livery. Only one in town."

"I see. Obviously a slick operator."

"What can I do?"

"You can keep Dobbin up, give him a daily tonic, and hope he starts eating. That, or do what was done to you. Give him a little arsenic each day and trade him off to the first stranger that comes by."

"Where would I get the arsenic?"

"From the drugstore in town."

"But what would I tell the druggist? He might think I'd give it to my wife."

"That's easy. Just tell him it's for your rich uncle, who's just named you the sole beneficiary in his will."

Overman guffawed and then they were all laughing.

"On second thought," Billy said when the laughter died, "take Dobbin back to Tolliver. Tell him you're on to his trick and want him to take the horse back and give you twenty-five dollars. That way Tolliver will make ten and you'll be rid of the horse and Tolliver can trade him off again. I doubt that he would take the horse back and return your thirty-five dollars. No trader would."

"Hmmnn," Overman mused. "I'll try that. I've been skinned before by Tolliver. Once he traded me a mule with the heaves. Even tried to sell me a broken-down racehorse which he claimed he'd just brought in from Kentucky after winning big back there. For once, I didn't bite."

Dude's interest quickened. "Did you say a racehorse?"

"Yup. Tolliver has a racehorse or two. He's as slick at racing as he is at skinning us farmers. His stud Keeno has taken the slack out of everything from here to the Nebraska line."

Dude caught Coyote's nod and the forked-tongue sign and each nodded: *Tricky white man. Good. Heap good. Just what we need.*

"If it's any consolation to you, Mr. Overman," Billy said as they were leaving, "remember that a horseman is the only animal that can be skinned more than once."

"You mean a farmer, don't you?" the woe-begone Overman called after them.

By early afternoon Blue Springs lay spread out before the outfit, a church steeple rising above the scattering of trees and neat white houses, an orderly little town on the rolling Kansas heartland.

Dude motioned Coyote to halt the wagon and rode back to Uncle Billy in the buggy. "Uncle,

51

what do you say we slick Texas Jack up a little and put the pack on the Judge? You heard what Overman said about Tolliver's racehorse."

The old man sat back, his vitality of the early morning all but gone. "Now, Dude, I said I'd come along and we'd match a race now and then, but the main reason for this expedition, as I see it, is to trace the Judge's breeding. I'm all for that. We owe it to a top runnin' horse. Trouble is, I'm still off my feed, still a mite poorly."

"You were your old self back there when you figured out that arsenic trick." Yet, Dude thought, Uncle did look kind of peaked, and he still wasn't taking to his vittles the way he should.

"Had to help that poor fella, didn't we? Seems this Tolliver, who obviously knows all the old tricks of the trade, takes particular delight in gettin' the best of farmers, who as a rule are pretty gullible." There was a flash of the old Uncle Billy as he added, "I hate to see a man get skinned . . . unless I'm the one doing the skinning." And Dude had to grin at the improvement.

Then the old man seemed to give in to himself once again, saying, "It's up to you and Coyote. I'd better stay out of this one till I get on my feet."

"What do you think, Coyote?" Dude called, knowing the answer.

"Like Grandfather says, the Judge too much weight carries. Race he needs."

"That settles it," Dude said.

So they curried and brushed Texas Jack to glistening show-ring smoothness. And he was a pretty horse. All he lacked was the heart to run. Then, taking a worn canvas pack from the wagon, he draped it over Judge Blair's short back and cinched it and stepped back to admire the results. The Judge still looked too smooth. So he rubbed peroxide on the long, sloping shoulder and along the powerful hindquarters for harness marks, and looked again. Still not satisfied, he rummaged in the wagon for a flour sack of cockleburs and ruffled up the Judge's black mane and tail and stuck in a few burs.

Blue Springs turned out to be a busy county seat, with its gray stone courthouse crouching in the square not unlike a community watch-dog overlooking the environs. Passing the variety of high-fronted stores, Dude, riding Texas Jack, sensed an air of stability, not uncommon in the Sunflower State, thanks to its thrifty farmers. Toward the end of Main Street, Dude located what he sought, a giant red barn, across its broad face these huge black letters:

HONEST ABE TOLLIVER
I Buy, Sell & Trade Horses & Mules

Dude tied up at the hitching rack in front of the barn. Seeing a man lounging in the sun by the barn's breezeway, Dude went up to him and said, "Good afternoon. Can you direct me to a good campin' place for the night?"

The man was small, but not slight, his bony, wrinkled face the color of an old saddle seat, his sharp eyes like black buttons, his long hook of a nose seeming about to catch the thin lips. There was something monkeylike about him: the hunched, powerful shoulders, the extra long arms and long-fingered hands, about the biggest hands Dude had ever seen. He might as well have spoken to a mule, for all the man said or any expression he showed. At last he answered, lips hardly moving, "Can."

Dude heard a stir inside the barn's office and a man stepped out. He was all smiles, hand outstretched, as friendly as an old hound dog. Dude took the hand, noting the wide, mobile mouth in the moon face. A short, rotund individual, as round as a beer keg, pink of cheek, around fifty. Dude kept coming back to the eyes, eyes of experience.

"I'm Abe Tolliver. How can I oblige you, friend?"

"Our little horse outfit is just passin'

through," Dude said, getting that in first, and then gave his name. "Need a campin' place. Might stay a few days. We've come far."

The experienced eyes flicked from the hitching rack to the wagon, seemed to focus on Texas Jack and the Judge. "Anything to trade or sell?"

"Nothin' with any hidden defects I'd like to get shed of right now," Dude said, and they both grinned, Tolliver raising one eyebrow. "If there's a track around here, we'd like to camp nearby. Want to work our runnin' horse."

Tolliver made a broad sweep with his right hand. "You've come to the prime place, friend," he emphasized, heavy on the "friend" approach. "Go on out to the east edge of town. There's a right nice little park out there by the county fairgrounds and plenty of good well water. There's an oval track and a short straightaway. We're proud of our track and call it Sunflower Downs."

"There's nothin' like true civic pride," Dude said, nodding his thanks. Then, as if suddenly remembering something, he snapped his fingers. "Almost slipped my mind. We could use a couple of sacks of oats."

"Should've thought of that," Tolliver said.

At that the big-handed little man rose and disappeared inside the barn. While he was loading the feed into the wagon at Dude's direction, Tolliver eyed the two haltered horses. "I can see which one is your racehorse," he said, indicating the smooth Texas Jack.

"He's just gettin' over the colic," Dude replied, not wanting to sound eager.

"However," said Tolliver, eyeballing Judge Blair, "your ol' packhorse's conformation is equally good."

"Takes more than conformation to make a racehorse. That's why Hoot Owl is a packhorse." Judge Blair stood head hanging, as he usually did with the pack or a stock saddle. But once the light racing saddle was cinched on him, he became a different horse, head up, that eagle look in his eyes, cocked to run. Dude snapped his fingers again. "Guess we could use a couple of bales of good prairie hay," he said to keep the talk going.

"Should've thought of that, too," Tolliver said, full of apology. "But didn't want to push. Always like to be neighborly, even to strangers passing through. Never know, they might come back someday." He turned toward the barn, where the little man had returned to his station by the breezeway. "Two bales of our best hay, Big Hands."

"Big Hands?" Dude inquired. "The name fits."

"Big Hands Burns," Tolliver explained. "Also

rides for me, which ain't often. Not many racehorses around here."

"Too bad," Dude sympathized. "Folks are sure missin' a heap of fun."

Burns loaded the hay, turned, and asked, "All?" Dude nodded. When Burns had left them, Tolliver said in a low voice, "He's not one to use two words when one will do."

"I'm for a man who can hobble his lip," Dude agreed. "How much do we owe you, Mr. Tolliver?"

Tolliver squinted up at the blue sky, lips moving, calculating. "A dollar and a half will cover it. Hope that sounds about right?"

Dude paid him, thinking he'd never heard a man apologize so much. Seeing Uncle Billy in the buggy, looking straight ahead, removed from the roundabout palaver, Dude said deliberately, hoping to draw Uncle into this, "Mr. Tolliver, I want you to meet our outfit. That's Dr. William Tecumseh Lockhart of Kentucky there . . . and that's Mr. Coyote Walking, our rider."

Tolliver couldn't get over to the buggy fast enough. He pumped Billy's hand till the old man winced and withdrew it, then shook Coyote's hand again and again, and came back to Dude. "Did I hear you right, friend? You said *doctor . . . Dr.* Lockhart?"

"Dr. Lockhart is a veterinarian of national repute back in Kentucky. With Cedar Crest Farm. Out here on a little junket for his health. I'm glad to see that he is on the improve."

"Cedar Crest Farm?" Tolliver seemed to roll the words around in his mouth. "Can't say I've heard of it and I've been through Kentucky several times. I'm acquainted back there."

"It's right out of Lexington," Dude supplied, simulating surprise, at the same time catching Uncle's warning look. But on he went, rolling out the first fictitious name that jumped to his mind. "Their foundation sire is none other than the great Old Kentucky Home. Must be you've heard of Old Kentucky Home, sir?" He regarded Tolliver inquiringly.

"Guess I have at that — comes to me now," Tolliver gave in. He looked at Billy, put down his head and a sheepishness crept into his voice. "Seeing as how you are a doctor, I might as well tell you gentlemen about an old trick that was played on me only last week. A stranger drifted in here with a bay gelding workhorse. The horse moved smartly and checked out every way — I thought. So I traded for him. . . . Next day I remembered I hadn't looked at his nose. Sure enough, I found sponges stuffed up each nostril. I pulled them out and he started roaring and whistling. Doc-

58

tor, can anything be done for a horse with the heaves?"

"One teaspoonful of lobelia once a day given in the feed for a week will often relieve the sufferer," Billy said, giving him a crafty smile. "But the only proven course is to stick the sponges back up the nostrils and look for a trade, say to some rube farmer."

"Oh, I wouldn't do that to one of my farmer friends. I have to live around these people."

"Why, of course not," the old man said, his tone shedding mockery. "Well, Dude, we'd better get along if we aim to make camp early." He lifted reins, chirruped "Giddup," and the blind trotter took him rapidly down the road, Coyote following with the wagon.

"When the doctor says go, we go," Dude told Tolliver and rode off, taking with him the insight that Uncle hadn't given the barn trader the usual heaves remedy that was always "good to trade on" — two ounces each of Spanish brown, gentian, and lobelia, three ounces of resin, and eight ounces of Jamaica ginger. He wondered why and then realized that Uncle had taken a special dislike to Tolliver. Were the trader a farmer who'd been skinned, Uncle would have passed on the sure-fire trade concoction.

Dude rode up alongside the buggy and, out

of earshot of Tolliver, the old man said, "Don't believe Honest Abe will match us. He's so slippery himself he's afraid to because Texas Jack looks so smooth."

"We can wait a day or so."

"Not if we expect to reach Illinois soon, poorly as I am."

"Believe you've overlooked the first lesson you schooled me in when rockin' back and forth to match a race."

"What's that?" Billy sounded tired and a little crabby.

"Never appear too eager to match your horse."

"Now, did I say that still didn't hold true?" In a tone that brushed the matter aside as if of no importance now, he said, "Time we went up against that crooked banker Lightfoot, you brought up Cedar Crest Farm, of which there is none, and Lightfoot caught it. You did again back there, and Tolliver questioned it. There is a Crestwood, but no Cedar Crest. Try to remember that. Or don't use it a-tall."

"Yes, Uncle."

"And I don't recall a stud called Old Kentucky Home."

"Yes, Uncle."

They made camp in a pleasant grove of elms not far from a hand pump that brought up plenty of sweet water. Afterward, the threesome looked at the track, a half-mile oval that Texans called a "bull ring," with sharp turns. The straightaway covered 300 yards. There was a fenced paddock near the unroofed stands.

"The inside horse would have the advantage going two turns," Billy observed. "Too, he might veer wide into the outside horse."

The next day passed without sign of Tolliver, and Dude, who had expected the barn trader to come slyly talking match race, could see that Uncle was becoming restless. At breakfast the following morning, the old man, fretting, said, "I don't like waiting much longer, as poorly as I feel."

"Well . . . ?" Dude ventured.

"You'll have to make the first approach. Take the bull by the horns without appearin' to do so."

"How?" Dude asked, playing mystified.

"We could use a sack of bran. That's excuse enough to go to the barn."

"You mean just buy a sack of bran and say, 'I'd like to take a gander at your racehorse?' We're not supposed to know he has one."

The old man looked pained. "I can see now I've wasted most of my time on a certain Alamo Texan. I'll have to handle this if we're ever gonna get down the trail to Illinois." Resigned, he pushed up from the cane-bottomed chair, reached for his cane, and Dude winked at Coyote: *Good. Heap good. He's gettin' interested.*

They had scarcely pulled up in front of the big red barn, Dude riding with Uncle in the buggy, when Tolliver fairly bounced out of the office. He started shaking hands thirty feet away, the ever-present horse trader's smile of welcome pasted on his moon face. "Well, friends, I figured you had drifted on."

"Restin'," Dude said, taking the eager hand. "Need twenty-five pounds of bran."

"Should've thought of that the other day," Tolliver said, reeking apology. "Since you're here, I'd appreciate it if Dr. Lockhart will look at one of my horses?"

"Glad to," Billy said. "What seems to be the problem?"

"Few days ago he had heat in his left cannon bone."

Wrapping the reins around the whip socket, Billy stepped down. Dude, joining him while Tolliver led the way to the barn past the lounging Big Hands Burns, noticed that Uncle had left his cane in the buggy. Tolliver took them through the dimness of the cavernous barn to the last stall, where he opened the door and led out a rangy chestnut gelding.

"Let me look him over first," the old man

said, his voice professional. He circled the gelding twice, nodding approval as he did, the old wrinkle, Dude recognized, to make the other horseman feel good about his horse. Then, speaking softly to the horse, Billy ran his hand down the left front leg and picked up the foot, peered at the frog, set the foot down, and gently felt the cannon bone between fetlock and knee, running his hand up and down. Pushing his spectacles back, he looked up at Tolliver. "I find no heat whatever. You've rested him enough. Your horse is sound."

"Now that's good news," Tolliver said. "Maybe I can run him a little."

Ah, Dude thought, the approach. And a slick way to go about it. It was always better if the other side made the first move.

"He has the lines of a racehorse, all right," Billy said, complimenting. "Noticed that right off."

Tolliver hung his head in that good-ol'-boy manner, which Dude perceived by now was characteristic of the man when leading up to something, and let drop, "Just wonder if we might dicker about a little match race, now that Keeno is fit to run?"

"Texas Jack is Dude's horse," Billy said, staying out of it.

Dude hitched thumbs in belt and looked

about indifferently. "Can't say right off. Can't run far when he's just gettin' over the colic. About how far would you want to go?"

"Not far," Tolliver said, matching Dude's casualness.

"Say two-twenty?"

"A tad more?" Tolliver was all smiles.

"Not more than two-fifty?"

"Me either."

This man was too agreeable, Dude sensed. "About how much you want to bet?"

"Not much. Been a lean year."

"And travelin' expenses are high. What say, twenty-five dollars?" Why bet much when you knew your slow horse was going to lose so you could set up the switch with odds?

"I could go thirty-five."

"All right," Dude agreed. "Two hundred fifty yards for thirty-five dollars. When do you want to run?"

"Saturday is always a good day, when folks come to town."

"It is. Now we need a starter."

"Dr. Lockhart would be fine with me."

Dude almost choked. You *always* favored a starter who would give your horse the edge at the start, at least an even break; if there was a neutral starter, you hoped he really was neutral. Most times, with both sides pressing for the advantage, you had to flip for the man. Tolliver was just too agreeable.

"What about finish-line judges?" Dude asked.

"There'll be plenty of honest farmers, once word gets around there's a race."

"Suits me. What time do you want to run?"

"Two o'clock agreeable with you?"

"It is," Dude said. "We haven't talked about weights. Catch weights all right?"

Tolliver nodded and they shook hands on all conditions of the race.

Burns, at Tolliver's direction, loaded the sack of bran onto the buggy and when Dude asked how much, the barn trader dug the toe of his right boot into the dirt and hesitating, said, "A dollar. No, make it four bits. Hope that sounds about right?"

"I've never seen a man so agreeable about matchin' a horse race," Dude said after they left the barn. "What did you make of Keeno?"

"Best as I could tell, dark as it was back there, he's a tolerable-looking racehorse. Has sickle hocks, though, which limit the extension of the hind leg and don't make for long strides. Yet, some good horses have sickle hocks. And he toes out in front, which means he could strike himself while runnin', or he could strain other parts of the leg . . . the ankles or the knees. Yet, some horses with conformation defects have brilliant speed. I'd say Tolliver is wise to match him short. But I doubt that he's had heat recently in the left cannon bone. That was only a lead-in to match talk."

"I notice you forgot your cane when you walked to the barn," Dude guyed him.

"Yes, I did," came the testy reply, "and my joints hurt like all get-out."

CHAPTER 3

One Good Race

Dude was observing the flow of wagons and buggies, horsemen and townsmen on foot filling the little park. Farm families had brought picnic baskets and were having dinner under the elms. "Guess word got around fast," he said.

"Next to a circus," Billy said, "a horse race is the best entertainment there is. It's a family outing. And in a town this size, starved for amusement, even an arm-wavin' preacher draws a good crowd."

Not long before the two o'clock post time, Homer Overman drove up in a spring wagon, the sad gray workhorse trailing on halter. Dude shook his head at the sight of the faltering old horse.

"As you can see," Overman said, stepping down, "I still have poor Dobbin. I just came from the barn. Told Tolliver I was on to his trick and how old Dobbin really is and suggested he take the horse back, keep ten dollars, and there'd be no hard feelings. Oh, he apologized – nobody can apologize like Tolliver and skin you at the same time – but he said a trade's a trade and wouldn't budge. Claimed he'd put the money out on another deal."

"I expected that," Billy said. "Did you tell him how you learned about the arsenic trick?"

"Nope. I let him wonder about that and he didn't deny it."

"What do you plan to do with Dobbin, if I may ask?"

"Take him home and let him finish out his days."

"You didn't get any arsenic?"

"Don't have a rich uncle," Overman said, guffawing, slapping a leg. He sobered. "No, Doctor, I couldn't do that. Wouldn't be fair to Dobbin."

"He looks pretty gaunted right now. I'll stir up a little potion, I mean tonic, for you to give him before you start home. It will put sparkle in his eye and zip in his step. He'll act so spirited you may be able to trade him off to some stranger between here and the farm."

The old man, forgetting his cane again, turned to the rear of the wagon and, shortly, Dude could hear bottles clinking. Once, Uncle came out of the shade and into the sun and squinted keenly at the contents of a measuring cup. And, last, Dude caught the *thung* of the cob stopper on the jug of sour mash. In moments Billy returned with a pint fruit jar containing a murky-looking mixture, which he handed to Overman. "Give this to Dobbin all in one dose."

"How do I go about that?"

Looking amused, Billy seemed to call on all his patience. "You open the horse's mouth and pour it in."

Overman grinned. "I mean how am I gonna hold his head up and open his mouth and give the medicine all at the same time?"

"Just trickle a little in his mouth. He'll like the taste of it and ask for more."

The farmer unscrewed the lid and sniffed the contents. "Why, Doctor, this smells like whiskey! Think he'll take it?"

"Ever know a horse that didn't like corn?" the old man retorted. "But it's not all whiskey." Taking a memorandum book and a stub pencil, he put down four decisive lines, tore out the page, and gave it to Overman. "Here's a prescription for Dobbin if you haven't traded him off to that stranger before you get home. Professor Gleason's Original Sure-Shot Conditioner. Mix well and give ten drops daily in a bucket of water."

"Professor Gleason?" Overman was dubious.

"An old contemporary of mine, now gone to his just reward, where the horses run fast and far and there are no cloudy days. If you doubt the effectiveness of this, good neighbor, let me tell you what happened to an old acquaintance of mine who took a dose of it by mistake."

"He took horse medicine! What happened?"

Uncle Billy gazed away, a remote smile moving across his mouth and eyes, letting Overman wonder. A moment more and he said, "My old friend got so lively around the house his good wife made him sleep in the barn for a week and take his meals on the back porch. You may have to pen old Dobbin."

Overman exploded into a series of coarse guffaws. "Might take a spoonful of that myself," he said.

Dude listened to all this with growing gratification. Whether Uncle realized it or not, he was on his way back: mixing "potions" again from the off-limits medicine chest; handing out free remedies, and telling stories; uppermost, always, his love and concern for horses.

"What do I owe you, Doctor?" Overman asked, still chuckling.

"Not a thing, good neighbor. Just take care of Dobbin."

Soon after, Dude noticed picnickers turning to look at two horsemen coming from town. It was Tolliver in the lead, ponying Keeno, ridden by Big Hands Burns. Tolliver waved genially at Dude and rode on to the paddock. By now Coyote had saddled Texas Jack. Dude mounted Blue Grass, Billy climbed into the buggy, and they all set out for the paddock, gathering a crowd as they went. Billy parked and tied Amos at the paddock fence.

"Ready to pick our finish-line judges?" Tolliver called out obligingly as the outfit came inside the paddock. Dude nodded and Tolliver faced about to the men leaning on the paddock fence. "Would three of you gentlemen like to act as finish-line judges? We'd sure appreciate it."

Two men raised hands at once, a third, hesitantly.

"All right?" Tolliver asked Dude.

Dude gave him a nod, not till then seeing that the third man was Overman. When Coyote rode to a stall and dismounted, Billy, speaking in a low voice, said, "I'm surprised Tolliver would agree to Overman, after the way he skinned him. If I were Overman, I'd think twice before I'd give him the benefit of the doubt in a close finish."

"That is a little unusual," Dude agreed. "In

the first place, a local horseman always has men he prefers as judges."

"— and as the starter."

As part of the customary ritual for the paddock watchers, Dude unsaddled Texas Jack, brushed him off, and paraded the smooth-looking bay gelding around the enclosure three times, raising murmurs of approval. Resaddling, making a play of settling the blanket on just so, and of checking the cinch on the light racing saddle, Dude said quietly, "I hope these farmers don't lose too much. I take it they'd like to see Tolliver get beat."

Tolliver and Burns had finished fussing over saddling Keeno and Tolliver gave the jockey a leg up and they were ready for the post parade. Seeing that, Coyote rode over there and Billy, following, told them, "It will be a lap-and-tap start. When I tell you riders to approach the line, you will walk your horses up, and when you are closely lapped, I'll bring my hand down and tap you off by shoutin', 'Go!' Any questions, Mr. Burns?"

"Nary."

"Mr. Coyote Walking?"

Coyote shook his head. Today he was playing the role of a silent reservation Indian dressed in white man's shirt and trousers, only moccasins and headband his native garb.

Tolliver and Burns were first out of the paddock onto the track. Dude thought the chestnut Keeno looked smooth and ready to run, prancing and tossing his head. An easy winner against Texas Jack. Dude followed, leading the bay. They moved so slowly past the stands, Texas Jack so pokily, that Dude, keeping his voice down, said, "Touch him up a little, Coyote," and the Comanche, unseen by the spectators in the stands on his right, slipped his left foot out of the stirrup and nudged the gelding's flank. Instantly, Texas Jack lurched and started a mild bucking, and Dude, appearing to take a firm hold on the lead shank, hollered, "Hold 'im, Injun! He's tryin' to bolt!" A couple of jumps and the bay settled down, Dude making a show of holding his head up.

"He sure looks like a runner," said a farmer leaning on the rail.

"Sometimes," Dude said. "But don't bet the old homeplace."

Circling now, he caught sight of Billy heading down the track in the buggy for the starting line. Once past the stands, Dude released Texas Jack and crossed over to the infield near the finish line, marked by posts on each side of the track.

The two horses, at a prancing walk, seemed

to take a long time reaching the head of the track. Dude saw Uncle motion the riders back to begin the approach. Now they turned and walked forward. But as they drew near the starting line, Texas Jack was too far ahead and Billy waved them around. Again they turned together and approached. This time they looked fairly lapped. Billy dropped his hand, his shout lost on the wind.

They were off!

To Dude's surprise, Texas Jack took the break by half a length and shot ahead. That was the thing about him: Though not a Judge Blair, he wasn't a sorry runner the first hundred yards. At least he looked convincing at that distance, which helped set up the switch. But once he got thereabout, he would start fading, his heart not in it.

Dude watched, prepared for Keeno to stride ahead.

Strangely, there was no change. Dude saw Texas Jack slacken a bit, yet he continued to hold the lead, now widened to a full length. Burns went to the whip and Keeno responded, moving up to the bay's hip. There he stayed, running stubbornly.

Coyote glanced over his shoulder, as if in alarm, and gave his mount a couple of whacks across the hindquarters.

Dude grinned to himself. Some playactor, that Comanche. You had to make the race look bona fide, even though you knew your slow horse always lost.

But at two hundred yards, suddenly, Texas Jack opened daylight. Keeno was fading. Dude couldn't believe his eyes, because Texas Jack had never won a race, had yet to "break his maiden," as they said of a winless runner in the jargon of the organized tracks.

They were pounding for the finish poles. Dude could only stare in open-mouthed astonishment as Texas Jack crossed the line, Keeno struggling two lengths behind despite Burns's frantic laying on of the whip.

Dude sat his horse a while longer, too stunned to move, realizing that the switch wouldn't work now. Even so, mulling over the race, he found himself smiling, glad, in a way, that Texas Jack had finally won. He was a nice horse. Easy to handle. A good keeper. Intelligent. A calm disposition. A friend.

Well, he decided, seeing Coyote bringing the winner back at trot, let's do this right. And Dude, grinning broadly, as befitted the happy owner, dismounted to greet the victors in front of the stands where the winner's circle would be if the track had one. Applause rippled as Coyote rode up, whip held high. He slipped down and Dude shook his hand and slapped him on the back and rubbed Texas Jack's nose. Glancing about, Dude saw Burns already riding for town.

Coyote and Dude were leading their horses back to camp when Tolliver rushed up. "Here's your money, friend. You had it on us today. Keeno just didn't take to the track. He seemed a little off his feed yesterday, but I didn't think anything about it. Sometimes he's a picky eater." Tolliver hung his head in that self-deprecating way. "First time he ever lost. I know he can run better. Would you . . . maybe . . . listen to a rematch?"

Dude might have been hearing himself talking while trying to set up the switch at high odds had Texas Jack lost. "Might," he said, surprised. "Come by in the mornin' and we'll powwow about it."

"That's mighty sporting of you, friend." Tolliver insisted on shaking hands with both Dude and Coyote.

Watching him go, Dude said, "I never saw a man pay off so fast and never saw a loser act so friendly. Almost the same as if he'd won."

Billy drove up grinning like a tomcat. "I've always said there's one good race in every horse, no matter how slow he is. Same as there's one explosion in every horse, no matter how tame he is." He was chuckling. "What happened, Coyote? Did Burns pull his horse?"

"Too far ahead I was to see," Coyote grinned, playing proud.

"Did Texas Jack seem to run any faster than usual?"

"Run the same, he did. Start off pretty good. Then slow he ran, like always. But no slower, no faster."

"He's such a nice-looking horse, he seems fast when he's slow. It's what you call form. I figure he ran that two-fifty in about what a good horse would three hundred yards. Say around seventeen or eighteen seconds."

"From what I could tell," Dude put in, "Keeno didn't fire. I watched them all the way. Burns didn't pull him. He used plenty of whip."

"It's a little odd," Billy said. "A horse with his record going that slow. An unbeaten horse at that. Well, I'd say now we can be on our way to Illinois."

"Not yet," Dude said. "Tolliver wants to run at us again. He paid off right after the race. Said his horse didn't take to the track. I told him to come by in the morning and we'd talk. How do you figure a rematch?"

Billy considered. "Keeno couldn't have outrun a three-year-old terrapin today. . . . And he wasn't pulled. I wouldn't be too eager, Dude, pardner."

When Abe Tolliver arrived next morning, the old man sat in the cane-bottomed chair, perusing a heavy medical "tome," so engrossed he no more than glanced up. Coyote was braiding a horsehair hatband. The barn trader shook hands with Dude, then opened with, "Keeno kicked up his heels this morning after his early feed. Acted like his old self, which is more than I could say for him yesterday."

"Glad to hear it," Dude said.

"Which brings up the proposition, friend McQuinn. About how far would you like to run this time?"

"To be honest, I haven't thought much about it."

"Well, *would* you think about it?"

"Might. Though we're headin' back East and don't want to linger by the wayside where the wild flowers grow." Dude figured Tolliver would rock back and forth for a short race; therefore, the wise slant was to match him long.

"Cite me a distance, friend McQuinn."

Dude shrugged, the epitome of indifference, and took a hitch at his belt. "What say six furlongs, friend Tolliver?"

"Six!" Tolliver's voice peaked to a howl. "Keeno is no long-distance sprinter. Come again, friend."

"Five?"

"You're still way out yonder where the tall corn grows."

"Four furlongs?" Since Texas Jack had widened his lead the farther they ran, Tolliver was a fool to match Keeno long. Even two-fifty was long for him.

"I would go you at that," Tolliver said and winked, "but I'd have to have odds."

"Odds?" Why, the man sounded like Dude McQuinn maneuvering for the switch. "I never give odds."

"Why not, friend McQuinn?"

"It's like this," Dude explained, thinking if they kept up this *friend* stuff, before long they'd be hugging. "I never bet more than I can pay off."

"A sound fiscal policy, my friend. Just the same, you must admit that, having daylighted Keeno, you should give odds to get me back on the track."

"You're askin' for the race, friend Tolliver. Not me." Tolliver had him doing it again.

"Me? Sure. I want to make my money back and then some." Tolliver slapped his leg and hung his head and cocked an eye. "Tell you what. Would you bet three hundred dollars and no odds?"

My, oh my, this Tolliver is eager, Dude thought. At the same time he started to feel a vague uneasiness and decided to get rid of him. "I won't go three, but I will go five," he said, hoping that would scare the barn trader off.

"You're on!" Tolliver replied, catching Dude by surprise. "When?"

Dude's jaw fell. But he had stated his bet and had it taken and would have to stand behind it. "We'll run you Saturday, four furlongs, same time, even money, no odds, catch weights — as before."

"You gentlemen may not get to run your race after all," a matter-of-fact voice interrupted. It was Billy, standing behind them, the spectacles pushed out to the end of his nose, holding the medical book.

Dude looked at him. "What do you mean?"

"Texas Jack's colic has returned. Not bad yet. Just enough to throw him off. I was looking for something quickly helpful when you rode up, Mr. Tolliver. In case it's more than mild indigestion, I'll give him a stimulant with some nitric ether and a tincture of opium."

"So the race is off," Tolliver grumbled.

"Unless . . . unless," the old man said, "you feel you just have to have a race?"

"All I want is a shot at getting my money back."

"In that event, Dude might run his ol' packhorse Hoot Owl at you."

"That ol' cockleburred packhorse?" Tolliver jeered, suppressing his laughter, and looked scornfully at Judge Blair, who stood head low, indolently tailswitching flies.

Dude remained silent but thought: *At last! Uncle is getting involved.*

"He's in the class of Texas Jack . . . no more," Billy said. "Only difference is he can go a little farther down the track. Believe I heard you two agree to half a mile. Think he can go that distance, Dude?"

Dude shrugged. "Hoot Owl can go a distance, all right, but he may have to lope the last hundred yards, or Coyote may have to tote him across the finish line."

"I'll run you," Tolliver averred, "either at Texas Jack or your ol' Hoot Owl packhorse, whichever is ready." There was still a note of mockery in his voice.

"It won't be Texas Jack," the old man said.

"That's still a far get-there for my ol' packhorse," Dude groused, playing uncertain. "However, I said what I'd bet and you agreed, friend Tolliver. I have a hunch your Keeno will start makin' up ground after the quarter mile."

81

He shook his head doubtfully.

"It's all agreed, then?"

"On all conditions except the starter and the finish-line judges. You saw Dr. Lockhart tap both horses off fair and square. I propose that he tap us off again."

Tolliver's ever-present smile thinned. "That the good doctor did, friend McQuinn, fair and square. Only I have another man in mind, a pillar in our fair city. A Mr. Dink Fargo."

Dude caught the change. Where was all that good-ol'-boy affability? "Let's flip for it. I believe you would trust Dr. Lockhart to handle the toss?"

"Should've thought of that myself," Tolliver apologized.

Uncle took a silver dollar from a leather purse, showed both sides of it, and said, "You call it in the air, Mr. Tolliver," and flipped the coin high.

"Heads," called Tolliver.

The spinning coin landed and bounced and settled. "Heads it is," Billy affirmed. "Your man is the starter, Mr. Tolliver. Now for the judges."

"Would you agree to taking our judges from the crowd, like before?" Tolliver, that eye cocked, looked slyly at Dude, who said, "Will — with each side pickin' a judge and flippin' for the third man."

Tolliver appeared to work that through his mind, in and out. "I agree, friend McQuinn. So we're all set." He shook hands formally, briefly, and pumped Dude's hand twice.

Uncertainly, they watched Tolliver ride away. Billy said, "I started to nix the race with that colic claim, but changed my mind to run. A little later I changed it again, when I threw in the ol' packhorse wrinkle, which has moss all over it, figurin' Tolliver would back off, cagey as he is. Instead, he jumped on it. This way we can run the Judge as is, without the switch to make him look like Texas Jack and vice versa."

"It's the money," Dude said. "He'd skin a widow woman out of her egg money."

"Another thing, Dude. We'll have to work the Judge" – he loosened a little smile – "that is, Hoot Owl, on the turns. I want to make certain he's changing leads going into the turns and again coming out on the backstretch and when he heads for home."

"He ain't been four furlongs in a long time," Dude worried.

"We'll lengthen him out with slow gallops. If friend Tolliver has a lookout watching, which likely he will, he won't see much speed. In this, we all forgot one important item – post position, which is mighty important on the turns.

Gives the inside horse the advantage. If he goes wide, he forces the other horse out. If he hangs close to the rail, he's saving ground. We'll flip for that at the paddock."

"What I can't see," Dude puzzled, "is why Tolliver would match Keeno long, after the way he struggled goin' two-fifty?"

"I'd say he knows something we don't. He figures he has the advantage. We'll see about that." The old man swung away, moving briskly to the rear of the wagon. He leaned inside where the medicine chest was; soon, Dude heard the stopper on the jug go *thung*. He glanced at Coyote, sharing conspirational smiles, and they nodded in unison: *He's back!*

CHAPTER 4

The Switch

Soon after daylight Sunday the outfit took Judge Blair to the racecourse. Coyote eased him off at the half-mile starting line and they galloped for the first turn, while Dude and Uncle Billy watched from the stands.

"He broke in the right lead the way he always does," said the old man, with keen satisfaction. He seemed in a euphoric world, absorbed in his total concentration and enjoyment of observing a good horse work. "He changed into the left lead goin' into the turn—good! . . . That turn is sharp. I don't like it. These bull rings are better suited for footraces. . . . Comin' out of the turn now. There! He changed back to the right lead. . . . He likes that backstretch. He's movin' out . . . but Coyote's got a tight hold . . . won't let him run. . . . Into the last turn now. That's it! Into the left lead! Good boy!" (Billy might be talking to the Judge, Dude felt). "Come on now. . . . Back to the right lead as you straighten out for home. . . . There! You've got it!"

A finishing gallop now. A much faster gallop. As Coyote took the Judge over the finish line, the two observers went down to the track, Billy matching Dude's long strides. It struck Dude then, quite sharply, that Uncle hadn't used the cane for two days. But a wise partner said nothing.

"Well —?" Billy asked on Coyote's return.

"He wanted to run like buffalo horse, this horse." The Comanche bared his teeth. "Those turns I hate — sharp, they are."

"But he made the lead changes."

"He did. Quick he had to make them too, and the track is fast, Grandfather. The feel of it he likes. It has grass here and there, like curly buffalo grass."

"The Judge is a balanced horse. That's why he can change with no loss of speed. In fact, when he changes he reaches out a little farther on the fresh lead foot and gains ground, mean-time resting the other foot. We'll breeze him out faster Wednesday. Get him primed."

Homer Overman, heavy and genial, was a welcome Monday afternoon visitor. "I'm feeling so good after winning back my thirty-five dollars off a town loafer, I thought I'd see how you're all making out today."

"All that money and Dobbin to boot," Dude joshed him. "How is the old fella?"

"Doctor's tonic perked him up. I turned him out. Plan to make a pensioner of him."

"You're just the man we need to see. We've matched Tolliver again on Saturday. Four furlongs this time with Hoot Owl, our ol' packhorse. We flipped for the starter and Tolliver won. Wanted Dink Fargo. Who's he?"

"Runs the biggest saloon in the town. Also waters his whiskey and the games are crooked."

"Tolliver claimed he's a pillar in the community."

"Depends on what you call a pillar. I wouldn't trust him as far as I could throw a bull elephant by the tail uphill against the wind."

Dude frowned. "That means they'll try for the advantage at the break. We hope we can count on you for a finish-line judge again. Tolliver picks one and we flip for the third man."

"I'll be here. Don't worry."

"What can you tell us about this Big Hands Burns? He strikes me as an experienced jock."

"He is, they say. I don't know much, other than he rode on the big tracks in St. Louis and

Chicago. Turned up in Blue Springs about two years ago. Worked for Tolliver ever since."

"Wonder why he left the big tracks?"

"Too fond of John Barleycorn. A periodic drinker. He'll disappear for a week or two, then won't touch a drop for months."

"How does he ride?"

"Rough as a cob. Very aggressive. Last Fourth of July a Topeka horseman brought in a fast little mare called Miss Tulip. I saw her work here at Sunflower Downs and believe you me she could run more than a little. Keeno drew the rail – blamed if Tolliver don't have more luck than anybody – and then Fargo gives Burns the break by half a length. But that little mare hung in there. . . . There was a little bitty ol' kid riding her. Couldn't have been more than twelve years old. . . . She hung with Keeno all the way to the homestretch turn, and as they straightened out, she closed on Keeno. She was hell-bent to pass when Keeno veered out, forcing the mare to break stride. That was the race right there. Keeno won by two lengths. . . . Oh, there was a big ruckus. The Topeka man cried foul. Big Hands Burns, just as innocent as you please, claimed he couldn't hold Keeno when he bore out. Claimed he was whipping Keeno righthanded to keep left. Truth is, he was pullin' on the right rein with his left hand at the same time. I saw that myself – was on the rail. . . . Well, Tolliver, he apologized and hung his head and said anything can happen in a horse race. The finish judges, all picks from Fargo's saloon, disallowed the foul and the Topeka man paid off."

"Interesting," Dude said, and Coyote, nodding, seemed to put it away in his mind.

"We expect to see Keeno work before long," Billy said.

"You won't see Keeno till race day," Overman said. "Tolliver never works Keeno here before a race."

"Why not?"

"He's got a track across the road from his house four miles north of town. It's just like this one, a half-mile bull ring. Always works Keeno at dawn, they say in town. Another reason I've come by is to tell you how they're betting."

"*They?*" Billy asked.

"The gamblers at Fargo's saloon. They're giving two-to-one odds on Keeno. I sure laid down my money."

"Keeno was daylighted . . . yet they're giving odds," Billy mused. "I don't savvy their logic unless, as Tolliver said, his horse was off his feed. Can happen. Too, there's a horseman's pride. Having an unbeaten horse lose his first race to an unknown."

There was a run of reflective silence after Overman left, until Dude asked, "Uncle, when would Tolliver send Keeno through his last work before Saturday?"

"I'd top my horse off about Wednesday – no later than Thursday – then let him loaf. After that, no more than a morning walk."

"What say we take us a little look-see that way Wednesday before dawn?"

The cagey smile of old rose to Billy's face. "You wouldn't take the words out of my mouth, would you, Dude, pardner? And, Coyote, pardner, will you sorta drift up that way tomorrow morning, making sure Tolliver is at the barn, and scout out where to tie our horses and where the best lookout is?"

"As you say, Grandfather."

"And don't call me Grandfather."

Minutes before dawn they rode through the freshening, grass-sweet scents of an awakening prairie world along the north road. When the blur of a large white farmhouse bulged dimly ahead, they turned into a scattering of oaks and tied their horses. At Coyote's direction, they crossed the road and, keeping to open pasture, walked toward the track. Atop a slight rise, Coyote stopped and they crouched down to watch.

Dawn broke, bringing streaks of dove-gray light, then a pinkish glow. They watched the house, a two-story affair with a porch running its length, and the red barn below the house. Minutes slipped by. By now it was broad daylight, and although they were fairly well hidden, Dude began to feel uncomfortable. No one left the house. Nothing stirred at the barn.

They must have kept the vigil for half an hour when Billy said, "He's not working his horse today. Let's go."

They eased back down the crest to the horses.

On the way to town, Dude asked, "What do you think now, Uncle?"

"He'll work Keeno tomorrow. If he doesn't, that's a new way to train a racehorse. Any horse needs a prep within the week before a race. Take the Judge. He's shed some of the extra weight I noticed at Painted Rock, but he still needs a stiff blowout. We'll tend to that when we get back in the morning. He's the kind of horse that thrives on work."

Once again they watched from the grassy crest in the early morning darkness. This time they had come earlier. As they had yesterday morning, Coyote rode the Judge and Billy was on Texas Jack.

A light flared in the house. In a few minutes Dude saw two figures leave the house and go to the barn; in a little while, they led out two horses. They mounted and rode past the house to the road and across to the track. There one of the riders trotted up the track and back, warming his horse. A brief pause and a horse took off, sprinting into the first turn, coming out of it rapidly on the backstretch, a speeding blur against the muddy light.

"Keeno is movin' faster now than he did against Texas Jack," Dude said, "and he took that turn tight on the rail."

The hoofbeats drummed louder and faster as the horse rounded the last turn and pounded down the stretch, the jockey not easing up until they passed the waiting second horseman. When the rider brought the runner back, the two riders crossed the road to the barn.

Billy was squinting at his stopwatch in the half light. "Keeno covered that half mile in fifty seconds flat, which is fast for a prep work around two turns. Boys, we've got a race on our hands."

"Never saw a horse improve so much in a few days," Dude said, drily amused. "Maybe friend Tolliver has gone to the arsenic treatment. How do you see this big change, Uncle?"

"I can't answer that unless, as Tolliver

claimed, his horse wasn't right. We could be up against a new wrinkle."

They rode back in silence.

As they entered the park, a man ran from their camp toward the racecourse stands. Dude heeled his horse into a run and shouted for the man to stop. He didn't and Dude took down his rope and shook out a loop as he kicked the eager saddler faster. Racing up, he sailed the loop over the man's head and around his shoulders, and jerked him down.

Dude was out of the saddle and going down the rope as if he had caught a calf. Before the man could rise, Dude jerked him to his feet. "What the hell you doin' in our camp?"

No answer. The man was surly, slack-jawed, long-haired, maybe forty years old. His eyes wouldn't meet Dude's. Yet he carried nothing.

"Don't come back," Dude warned. "Our Comanche jockey might take a notion to lift your long hair."

With another surly look, the man jerked free and fled toward town.

"What was that all about?" Billy asked when Dude rode back.

"I have an idea he was all set to spy on the Judge. When he found the camp empty, he decided to prowl. Didn't have time to take anything."

"It's too early to dope a horse, if that's what he had in mind," the old man said. "Good thing we rode the Judge this morning. Which brings up a rule that hasn't changed since the Darley Arabian arrived in England in 1704: Never leave your racehorse unattended. Never!" He made an upflung motion with his left hand, which was characteristic of him in the little outfit's earlier days, indicative of decision. So that gesture had returned, Dude noticed. Billy looked straight at his partners. "Tomorrow night we better take turns standing guard. We'll halter the Judge behind the wagon between Amos and Blue Grass. That's another advantage of having a blind horse. Because he can't see, his hearing and sense of smell are extra sharp. He makes a good sentry, as we all remember at Lightfoot."

Dude caught himself in a crinkling grin. When, unknowingly, Uncle had traded for blind Amos, his self-esteem had taken a nosedive, forgetting that in the deal he had traded off a broken-winded saddler to the other fellow. A disgrace, he'd said, for a horseman to get slickered into owning a blind horse, and an even greater disgrace to keep a blind horse. Now, Dude thought, there's not enough money in the wheat belt to induce Uncle to sell or trade the speedy blue roan.

"Let's blow the Judge out over the distance he'll go in the race," Billy said. "He needs a fast work to tighten him up. And, Dude, I wish you'd take the cockleburs out of his mane and tail."

Save for walking Judge Blair on the halter Friday morning, the outfit rested, and Friday night passed without alarm. By noon Saturday the park was crowded with the wagons and buggies of farm families. Overman came to the camp, hopeful as ever. "I passed word to my neighbors," he said. "Tolliver has skinned 'em all at least once, maybe twice, like me, and we're here to see Keeno get beat."

"How are the odds?" Dude asked.

"Fargo's gamblers are still offering two to one on Keeno. Believe you me, they've found some takers from us farm folks."

"Two to one sounds mighty confident. Hope your friends didn't bet their corn crops. Anything can happen in a horse race."

"They bet more than egg-and-butter money. I'll see you at the paddock."

Judge Blair, curried and brushed and the burs removed, his dark bay coat showing the shine of a ready racehorse, gazed about now and then at the stir of people and horses; otherwise, his head drooping a little, he might be a steady family saddler, Old Reliable, the

95

one the kids learned to ride on, as many as three and four on his back at a time, a horse of endless patience who *always* brought the little ones home. At the moment he was unconcerned about all the commotion. That would change when he felt the light saddle being cinched. For a discerning eye, on closer inspection, his racing features stood out: powerful front and hindquarters. That sloping shoulder. That deep girth of wind and heart. That short back and long underline. The short cannons and pasterns to bear the shock of pounding up front. The front and hind legs straight. Four white-sock feet. The handsome head with the blaze coming to a point between the flaring nostrils. The fox ears and the wide-spaced, intelligent eyes and the big jaws. A sound horse. A balanced horse. Some twelve hundred pounds of running horse.

Looking at his horse, Dude wondered whether they would ever learn the Judge's true breeding. This was probably the last race they'd match until they reached Illinois. Unless . . . he smiled an oblique smile . . . unless somebody offered odds.

As post time approached, Billy peered into the Judge's dark brown eyes — "the mirror of his inner self" — and examined the Judge's front cannons for heat. He nodded, satisfied.

"He came out of yesterday's work without any soreness whatever, and he's shed most of that pampered weight you and Coyote put on him. He's ready to run."

Racegoers were swarming toward the stands now. Coltish boys running here and there. Dude glanced at his pocket watch. Fifteen minutes yet. Coyote took his parfleche wardrobe case from the wagon and disappeared behind the wagon where the other horses were haltered. He was there several minutes.

Dude gaped when Coyote came out. Once again a Plains Indian. A golden eagle feather in his blue-black hair, which hung to his shoulders. Naked above the waist, wearing only breechcloth and beaded moccasins with buckskin fringes. The fringes, Coyote had pointed out once to Dude, were the distinguishing mark of Comanche moccasins. He did not wear his hair braided, wrapped in beaver fur, like the old warriors, Coyote had explained further, for fear in a race the other jockey might grab a braid and jerk him off the Judge. However, in keeping with the ways of his people, he groomed his hair with brushes made from the tails of porcupines. He never shaved; instead, he carefully plucked all hair from his face and eyebrows with tweezers made of bone, and his copper-bright skin was smooth and unlined, despite his twenty-some years of constant exposure to Grandfather Sun. Although not a tall man, he was straight and deep-chested. His eyes had the distant quality of one who was accustomed to gazing far off. His mouth was evenly cast, his aquiline nose curved like an eagle's beak. His legs were slightly bowed from riding since early childhood and he moved awkwardly afoot, but when mounted he seemed a part of the horse and its fluid motion. A Comanche warrior, Dude saw now, admiring him, aware of pride and affection for him. They had been through a great deal together. Good times and hard times, not forgetting some close scrapes. Not many years ago Comanches and Texans had shot each other on sight.

Uncle had bridled and saddled Judge Blair. Coyote sprang to the saddle and took up the reins. At that, the Judge tossed his head, even more alert. Dude mounted Blue Grass, Uncle Billy stepped to the buggy seat, and they all angled slowly through the crowd toward the track.

The paddock was empty and it was two o'clock.

"Old stuff," Billy sniffed. "Tolliver hopes our horse is nervous. Wants the Judge — I mean Hoot Owl — to start sweating. Some horses sweat out their race in the paddock."

Overman joined them while they waited.

Tolliver was fifteen minutes late. "Took time to get through the crowd," he apologized, waving, while Burns rode Keeno to a saddling stall. A man hurried from the crowd to hold Keeno's reins. Tolliver strolled over to the outfit, all neighborly smiles. "Seeing as how Keeno got daylighted last time, friend McQuinn, reckon you'll give us the inside position today?"

"No such thing." Dude was blunt. "We'll flip for it."

"I don't mind. You handle the flip, Dr. Lockhart."

"You call it," Billy said and flipped a silver dollar high.

"Heads," Tolliver called.

The coin bounced and lay still. "Your lucky call again, Mr. Tolliver," Billy said. "Heads it is."

"I always call heads," Tolliver said. "The head of a horse is always smarter than the tail," and he burst into a braying laugh.

"Now for the third finish judge," Dude hurried him. "I've already picked Overman."

"My other judge is at the finish line. Dr. Lockhart has brought me luck so far with the flip. I believe he will again. Flip it, Doctor."

"All right, Mr. Tolliver, and you call it again." Billy flipped the dollar, Tolliver called,

"Heads," and the coin dropped.

"Heads again," said Billy.

Tolliver started off, but Dude's voice checked him. "One more little thing, friend Tolliver. The payoff will be right after the race. No beatin' around the bush and no disappearance acts."

"Friend McQuinn," Tolliver said, feigning shock, "how you do hurt a fellow horseman's feelings. In turn, I remind you to keep your money handy." He moved to the paddock fence and called, and a man showed himself. They exchanged words and the man nodded.

"That's one of the bartenders from Fargo's," Overman said. "Any man who waters whiskey will cheat on a close finish call."

"There'll be hell to pay if he does," Dude swore. "Uncle and I will both be at the finish line. I'm more worried about the start."

A handlebar-mustached man with morose features entered the paddock and spoke to Tolliver and, motioning Burns to follow, strode over to the outfit. "I'm Dink Fargo, the starter," he said. "Figured I'd better tell you how I start a race." He looked in question at Coyote, and Dude said, "This is Mr. Coyote Walking, our jockey," and then introduced Billy and himself.

Fargo shook hands limply. "This will be the old lap-and-tap. When the horses are even, I'll bring my hat down and shout, 'Go!' "

"All we expect is a fair start, an even get-away," Dude emphasized.

"You'll get it," Fargo replied and left them. Tolliver lingered, for the first time giving Judge Blair a close look. "Your ol' packhorse has perked up."

"Any horse looks better when you take the pack off," Dude said.

"We're ready for the post parade when you are, friend McQuinn."

More horse trader's hot air, Dude said to himself, and said, "Go ahead, friend Tolliver. We're ready." It struck him worriedly how confident Tolliver sounded. Dude missed Uncle and found him coming back from Keeno's stall. Billy's expression was grim. "I thought there was something different about Tolliver's horse," the old man said. "Remember, the horse we saw at the barn had sickle hocks and toed out? Well, this horse has straight hocks and is straight in front. Has the excellent conformation of a sprinting Thoroughbred. This is the real Keeno. Tolliver's pulled the switch on us."

Dude swallowed hard. "So Texas Jack beat Tolliver's slow horse?"

"Exactly, and we've got a tough race on our hands." Billy turned to Coyote. "Look for Burns to pull something on the turns. He'll try

101

to intimidate you. So be on the lookout, Coyote, pardner." The old Uncle Billy was talking now.

"Do that I will, Grandfather." He leaped to the saddle before Dude could give him a hand. Dude mounted and attached the lead shank to the Judge's bridle, a totally unnecessary precaution as gentle as the bay gelding was, but ponying a runner was part of racetrack protocol and the crowd liked it, particularly when a runner pranced and arched its head.

There were oohs and much gawking when the people in the stands sighted Coyote. A venturesome boy ran out on the track and up to Coyote, yelling, "Are you a real Indian?" and Coyote made as if to grab the boy's hair and the boy took abrupt flight. Fleeing to the rail, he looked back and Coyote grinned at him. "Heap good boy. Me like."

The starting line, midway of the stands, was also the finish mark for today's half-mile race. Dude spied Overman standing at the pole-marked line with the judge Tolliver had called from the crowd at the paddock. This man spoke to another beside him and Dude gave a start. It was the camp prowler, evidently the horse trader's other judge. Well, the outfit had had no luck so far, losing the inside post position and the starter, and now Tolliver had a two-to-one margin with the judges if the race came down to a nose-to-nose finish. His concern deepening, Dude released the Judge and rode to the infield to watch the race from horseback.

There had been scant time for Dude to eye Keeno in the saddling paddock. From here the chestnut gelding had the leggy lines of a long-striding sprinter. A good-looking horse. Also high-strung and starting to sweat. So the noisy crowd bothered him. Another reason for Tolliver's late arrival.

After the track was cleared of spectators, Fargo motioned the riders to circle back and move to the starting line. As the horses turned toward Fargo, Dude saw Burns look at Coyote, his mouth working. Coyote ignored him.

They pranced nearer the line. All at once the Judge broke ahead and the taut Keeno broke also, sprinting down the track, while Burns fought the reins. Keeno ran almost to the turn before Burns had his horse under control. Meanwhile, Judge Blair, unruffled, under a tight hold, head high, and that look in his eyes, had loped only some fifty yards. Coyote reined him around and trotted back as if nothing had happened.

Dude felt a smile split his face. Coyote had deliberately broken ahead to draw Keeno off, knowing Fargo wouldn't call it a start. That was one way to wear down the other horse, and to offset the disadvantage of drawing the outside position.

Tolliver rushed up to Fargo and spoke, his words lost in the murmur of the crowd, and then Fargo spoke to Coyote, who shrugged stoically and pointed at his horse. Burns's mouth started working again the moment he took his horse back for another walk-up. Again, Coyote ignored him.

Burns, still mouthing, walked Keeno faster. Coyote kept the Judge even. Fargo held both hands up to slow the horses. They were nearly at the line. That was when Burns, suddenly, heeled his horse ahead and Fargo shouted and brought his hat down.

Dude's anger soared. The start should be called back. Fargo had allowed Burns a half-length lead at the break. It was all planned.

Even so, Coyote had Judge Blair's head at Keeno's withers and the race was on. That margin held going into the turn. There, the Judge changed into the left lead, but so did Keeno.

Coming out on the backstretch, Judge Blair changed back to the right lead and closed the gap. Little by little, Coyote began to move his mount ahead. He had a length on Keeno when they sprinted into the far turn. They seemed like dancers as both horses changed leads almost together, Keeno, on the inside, regaining what he had lost on the back straightaway.

Dude worried. Keeno could run.

As the horses turned for home, running head to head, Dude saw the Judge change leads and, quite suddenly, move out a head. He was going to pass Keeno.

Then Dude could see it happening, just as Billy had feared. Keeno, feeling Burns's whip, charged up and closed on Judge Blair. In another moment Burns was drawing his horse to the right side, forcing Coyote wide toward the outside rail so the Judge couldn't pass. The horses brushed, nearly colliding. The same tactic, Dude caught, that Burns had used on Miss Tulip.

His concern shot up when Coyote seemed to ease his horse off the pace a little, though not breaking stride, which would have ended the race right there. Instead, Coyote let Burns drive past, still coming out into Judge Blair. Was Coyote yielding to save his horse from injury? The thought flashed through Dude, when Coyote, unexpectedly, swung his horse to the inside for the rail. At the same instant Dude heard the Comanche's screeching whoop and saw Judge Blair, with open track before him, find his footing again. A few jumps and he was running like a wild horse.

Burns, with a startled sideways glance, straightened his horse.

There was about a hundred yards of track left when the horses headed each other again. The crowd was screaming. An open horse race now, Dude saw. Keeno came flying under Burns's desperate, unbroken whipping, but Coyote was whooping at every jump of his horse.

Along the inside rail, Judge Blair seemed to flatten out, eyes bulging, mane flying, his white-sock hooves barely skimming the track, nostrils flaring, ears laid back, running straight. One of Uncle's lines leaped to Dude's mind: *Like an arrow from a bow.* And Coyote's own highest praise for the horse he rode: *Like buffalo runner.* This dark bay horse of unknown breeding with the brilliant speed and the great heart to match.

Stride by stride, Judge Blair was drawing away. Half a length now. A length. A length and a half. And there the hard-charging Keeno hung, despite Burns's frantic whipping.

Dude had tears in his eyes as they tore across the finish line, as he saw Coyote glance back at Burns and make the sign for scalped.

Dude rode over to Billy, who called out in a happy haze, above the still-noisy crowd, "This is what it's all about, Dude, pardner. Why, I feel thirty years younger. Did you ever see the Ju — I mean Hoot Owl — run better or show more gameness? Or Coyote ever ride a smarter race? They ripped that half mile apart in forty-six flat, after forced wide and losing ground. I clocked 'em." The clear blue eyes hardened, the saintly features firmed. "I'd like to take that Burns down a notch or two — will, if I can find him. You bet I am." He slapped the breast of his coat, and Dude saw the bulge of a handgun.

"Never mind," Dude said carefully, to assure him. "I'll take care of that. There Burns goes now, headin' for town. And where's Tolliver? I want our money and I want it now, like we agreed."

A jubilant Overman joined them. More farmers crowded around. "A great day for us farm folks. Tolliver finally got skinned and it was done fair and square, which makes it all the sweeter. Oughta run 'em both outa town after the way Burns tried to force your horse into the outside rail. Same stunt he pulled on Miss Tulip."

Dude was scanning the crowd. "I don't see Tolliver anywhere."

Overman said, "I saw him run to his horse just after the horses crossed the finish line. Bet he skedaddled to his office."

"He's welchin' on his bet. I'm goin' after 'im!" Billy was in motion with Dude's words, darting through the crowd for his buggy on the other side of the track. Overman shouted after him, "Hold on, Doc! I'm going with you. We're all going!"

Dude reached the barn first. In the distance, he could see Burns loping Keeno out of town in the direction of Tolliver's farm. Billy dashed up in the buggy, Overman seated beside him, after them a straggle of farmers in wagons, buggies, and horseback.

Dude ran to the office, followed by Billy and Overman. It was empty. He lurched out into the long breezeway and strode rapidly along it. A horse stirred in a dark stall. A saddled horse, he saw. Stepping in, he felt the saddler's shoulder, and his hand came away wet with sweat. So Tolliver was around here somewhere.

Walking slower, Dude looked in each stall, passed what he took to be a closed grain bin, and went out to the corral, occupied by two worn-out draft horses, and came back. By now the barn was overflowing with talkative farmers. Dude paused. He was considering searching the hayloft when he remembered that he had gone past the storage bin without looking inside. Its door was closed. He jerked on the handle; the door wouldn't budge. He yanked again, more forcibly, and felt the door give a little and spring back, as if someone were holding it. This time he jerked with both hands and the door flew open. Tolliver stood before him, trying to look puzzled at all this.

"Come out," Dude told him.

"You're trespassing, McQuinn."

"Whatever happened to *friend McQuinn?*" said Dude, sarcastically. "I want the five hundred dollars you owe us."

Tolliver's round face turned green in the murky light. "Your horse is a ringer. You pulled a ringer on me." He stepped out of the bin and started to walk off.

Dude caught him by the shirt front and spun him around and threw him against the bin. "Our horse is the same horse you first saw with the pack on him. And you – you switched horses on us. Texas Jack beat your look-alike slow horse. When we bet big, you switched to the real Keeno. Besides, Burns tried to force our horse wide into the rail. Now pay up!"

Overman got into it. "If you expect to stay in business in Blue Springs, Tolliver, you'd better pay up. You've skinned folks along enough." A supporting chorus backed him up.

In actual pain, Tolliver took a roll of green-backs from the front pocket and peeled off some bills. His face was sickly when he handed

109

them to Dude, who counted each one carefully. "You're fifty dollars short, *Honest Abe.*"

Hurting even more, Tolliver removed another greenback, and as he grudgingly passed it to Dude, a bafflement rose through his voice. "All I can say is, that's some ol' packhorse."

"Hoot Owl runs a heap better with the pack off," Dude said. "Let's go, Uncle."

CHAPTER 5

Just an Ol' Wagon Horse

At last, there in the sunny distance lay the little farming town of Petersburg, sprawled on the rolling Illinois prairie. Like an oasis, Dude thought. Their long journey had been interrupted only once since leaving Blue Springs, when Judge Blair, matched against the local favorite of Sedalia, Missouri, had won by daylight at 350 yards, running, for a change, under his real name. Also for a change – Dude had to grin at the comfortable memory – the outfit had collected the bets leisurely and had not had to hurry out of town looking back.

The outfit halted and Billy said, "Now, Dude, I recall one time you said a little molasses never hurt anybody. Such as the time you put in the paper that my family tree dates back to the Plymouth Colony, which got me in a peck of trouble with a certain determined widow woman. Well, we're in foundation quarter-horse country now, where the boss runners came from. So I don't want you introducing me as so-and-so the great horseman, or the veterinarian of some high-sounding, never-was horse farm. They'd catch on in a minute. Savvy?"

Dude put on a penitent face. "Whatever you say, Uncle."

"All we have to go on is the name of this Si Eckert fella. Didn't that Texas cowman tell you any more than that?"

"Like I said, all he knew was that the Judge had been shipped down to Texas from Petersburg in a carload of workstock to a road contractor and the Judge showed collar and trace-chain marks."

"Pretty obvious," said Billy, suspiciously, "not all those horses were workstock. Did he say this Si Eckert shipped the horses?"

"He didn't say. Just gave me Eckert's name."

"That maybe Eckert would know something?"

"Didn't even say that. Just said, 'Here's a name you might find interestin',' and he seemed to hold back on that."

"Hold back?"

"Like he wasn't sure he should."

"There was some skullduggery somewhere along the line, else why would a once-in-a-lifetime horse like the Judge be sold with a bunch of workhorses, and let's add some saddlers."

"Right, Grandfather," Coyote added.

"He's a compact horse with a powerful butt," Dude said. "He can pull a wagon. A man wouldn't know he could run unless he just happened to try him."

"Well, he's sure not a draft-horse type. He shows excellent breeding. A fine head. Good balance. Good bone. Beauty and style. Smooth shoulders and hindquarters — and that look of eagles."

"When he's not in harness or a pack on 'im," Dude qualified.

"What you're saying is, Dude, that he doesn't look like a rangy, long-legged Thoroughbred. True. But keep in mind that the great Janus, recognized as the forefather of the quarter horse, a Thoroughbred imported into Virginia in the 1750s, wasn't a rangy type either, standing fourteen and three-quarter hands." The old man's blue eyes began to shine in that way he had when feeling an oncoming lecture. "The old-time broadsides describe Janus as having great muscle and bone, very compact, powerful quarters, and very swift. A bullet horse. He passed those desirable qualities onto his progeny. They say his stamp was so unmistakable, you could tell the Janus blood at a glance. He not only sired sprinters who could run a hole in the wind, he sired stayers when clean-bred mares were brought to his court. You know, a horse doesn't have to stand sixteen hands to have bottom. Now, take the Judge. We've never sent him out to go more than six furlongs. But I'm confident he can handle a distance of ground, a mile or more, if we lengthen him out. Why? Because speed always helps out bottom, as the old saying goes. So does his twenty-five-foot stride and his ability to change leads." He shook his head, chuckling. "Got off the subject, didn't I?" and slanted a condoning eye at Dude. "If we don't do all the talking, maybe we can pick up a lead listening around the horse barns and the wagonyard. Meanwhile, maybe you can find that cigaret paper you wrote the password on."

With Texas Jack and one of the sorrels tied to the tailgate, and Judge Blair now a member of the wagon team, the outfit drew into the town's wagonyard, a larger than usual enclosure for vehicles and teams run by a typical sociable proprietor, a thickset, ruddy-faced man in patched overalls and peaked straw hat who said his name was Ike Arnold. For an opening to conversation, Dude purchased oats and hay.

Arnold, a keen eye on Texas Jack, remarked,

"I'd say you carry a nice running horse."

"Oh," said Dude, as if it mattered not, "he can run a little when the wind's behind him and his feet don't hurt."

"This used to be the hub of short racing." Arnold was proud. "Though most of the old studs, like Dan Tucker and Peter McCue, were sold to southwestern horsemen, there's still plenty of fast runners in this part of the state. Come Saturday, there'll be horsemen in town. You can match a race quicker'n you can work up a sweat. Be glad to pass the word about your horse."

Dude shrugged. *Never act eager.*

"Just passing through?" Arnold pried, affable about it.

"Just travelin' around for my health. You know . . . the open sky, campfire cookin'. Does wonders."

Dude and Billy walked back to the wagon. The old man spoke, reprovingly, "You can't help telling those stretchers, can you, Dude, pardner?"

Dude slid an affectionate arm around the thin shoulders. "Only this time it was on myself, instead of William Tecumseh Lockhart." He would never say again, as he had in the past, they were traveling because "Dr. Lockhart" was "poorly."

During the afternoon, while Billy napped and Coyote read, Dude strolled to the main part of town, hoping for some clue to Si Eckert. He idled down Main Street and back, up and back the principal side streets, looking at the signs on the storefronts. There were two livery barns, neither bearing Eckert's name; likewise the one blacksmith shop.

At the Union Saloon, where he found himself the lone customer at this hour, he ordered Old Green River whiskey. "You got a right nice little town here," Dude said to open the conversation.

"We like it," the rotund, middle-aged bartender said, full of local pride, blowing on a glass prior to shining it with a towel. "Naturally, Saturday's our big day. A horse race or two. Livestock auction. Reckon you noticed our new pens, just east of town." Dude nodded agreeably, though he hadn't. "All that blowin' and bettin' sure makes throats dry. Rest of the week you could fire a cannon down Main Street and not hit a soul."

"Reckon considerable horses change hands at the auction?"

"Some. More cows than horses. Folks tend to hang on to their good horses." He displayed a toothy smile. "Unless somebody comes along with the right amount of money."

"Many horses shipped out of here?" Dude asked, working around.

"Now and then."

"I mean is there a local man that buys horses, mostly workhorses, mixed in with other horses, say, and contracts the horses out of town? Reason I ask," Dude amplified, "I'm travelin' through with a little horse outfit and I might sell a stout wagon horse I bought down the road. Sometimes there's a big demand for heavy horses where there's a lot of road buildin', and to fill a contract a man buys up quite a bunch."

"In here," the barkeep said, "what I hear mostly is whose horse won and whose horse lost and who's gonna run next Saturday."

Dude finished his Old Green River, had another, and leaning on the bar, friendly like, asked, "Can I buy you a drink?"

"Thank you, sir, but it's against the rules of the house. However, I will have a mild cigar," and he reached into a box of Pittsburgh Stogies and took out a frazzled cigar and stuck it in the pocket of his shirt. The house cigar, Dude knew, which would go back into the box when he left.

"I well understand your forbearance, sir, in the face of temptation," Dude said, and re-marked further, "You know, the more I see of your town, the better I like it. Be a likely place for a man to settle down for his sundown years."

"You couldn't pick a more Christian place. I reckon Petersburg has more churches than most towns this size. The boys used to run races down Main Street, but things got a little rowdy and the town folks, urged on by the preachers, cut it out. Now we run north of town, and you should see them same preachers sneak out there to watch the horses run."

Dude was chuckling. "Any preachers ever sneak in the back door for a little toddy?"

"One did, and it wasn't just for a toddy. Straight whiskey. Always slipped in early. He called it his morning phlegm cutter, medicine for his catarrh. The good reverend is no longer with us. Up in Chicago. I hear tell he's got him a big church and drives a fancy trotter."

"Well, I never heard of anybody that got hurt goin' to church," said Dude, piously. "I understand this is mighty fine farmin' country, too. Cornstalks so high a farmer has to get on a ladder to pull the ears."

"Just maybe on a footstool," the bartender said, pleased at the exaggeration.

Dude finished his whiskey, figuring that he had broken the ice and now was the time to spring his big question. "Yes, I do cotton to your town, all right. Which reminds me. A friend down in Texas, on the Salt Fork of the Brazos, said if I went through Petersburg to look up an old friend of his by the name of Si Eckert. Reckon you know 'im?" he waited expectantly.

"Eckert, Eckert?" the man repeated and shook his head. "Never heard of 'im."

"My friend will be disappointed. They were bosom pals."

"I've lived here all my life and never heard of a Si Eckert."

"Maybe he had the wrong town," said Dude, crestfallen. "See you again, friend." He paid for his drinks and the house cigar and then left.

Entering the wagonyard and noticing Ike Arnold bent over a ledger in the office, Dude stopped in the doorway. Arnold looked up, his face obliging.

"Been meanin' to ask you about a man here," Dude said. "A Si Eckert. I was told down in Texas that he handles a lot of good horses. Ships some out of state. I'd like to see what he has for sale."

Eyes narrowing in thought, Arnold looked down and up. "Si Eckert? Afraid I can't place him."

"Maybe he was here some years back and moved?"

"There was a farmer out west of here. . . . No, his name was Edelman. . . . Still don't place a Si Eckert, and I've been here thirty-odd years."

"Looks like my friend was wrong. Much obliged, anyway."

"That's odd," said Billy, when Dude reported his findings. "In a town this size, everybody knows everybody and everybody's business."

"Well, one swaller sure don't make a summer," Dude said. "Or . . . somethin' like that. How does that go, Coyote?"

"I believe it is, 'One swallow alone does not a summer make,' if quoting you are Miguel de Cervantes?"

"Cervantes, sure. That's exactly the *hombre* I had in mind."

Coyote smiled forgivingly. "Close you were, white father."

"What I mean is, that bartender and Ike Arnold may know everybody in town, but they can't know *every* horseman that comes to town throughout the whole county."

"Let's keep our ears to the ground," Billy said. "There'll be horsemen in town Saturday."

After breakfast Saturday morning the outfit curried and brushed Texas Jack and posted him at the wagon, out where passersby couldn't miss racy-looking horseflesh. Judge Blair, showing harness streaks from the peroxide treatment, was tied in front also with one of the sorrels. Presently, the first arrivals passed on the dusty street. Later, wagons, buggies, and horsemen grew to a steady stream, some farmers leading horses and mules, some driving a few head of bawling cows. Everybody seemed to enjoy the sight of the sleek bay racehorse, but nobody stopped.

Past eleven o'clock a farmer driving a light wagon trailing a chunky, high-stepping gray horse came by the wagonyard. The man glanced at Texas Jack, held the look, and pulled up, still looking. As if on impulse, he reined the team across the street into the wagonyard and drew up. Stepping down, he came over to where Dude and Billy were watching the incoming trade crowd.

"Morning," the man said. "Couldn't miss noticing your horse. Looks like a runner."

"Same for your smooth gray geldin'," Dude said. "Looks like he might scatter the dust a little."

The farmer seemed to puff up a bit at that. "Gray Boy won here last week. Daylighted the Springfield Mare. My name's Bert Hooker." He held out his hand and Dude gave his name and introduced Billy.

Hooker was a spare man, his brown, bearded face sharply cast. Yet he seemed almost shy in his approach. A manner, Dude figured from experience, behind which Hooker hid the keen mind of a sharpshooting trader and fast-horse owner.

"Mind if I take a look-see at your horse?" Hooker asked, still shy, and when Dude said, "Go right ahead," Hooker took a slow turn around Texas Jack, clasped his hands in thought, and drifted back to Dude, saying, "Your horse looks as keen up close as he does at a distance."

"Well," said Dude, heavy on the regret, "I wish I could say the same today for his runnin'. He's all sored up."

"You mean he can't run?"

"Afraid so."

"Sorry to hear that. I was hoping maybe I could run Gray Boy at you."

Dude rubbed his chin, hitched at his wide belt, and puckered his lips. He said nothing for a short spell, then he sighed. "If you're hankerin' for a race, I might slap a saddle on that ol' bay wagon horse there."

Hooker turned that way. Judge Blair stood head drooping, indifferent to the commotion of horses and mules passing on the street, the jangling of harness and trace chains and the rumbling of wagons.

"You'd run *him?*" Hooker said, surprised.

"Funny thing about that ol' horse. He can pull a wagon, you can work cattle on him, and he can run down the road a piece when the spirit moves him. He's also a good kid horse. He's what we call a usin' horse down in Texas."

Hooker showed further surprise. "You've come all the way from Texas?"

Dude nodded. "From the Salt Fork of the Brazos."

Hooker pondered, and bit by bit Dude recognized the emerging expression of a horseman who figured he had the advantage. Hooker then said, "How far would you aim to run?"

"First, that is if you're sure you want to run, I'd better take a look at your horse." Hooker agreed to that with an inviting wave of his arm, and Dude and Billy moved across to the chunky gray, which turned out to have hocks too close together and a shoulder that sat too straight. Otherwise, Gray Boy met the eye favorably, being well muscled and sporting a fine, proud head. While they circled to the far side of the gelding, Billy murmured, "Match him long. This horse runs short."

Drifting back, Dude drawled slowly, "Maybe we can treaty with you." From his detailed inspection and Billy's tip, Dude judged that Gray Boy's best distance was probably not more than 250 yards, 300 at the farthest.

Hooker, eagerly, his pride puffing up again, asked, "What do you make of my Gray Boy?"

"A fine individual, sir," Dude said, laying it on. "Perfect conformation. A fine head. Unless my eye fails me, I'd say he carries Steel Dust blood."

"His grandsire was Gray Fox, a son of Steel Dust."

"Now you're talkin' racehorse. Makes me want to back off. A wagon horse against Steel Dust blood! Neighbor, you better be generous or we can't begin to treaty. How far might you want to go?"

"Two fifty."

"It takes a wagon horse a while to get goin'," Dude countered, minding Billy's appraisal. "What say we run on down there for a full quarter mile?"

Hooker stood back, his face changing. "Can't do that. Tell you what, being neighborly, I'll raise the distance to three hundred yards. What say?"

Dude lifted a light laugh. "Guess we'll just have to pass, Mr. Hooker," and he started to walk off to the other side of the wagon. He had taken only three steps when

Hooker's eager voice caught him. "I might go three-fifty. Not an inch more."

"Uncle," said Dude, drifting back, "Do you think we ought to match this race against Steel Dust blood? I feel a mite weak."

Billy spread his hands. "Your horse, Dude. The match is up to you. However, I wouldn't bet the wagon. I'd hate to have to walk back to the Salt Fork."

Dude turned to Hooker. "How about fifty dollars at three-fifty?"

The farmer sniffed. "It's a long way from my place to Petersburg. Fifty dollars ain't worth the trip. I won't bet less than a hundred."

Dude kicked at a clod on the ground. "All right. A hundred dollars. Catch weights?"

"Catch weights." Hooker liked that. "Two o'clock all right with you? The track's north of town."

"Two o'clock is fine. That leaves the starter and the finish line judges."

"The mayor starts all the races. That way there's no argument. Both sides pick one judge and flip for the third."

"Dr. Lockhart will be my judge. You toss the coin, Mr. Hooker, and I'll call it." When the farmer looked surprised, Dude said, "I trust you, Mr. Hooker."

When Hooker flipped a half dollar, Dude

called, "Heads." The coin hit and flopped and Dude, seeing "tails," wondered where his luck had gone, starting with Blue Springs.

After Hooker had rattled off down the busy street, Billy said, "Reason I said match him long is because a horse with a straight shoulder has limited reach. He's not a long strider, which makes him work harder than a horse with a good sloping shoulder. He can't go a distance of ground. Same for a horse with the hocks in too close. Still, those defects don't rule out speed and heart. I'd like to know the distance when Gray Boy daylighted the Springfield Mare."

Dude listened with a sense of encouragement. Except for his thinness, Uncle was now about where he was in the early days of the outfit, seeing at a single walk around a horse what many horsemen would not detect; then discussing what he had found in a logical way, drawing on his long experience as a horseman and veterinarian – maybe self-taught . . . Dude would never know – Uncle not forgetting the unfathomable: what made a horse run.

"Kinda like at a country dance," Dude said. "Sometimes the girl with the plainest face is the best dancer."

Billy regarded him as he might a small boy.

"I guess that's not a bad analogy for an Alamo Texan."

To Dude's wonder, the crowd overflowed both sides of the long straightaway, augmented by the usual half-mile bullring track.

"I believe the whole town is out here and half the county," Billy observed. Kids ran loose, as frisky as yearlings in a pasture, and bonneted women and straw-hatted farmers watched from buggies and wagons and the planked grandstand, which boasted an exception to the usual country racing track — a roof.

In the paddock, ringed by chattering spectators, Hooker was walking a tense Gray Boy about. As Dude, Billy, and Coyote took Judge Blair to a saddling stall, Hooker led his horse in next to the outfit. Immediately, a man strode briskly over, officious from his broad hat to his black suit and polished boots.

"I'm Mayor Gregg, the starter," he informed them, his tone formal. "I start everything lap-and-tap. If one horse breaks ahead before I say 'Go,' I call 'em back with this whistle." He blew it shrilly, causing Gray Boy to dance. He cleared his throat. "Mr. Hooker has heard me say this before, but I always point it out to visiting horsemen as a matter of civic pride. That on this track the great Peter McCue ran the fastest quarter mile ever recorded, twenty-one seconds flat. Two officials caught him in that, a third clocked him in twenty-one and a fifth."

"A truly great horse," Billy said, reverently.

"All right, gentlemen," Gregg said. "Take your post parade and I'll meet you at the starting line."

Dude was ponying Judge Blair out of the paddock, past the noisy spectators, when a burly man wearing a yellow-and-white checkered coat and a brown bowler left the crowd and stared hard at Judge Blair. Excitement flared in his eyes. He snapped his fingers and faced the crowd, his voice high. "Anybody want to bet on the gray?" Voices answered at once. "Over here! Here! I'll bet two-to-one on Gray Boy! I'll bet three-to-one!"

"Taken!" the man with the checkered coat called back, waving a roll of greenbacks.

Looking at him, Dude was reminded of a whiskey drummer.

Gray Boy was already on the track, a light-weight lad in the irons, Hooker on a bay pony horse.

"Look at that ol' wagon horse!" somebody jeered as Judge Blair appeared in front of the stands, the peroxide rubbings still showing as harness marks on his hindquarters. Dude tipped his big white hat at the crowd and displayed his rodeo arena smile, while Coyote, naked to the waist, dressed again like a Comanche warrior, ignored the scoffing and stared straight ahead, impassive, arms folded, letting the looped reins hang free.

"Why, that's a real live Indian!" a woman cried, and Dude, smiling broadly and raising his hat in salute, said, "We're all real, ma'am," which evoked her laughter.

The post parade completed, Dude released Judge Blair and found Billy on the infield side of the starting line. He looked nervous and concerned, which brought out his leanness.

"You all right, Uncle?"

"I never take winning for granted, even with the top horse. Anything can happen in a horse race, even if you're matched against a dray horse. I think Gray Boy is a flat-out sprinter, conformation defects and all."

Looking down the long straightaway, Dude saw the riders turn the runners and move toward the starting line, where Mayor Gregg awaited them, an intimidating figure of authority, as if daring a jockey to jump his horse off too soon. The horses looked fairly lapped, but not enough, the Judge in front. Gregg's shrill whistle sounded. The horses pranced back, wheeled, and came on again.

Suddenly they were off, an even break.

At the same moment, to Dude's alarm, the ground seemed to break out from under Judge Blair, and he broke raggedly, off stride. Gray Boy was off quickly, running like a deer, already two lengths in front.

Coyote straightened his horse, got him righted, and took up the chase.

For another hundred yards the distance between the horses stayed the same, Gray Boy striding evenly, Judge Blair apparently struggling to find himself.

Dude waited for Coyote's whoop. It didn't come. And Dude worried. What was wrong? The Judge appeared to be laboring. Had he hurt himself when the ground gave way under his usual powerful lunge at the break? That fear persisted.

Come on, Coyote. Don't wait too long. Get him goin'!

In moments, Dude saw why Coyote had not rushed his mount. Judge Blair was beginning to stride more smoothly, to take to the track. Coyote was settling him, bringing him on, giving him a little time before he made his run.

It happened at the two-fifty pole, as Dude heard Coyote whoop. At once the pace of the dark bay gelding quickened. Dude could see him flattening and straightening out as Coyote took dead aim at the fleet Gray Boy sprinting down the middle of the track.

Coyote whooped again, and when he did Judge Blair seemed to take off, those fox ears laid back, at last himself. With a burst of speed, he cut Gray Boy's lead to one length. He was running full out by now. He was, Dude realized, running the other horse down. The boy on the gray must have heard the bay coming, because he jerked his head and snapped a backward look and started whipping righthanded. The two horses drew abreast and for a moment Gray Boy ran with the Judge, stride for stride, two game horses fighting it out. Then the bay horse put his head in front.

About fifty yards from the finish line Judge Blair was opening up daylight with every twenty-five-foot stride. He ran so low his hooves seemed to be skimming the track. No lost motion. The crowd was shrieking for Gray Boy to come on. All at once the shouting raveled off.

Judge Blair was still drawing away when he crossed the line.

Dude, breathing hard, watched as his horse tore on another hundred yards before Coyote could bring him to hand, still full of run, fighting the bit to run some more.

The horses were trotting back to the line

when Dude, hearing an extremely loud and raucous voice, caught sight of the man in the checkered coat and bowler on the other side of the track at the foot of the grandstand. He was waving his arms and shouting and laughing, a chortling laugh. "Call that bay an ol' wagon horse. Folks, that's none other than Judge Blair — fastest quarter horse in the Southwest. I saw 'im beat the great Mexican speed mare, Yolanda, in Juarez, Mexico. The Indian was on 'im. I'd know those two anywhere. Just an ol' wagon horse? Ho, ho!"

In the following confusion and gabbling, Dude finally sighted Hooker still on the pony horse and rode over to him for the payoff.

"Your horse is a ringer!" Hooker shouted. "Damned if I'll pay off!"

"You'll pay off here and now," Dude told him, aware of the crowd gathering around them.

"But your horse is no wagon horse. I've heard of Judge Blair. Wouldn't run if I'd knowed."

"Now, look here, Mr. Hooker," said Dude, speaking reasonably, "I never said he wasn't Judge Blair, did I? I did not. I said he was a wagon horse, and he does pull the wagon sometimes. And he can work cattle and kids can ride him, like I said. He's an all-around horse. Furthermore, the ground broke out from under him at the break — you saw that. He won despite that. We beat you fair and square."

"That's right, Bert," a farmer spoke up. "It was fair and square and then some. A great race. Ain't been a horse like that around here since Peter McCue. Did anybody clock the race?"

"I did," a voice replied and a man pushed forward. "He ran on down there in seventeen and two-fifths."

The first farmer whistled and then Hooker, subdued, unhappy, in silence, took out a worn leather wallet, paid Dude a hundred dollars, and rode off, followed by the youngster on Gray Boy.

Billy was there in the crowd milling curiously around Judge Blair and the old man went up to Coyote. "I saw the ground break out from under him."

"The track was soft," Coyote said, dismounting. "I think the Judge hurt himself. Limping, he is. Favors, he does, his right hind leg."

Billy moved with Coyote's words, eyeballing the horse, peering and muttering, while he carefully, gently ran a hand down the muscles of the leg in question. He stood back. "I see it now. Cut his right cannon. Did that when he almost went down and had to change leads. Let's cool him off and take him back to camp.

You took your time getting him settled, Coyote, pardner. That was the only way. He had to start his run all over again. We'd have lost a much shorter race."

The crowd was breaking up, still gawking wonderingly at the dark bay runner, still talking about the race. Before the outfit could make its way through, an old man about Billy's age, and just as lively, strolled up, saying, "Well, Billy, I see you haven't lost your touch with runnin' horses."

Billy jerked around. For a fraction there was no recognition in the clear blue eyes. That, and for another interval it struck Dude that Uncle wished himself elsewhere, followed by a smile, a sort of tentative smile, and he thrust out his hand in a manner that swept away the gap of years and said, "Howdy, Poge Yates. Like olden times. How are you?"

"On the lead. On the lead."

"Same old Poge. I don't own the horse. My pardner here does, Dude McQuinn."

Poge Yates was short and wiry, wide in the shoulders and slim at the hips, a banty-rooster man, whose brown eyes set deep under thick, gray brows, projected a certain mockery, a cockiness. Gray stubble fringed his square jaw from ear to ear. He looked neither prosperous nor down on his luck. More like nondescript in his worn felt hat, blue shirt, and gray trousers on suspenders. Dude guessed him a former jockey.

"After today," Yates said, "guess you know you can't match this Judge Blair around these parts anymore? You beat a good horse. By this time tomorrow you couldn't match Judge Blair from here to Springfield. Y'know, moccasin telegraph as they used to say. Nothin' spreads faster than word about a fast horse. Hell, he's another Peter McCue."

"No matter," Billy shrugged. "We'll be drifting on before long."

"Which way?"

Billy shrugged again.

Yates waited until the crowd had thinned some more around Judge Blair. "But there is a way you can run him anywhere," he said, lowering his voice. "All nice and proper. Matched or on organized tracks."

"How's that?" Billy asked, slanting him a dubious look.

"Come out to my place in the morning and I'll show you. Two miles east of town. You'll see my mailbox." He strolled away, a swagger to his walk.

"Same old Poge," Billy said. "Some folks never change." Whatever Uncle was thinking, Dude sensed, he didn't like it.

CHAPTER 6

Si Eckert, Where Are You?

They rode in the buggy out to the Yates farm and turned at the mailbox into the lane. Observing the white house tucked away in the grove of oak trees, the fat red barn and big corral, the numerous sheds, and the well-kept rail fences guarding the fields, Billy said, "Looks like Poge has come up in the world since I first knew him."

Dude waited for the old man to say where, and when he didn't, Dude, prying, said, "That's interesting. And where was that, Uncle?"

"Now, did I say?"

Expecting that, Dude reckoned it was another promising sign of Uncle's virtual recovery. Like in the early days of the outfit, when he guarded his obscure past.

Yates met them in the yard and invited them

into the house and led them through the parlor to the back porch, where he brought out a jug and glasses and gestured, "Help yourselves, boys."

Billy, taking his whiskey straight, smacked his lips and, with a taunting little grin, said, "Poge, this is better stuff than you used to drink," and Yates, equal to the remark, said, "Now, Billy, you know the old sayin': There's no such thing as bad whiskey. Some's just better than others."

"And, vice versa, some's worse than others. I recollect one time paying as high as twenty dollars for a bottle and I didn't mind a bit."

"Didn't mind? That's highway robbery."

"I didn't look at it that way. The local temperance society had made even bad whiskey scarce. That was when I learned the true value of good Kentucky Bourbon."

A prim little woman some years younger than Yates, her plain face wearing a pleasant smile, came out on the porch from the kitchen. Her dark brown hair was pulled back over her ears and knotted on her neck. Her gray, friendly eyes also revealed a directness, as if little escaped her notice.

Yates called her Elsie and, somewhat awkwardly, introduced the visitors.

Billy stood and bowed like a jackknife. "Pleased to meet you, Elsie," And Dude, likewise bowing, said, "It's a pleasure, ma'am."

She blushed like a schoolgirl. "Poge," she said, "these men are gentlemen. Not a-tall like some you bring around. Why, they even took off their hats."

"I knew Billy years ago. Him and Dude are pardners. Dude's horse beat Gray Boy yesterday."

"Whatever they are, they are just in time for dinner, which won't be long coming."

With that pronouncement, she left them.

"One thing about Elsie," Yates said, "is she puts it on the table at high noon sharp. No sooner, no later — and you'd better be there. No goin' down to the barn before you eat. No goin' to the outhouse. No sayin', 'I'll be there in a little bit.' She means now."

He passed the jug again and he and Billy chatted awhile about old-time horses and races, and when there was a pause, Yates went inside and returned with a folded sheet of paper which he handed to Billy.

After scanning it quickly, then intently, Billy looked in question at Yates. "This is the Certificate of Registration for the Duke of Dexter. Says he's by the Duke of Highlands, out of Trixie M."

"It is — and duly registered with the Jockey Club."

"So?"

"Did you read the description?"

"I did. A six-year-old dark bay gelding with a blazed face and socks on the hind feet."

"Does that sound familiar?"

"There are a lot of dark bay horses with white socks. Mighty pretty. The one I know best is Judge Blair, with four socks."

"But you can't match him around here anymore."

"Believe you pointed that out yesterday."

"But you could with Duke's papers. You see, he died two days ago. My stallion got into his paddock, attacked him, and Duke, who had periodic moon blindness, tried to get away and ran into a tree and broke his neck."

Dude got it at the same time Billy said, "Sorry to hear that, Poge. What you mean is run Judge Blair as the Duke of Dexter?"

"Why not? It's not unusual around here to have two sets of papers on a fast quarter horse. That way he can run as a Thoroughbred on recognized tracks. Remember Carrie Nation, how she could run like a singed cat? She held the world's record for five-eighths of a mile. On the long tracks she was campaigned as the Belle of Oakford, a little town north of here.

Won, too. Some Texan bought her."

Billy was silent for a while. "What do you think, Dude? The Judge is your horse."

"We can't run him if we don't, though I can't say I like the idea. However, it seems to be the way the game is played around here."

"Believe I'd like to know more about Duke's overall conformation before we take his papers," Billy said. "You happen to have a picture of him, Poge?"

"I do. I'll get it."

Looking at the photograph with Billy, a side view of the horse, Dude saw a blaze-faced, rangy individual with straight shoulder, whereas the Judge's was sloping, and a horse that had calf knees and was goose-rumped, defects the Judge did not have, and socks on all feet.

Billy frowned. "There are some very evident differences, and sure as hell some old fella who can't remember his own name will sidle up and say, 'The Duke of Dexter I remember was sixteen hands. This horse is fifteen. And the Duke I remember was rangy. This horse is compact.'"

"And what will you say to that?" Yates asked, with a conniving grin.

"I'll say, 'Why, mister, I bought this horse off Poge Yates, over in Illinois, and he was always tight with feed and worked his horses to the bone. The Duke looks compact now because we feed him the way you're supposed to feed a racehorse.'" Grinning at his *touché*, Billy sat back and rested his chin on his hand. "But I can't make up for Duke's straight shoulder and goose rump. Too, I'll have to black out the socks on the Judge's forelegs when we run him."

"Still carry a brush and some paint, don't you, Billy boy?" Yates asked slyly, and passed the jug, and Billy, after a round, replied, "Does a singer forget how to sing? Does a politician forget how to kiss babies? Does a clog dancer forget how to clog?" He checked himself. "What about the Duke's racing record? We should know that."

Yates pursed his mouth and rolled his eyes and looked up at the ceiling. "Duke had thirty-five outs, won four, placed twice, and showed once. That includes when I ran him now and then as a quarter horse under the name of Diamond Dick. I also sent him out a few times at Louisville as a Thoroughbred, but he missed the big money. Ran back in the pack."

"As a Thoroughbred he won what?" Billy asked.

"He placed once and showed twice."

"Wasn't exactly a ball of fire, was he?"

141

"He had tendon problems."

"Maybe he shouldn't have been run that often," Billy said, which was characteristic of him, Dude thought, thinking of the horse's welfare. Billy said no more and regarded Yates with puzzlement. "You and I didn't always see eye to eye in the olden days. One reason, you were always on the other man's horse as I remember. So why, why are you doing this for us?"

Yates laid a pitying eye on him. "You are gettin' old and forgetful, Billy boy. You think I'd forget a good turn, such as when you slipped me a fast horse to get out of town on? Don't tell me you don't remember."

"It's not Christian to remind another of the generosity you once showed him," Billy answered, affecting modesty. "Especially when he'd been accused of pullin' the favorite in a big race."

"Pullin' the favorite — me!" Yates assumed a profound expression of hurt. "Why, Billy, you wouldn't have sneaked me the fast horse if I'd done such a lowdown stunt as that."

"No," Billy replied. "For certain, not if it had been my horse you pulled."

Simultaneously, they broke into roguish laughter, and Dude said, "You two get me. Where did this happen and when?"

"Now, did we say?" Yates cackled, joined by Billy, and Dude, marveling, thought, *Two of a kind!* Shaking his head, he said, "Uncle, I'm afraid we've sorta lost sight of our main reason for comin' to Petersburg, which is not to match races." Ignoring Billy's go-easy look, Dude turned to Yates. "We came back here to find out the true breeding of Judge Blair. I was told he was brought into Texas with a load of workstock, his breeding unknown. That he carried collar and trace-chain marks."

"You wouldn't be pullin' my leg, would you, Dude? A fast horse like Judge Blair bein' worked?"

"Might — if we's matchin' ourselves a race, but not on this," and Dude discovered himself laughing coarsely with Yates just as Billy had. "I won the Judge in a poker game. The man who wagered him didn't know he could run. One day I matched him and found I had a once-in-a-lifetime horse. A real track-burner. Later, the Texas cowman I'd won him off of confided that a man named Si Eckert in Petersburg might know the Judge's breeding. That's why we're here, racin' is secondary. What can you tell us about Si Eckert?"

Yate's shrewd features seemed to gather and smooth and turn unreadable. He's going to beat around the bush, Dude decided, like the bartender and Arnold. Dude was unprepared when, instead, Yates responded in a recalling tone. "Come to think of it, there was a Si Eckert around here. Been in and out the past few years." He reached that point and paused.

Dude could hardly control his voice. "What did he do here?"

"Well," said Yates, still in that reminiscent vein, "it seems that . . . I mean the first thing you remember about a man is the horse he rode. He rode a smooth red roan gelding. Fine saddler. Had all the gaits . . . traveled fast. Fact is, I tried to buy the saddler, but he claimed it was an old family horse and he couldn't let him go. Sentiment, y'know. I made him a second proposition. Even —"

"What did Eckert do here?" Dude kept on.

"Let me see now," said Yates, ever so slowly. "He did buy and trade a little, but everybody does. This is horse country, y'know."

"I mean, did he buy and trade horses to sell out of state, say down into Texas?"

"Could have. I don't stick my nose into other folks' business."

Dude was sweating. "Where is Si Eckert now, Mr. Yates?"

"Like I said . ." He didn't finish.

"Does anybody know where he went?"

"I'll have to ask Elsie. Maybe she'll know."

144

Dude sensed evasion, even as Yates called to his wife. She came to the door and he asked, "You remember that fellow called Si Eckert?"

A thinking-back look rose to her plain face. "The man you said rode a big red roan saddler?"

"Yes. Did anybody say where he went?"

"If you'd brought him out here and he had manners, I'd remember him all right. But since Mr. Lockhart and Mr. McQuinn" — she smiled at them — "are the only ones you've brought out that had manners, I can't seem to remember him a-tall except for his horse, and I don't remember that anybody said where he went. . . . Now, I have to get back to my dinner, Poge Yates. Don't bother me again."

"Now, hold on, Elsie. Did you hear he went over into Missouri?"

"I told you I didn't hear."

"Was it down into Kentucky, maybe?"

"I told you I didn't hear."

"Didn't go to Kansas, did he?"

Her face reddened. "I *told* you —" She whipped around and went back into the kitchen.

"Don't believe she knows," Yates said, accepting the rebuke. He passed the jug again and they sat around in silence, Dude discouraged. Before long, Elsie Yates called them to dinner

145

and they washed up at a bench on the porch and filed into the dining room.

Billy made a show of seating the hostess, and she said, "I do declare I've never seen such manners around Petersburg. Why, I feel like a lady goin' to a ten o'clock ball."

"You are a lady," Billy said, inclining his head toward her. "A most gracious lady." After which he said, "Dude, will you give the blessing, please?"

Red of face, too startled to speak for a moment, Dude swallowed and began in an uncertain voice, "Bless, O Lord ..." and stumbled, and Billy, like a cuing prompter, said, "this food to our use." Dude picked it up with, "and to us thy service," only to falter again. Billy, without pause, provided, "and keep us ever mindful of the needs of others, for Christ's sake," and Dude, adding, "Amen," stared at Billy, astonished. Why the old codger knew every word!

"Thank you, boys," said Elsie Yates, lifting her head. "That was very nice. It's extra nice when two render it."

Dude hadn't sat down to such a dinner in years: fried chicken, ham with red-eye gravy, biscuits and cornbread and lightbread, mashed potatoes and milk gravy, black-eyed peas and butter beans with ham hock, plum jelly and blackberry jam and peach preserves. He ate with abandon. For dessert there was peach cobbler served with pitchers of rich cream.

"I can't recall ever having a feast equal to this," said Billy, bowing his head to the hostess.

"Reminds me of down home on the Salt Fork of the Brazos," Dude said, smiling his appreciation.

"You boys are just hungry," she said, pleased.

They visited awhile over coffee, and when it was time to go, the partners thanked their hostess again, retrieved their hats from the porch, and made their way, chatting, through the parlor to the front door.

"Thanks for the papers, Poge," Billy said, shaking hands. "Like olden times, seeing you again, both of us on the same side for a change. We'll see that the Judge puts some shine on the Duke's racing record."

"Where you headed next?"

"You've got me stumped there. Looks like we've lost the trail."

Elsie Yates rushed darting through the parlor, her face alight, exclaiming, "It finally came to me! Si Eckert went on to Indian Creek from here — over into southeastern Indiana."

Her husband turned upon her a look of surprise, a straight look also. "You sure that's right, Elsie?"

"Poge Yates, do you question your wife?" She was a little angry.

"Oh, no. Where'd you hear it?"

"Don't ask me where, but I heard it. It just came to me. It's been a while, you know." She looked at the partners, a further enlightenment rising to her face. "Furthermore, the red roan saddler had an almost perfect three-pointed star on his forehead and a pretty stripe running the length of his face."

Her husband gave her another straight look, but said nothing.

The partners thanked her once more and rode away. They were at the end of the lane when Dude, his thoughts crowding in, asked, "Now, why would she know and Poge didn't?"

"Poge knew, but didn't want to say and didn't think Elsie knew."

"However, Poge wanted to repay the favor you did him a long time ago by givin' you the Duke's papers."

A creeping smile creased Billy's face. "I can understand that. You see, folks who lost money on the horse Poge pulled were gonna hang him. I thought that was a little too drastic. He was back in the jockeys' quarters by then. Didn't know what was coming. I happened to be riding a fast horse. So I rode up, handed him the reins, and told him to clear out fast."

"Did you get your horse back?"

Billy didn't answer at once. "Come to think of it, I didn't. That slippery cuss. So long ago I'd just about forgotten."

"Why would a little farm lady like Elsie know about Si Eckert, and the bartender and Ike Arnold plead total ignorance?"

"Maybe they knew *of* Eckert, but didn't know where he went and didn't want to get involved. We forget we're strangers. People don't tell strangers everything they know."

"It's a cover-up, Uncle."

"If it is, why did Elsie tell us?"

"Because, maybe," Dude studied, "she's in the dark about what Poge knows. And our manners didn't hurt." He struck a puffed-up pose.

Neither spoke again for some moments, the previous levity gone.

"I'm beginning to have some uneasy thoughts about this," Billy said. "I think Elsie, unknowingly, let the cat out of the bag. Even gave us the identifying markings of the red roan saddler."

"So?"

"It's on to Indiana, Dude, pardner. It's the only lead we have. We owe it to Judge Blair, if nothing else. When a man has a good horse, he owes that horse something, same as you would your best friend, who's given much to you. Maybe, too, it's like a boy growing up an orphan out West and wanting to know who his folks were back East, and so he goes searching."

CHAPTER 7

Sin Takes a Beating

On the forenoon of the fifteenth day, from the top of a gentle hill, Dude saw Indian Creek as clearly in the brightness as if etched on the face of the attractive wooded land. A winding creek edged the little town, veining the rolling countryside.

"It's been a long trip, but good for the horses," Billy said. "The Judge is leaned down now where he ought to be, after those two tumbleweeds I know let him put on all that tallow. You don't want a runnin' horse to carry an ounce of extra weight. You're only handicapping him when you do."

"I'd like to run him against some fancy Kentucky Thoroughbreds," Dude said, a hint of challenge in his voice. "Louisville's not far away. Just over the Ohio. Forty miles or so."

Billy cut him a teasing look. "What was that

I heard about our main purpose not being racing?"

"Still holds. Only I'd like to see what he could do against a field of Thoroughbreds, suh."

Being short of supplies, they pulled up in front of the first grocery store they saw. The town seemed to drowse. A man dressed in funereal black walked by, hardly giving the outfit a glance, his dour face a portrait of repentance. An elderly woman, likewise somberly dressed, left the grocery and marched along the plank walk, her steps measured, her sharp features a likeness of gloom and approaching damnation.

Coyote noticed. "Something wrong here is. Everybody sad. Not happy like Comanches."

Billy checked the supply list again, and he and Dude entered the store. A young woman clerk greeted them with a nod. She wore a high-necked, simple gray dress. Her well-formed face bore not the faintest trace of powder or rouge, Dude judged, only the color of her youth, a sort of sun-scrubbed look. Her downcast eyes were blue-green and luminous against prominent cheekbones and her lustrous hair formed a dark helmet high on her head. Dude guessed her age at not a day over nineteen.

When Billy showed her the list, she bowed her head to him and called for Horace, and a plump man of glum countenance shuffled from the rear of the store and the two began stacking supplies on the counter and checking them off.

She's a walkin' picture, only nobody's ever told her, Dude reflected with regret.

"Now, ma'am," he said, touching the brim of his hat, as the clerk Horace went out the door with the last sack of supplies, followed by Uncle Billy, "I'd like a half dozen sacks of Bull Durham and that many books of brown cigaret papers."

As yet she hadn't smiled and she didn't smile now as she replied, "Sir, we don't sell tobacco here."

"That's all right," he said genially, "I can get some at one of the saloons."

"The saloons are closed, sir. Have been for two years."

He stared at her, shocked. "I've never heard of that before."

"Nevertheless, that is true in Indian Creek."

"My name is Dude McQuinn, ma'am," he said, sweeping off his hat. He paused for her to give her name, but she didn't, and he went on. "My little horse outfit is just travelin' through, lookin' over the country. Came in from Illinois. Now and then we match a race."

"Horse racing is not permitted here," she informed him.

"You mean just inside the city limits?"

"I mean, sir, in the whole county. It's against the law. Once there was racing and we had gambling and whiskey drinking and fighting. Wages were lost and families went hungry."

"Well," he drawled, trying to sound understanding, "I reckon whatever folks want is what they get." He donned his rodeo arena smile. "I don't believe I got your name, Miss . . .," waiting.

"You didn't, sir, because I didn't give it," she said in a shy voice that left him impressed, she was so modest and appealing and unassuming and so inclined to piety.

He said, his voice sincere, "I hope I didn't offend you, miss. We're not some fly-by-night outfit, here to skin some poor widow woman out of her fine trotter and leave her with a blind horse or a fancy-lookin' one with the heaves. We're not horse traders."

Her face changed abruptly, breaking out of its mask of piety. "Oh, sir, I didn't mean that you would. It's just . . . that, well, we are suspicious of strangers here." Her earnestness brought a pretty flush to her cheeks and sparkle to her blue-green eyes. "My name is Blossom Price. My father owns this store."

"You bring delight to my day, Miss Blossom," he drawled. "We don't intend to remain strangers very long. We'd like to camp here for a while, if that's all right?"

"Oh, it would be, sir."

"Where would you suggest, Miss Blossom?"

"Down along the creek. There's a good sweetwater spring, too. And there's grass for your horses and firewood."

"That will be perfect. Thank you." He gathered himself in to depart, then delayed. "By the way, Miss Blossom, it occurs to me that possibly there will be a dance in town Saturday night. If so, I would deem it an honor if I may escort you there?"

She blushed again. It was evident to Dude that she blushed at the merest excitement. "Sir, we don't have dances here. There's an ordinance against it. It's . . . well, it's considered frivolous."

"Now, that's a shame, Miss Blossom. You would enjoy dancing. Particularly the waltz."

"The waltz?"

"You know, where you go round and round. I would take your right hand in my left and I would place my right arm around your waist — lightly, of course. And away we'd go." He smiled broadly at the anticipation and saw her blush.

"I've never danced, Mr. McQuinn." There

was a hint of regret in the depths of the blue-green eyes, as if her true self were shining through. "I thank you just the same. It is nice of you to ask me."

"You are most welcome, Miss Blossom. Good day."

As he turned to leave, she said, seemingly on impulse, her shy voice reaching out to him, "Sir, you said you just came from Illinois. However, you don't sound like someone from there. I guess it's your . . . your drawl that's different."

"The truth will out. I'm from Texas, down on the Salt Fork of the Brazos. Down where the hoot owls holler and coyotes howl and the cowboys take their baths in buffalo wallows every spring."

She almost broke into laughter. Restraining herself, she allowed him an appreciative smile.

He went out in sadness, thinking, *My, she's pretty — and so blamed held in and subdued.*

The Indian Creek campground was as Blossom Price had said: a sweet-water spring that ran murmuring into the creek; the creek, in turn, singing over a clear, pebbly bottom. Plenty of firewood and a grassy stretch on which to picket the horses.

Dude had said very little since leaving the store. Billy, looking at him, said, "There's something on your mind. You haven't said three words since we camped. Believe that's more than a little unusual for one Dude McQuinn. What is it?"

"We'll never get past the first furlong with this Si Eckert puzzle by pussyfootin' around. We have to smoke him out somehow."

Billy looked tolerantly amused. "And just how do we go about that?"

"Mix with the people, and I don't mean just with the horse folks, if there's any left. I picked up enough from that pretty young lady at the store to find out that this town has been squeezed down to the very nubbins. No tobacco, no whiskey — all the saloons closed — no dancin', and no horse racin' in the whole county."

"On top of that, you lost the password."

"It'll come to me one of these days."

"If you were going to recall it, I believe you would have by now."

"I've tried too hard," Dude said, accusing himself. "Guess it's blocked off in my mind. I could kick myself for losin' that cigaret paper."

"Maybe you rolled yourself a smoke with it," Billy guyed him. "Anyway, put it aside. Something will touch it off. Maybe one word. Something said at a particular place and time."

"Trouble is," Dude lamented, "I never memorized it to start with. Just scribbled it down in the saloon."

They had no more than watered and picketed the horses, when a man, clad all in black except for a white shirt, came striding into the camp, nodding as he approached, but not smiling.

In a voice as hoarse as a hog caller's, he said, "I'm the Reverend Joe Bob Quincy of the Good News Church. You gentlemen are invited to our evening prayer service, starting promptly at six-thirty. You'll find us on Elm Street, just off Main." He was a man of strapping physical dimensions, with stern, deep-set eyes, and when he smiled, it was like a symptom of pain, Dude thought. The dominant eyes and the hoarse voice and the mouth, like a slash across his bush-bearded face, combined to project an intimidating presence.

Almost before Dude knew it, Quincy was gripping Dude's hand. Billy would have stepped away, but Quincy was already upon him, and Billy, openly reluctant, met his hand.

Noticing Coyote for the first time, Quincy stared at him, then let go. "An Indian! A genuine Indian!" He moved quickly to Coyote and virtually seized his hand, pumping it again and again, and asked, his voice wondering and deeply hoarse, "You speak American?"

For an instant Dude thought Coyote was going to fall back on his gibberish act, playing the role of a dumb Indian, saying, "Me no speakum white man's talk — no savvy," as he did when he wished to rebuke an unpleasant approach because of his race.

Instead, he bowed with grace and said, not without a trace of Indian hauteur, "Yes, Reverend, English I speak when with my white brothers conversing. I find it helpful quite, especially reading when the small print on treaties, which we call talking papers, stating how much the reservation of my people, the Comanches, will shrink if we affix our marks thereon. In addition to my native tongue, I also speak Spanish, Kiowa, Arapaho, Plains Apache, and a smattering of Cheyenne, and, of course, by necessity, eloquent I am in the sign language, sometimes called the Language of the Plains. My name is Coyote Walking."

"He's an honor graduate of Carlisle School," Dude put in for emphasis. "His daddy's chief of all the Comanches."

Quincy could hardly contain himself. "Wonderful! Mr. Coyote, you are just the person we need to speak to our young people tomorrow evening. Thank you for accepting." He turned before Coyote could refuse. "We'll be looking for all of you tonight at the prayer meeting.

You will come, won't you?" He fixed that intimidating stare on Dude.

"Thank you, Reverend," Dude said, not hesitating, "we'll be there," and saw his partners cringe. "This is Dr. William Tecumseh Lockhart and my name is Dude McQuinn."

Quincy pumped their hands again and departed in a rush, head high, remindful to Dude of the way a man might move while breasting the waves of sin.

"You've sure got us hemmed in now," Billy complained, and Coyote, who was wringing his right hand, said, "That white medicine man hard grip he has. I felt like a mean mule the way he grabbed me."

"But don't you two see?" Dude pleaded. "This gives us a chance to get acquainted and locate Si Eckert."

"I've a good notion to back out now," Billy said.

"And I," Coyote chimed in, "go not tonight or to young people speak."

"You two wouldn't make a liar out of your old pardner, would you?" Dude shot back.

The church was deadly quiet when the outfit arrived promptly at six-thirty and took seats at the rear, Billy wearing a dark broadcloth frock coat with vest and pantaloons to match, a white shirt, and a string tie, his bib beard and shoulder-length white hair carefully combed and brushed, all adding to his air of dignity; Dude in his best cowhide boots and gray pantaloons and his only dress coat, a light blue, and gray flannel shirt and wine-colored bandanna knotted at the throat, cowboy style; Coyote literally stuffed into his Carlisle School clothes, wrinkled and far too small for him now, the dark pantaloons riding high water above box-toed shoes. A stifling black tie and tight blue flannel shirt completed Coyote's attire. His straight black hair hung to his shoulders.

Dude, glancing about, had never seen such a meek and solemn gathering. Not one happy face. A young one caught his eye. A pretty face. That of Blossom Price, and his pulse jumped. She, too, looked glum and put down, sitting stiffly, staring straight ahead.

As if waiting for the outfit's arrival before beginning the service, the Reverend Quincy, arms wide, palms upward, motioned for all to stand for prayer. His hoarse voice gradually gathering volume, he prayed that the congregation would be "cleansed of sin" and would avoid "pitfalls of passion" and that Indian Creek would continue to "ward off sin." On and on he prayed, until Dude caught the sounds of a restless stirring. After about fifteen minutes, he reckoned, the Reverend said, "Amen," and everybody sat down, Dude hearing tactfully subdued sighs of relief.

"And now, folks," said Quincy, hoarsely, "I should like to introduce our guests. Dr. William Tecumseh Lockhart . . . Mr. Dude McQuinn . . . and Mr. Walking Coyote." Coyote gave a start at the transposition. The three stood and nodded around and when they sat down Quincy said, "Mr. Coyote, who is a member of the Comanche tribe, will speak to our young people tomorrow evening at six-thirty sharp. For which we sincerely thank him. Refreshments will be served."

Two hymns were sung without music, Quincy leading, swinging his right arm, and then, squaring his shoulders as if for an encounter, he spread a sheet of paper on the lectern and roared, "Sin comes in many forms!" and the congregation, not unlike by rote, answered, "Amen!"

"It comes," he roared, "in a bottle of Kentucky whiskey!"

"Amen!"

"It comes in a sack of tobacco with a picture on it!"

"Amen!"

"It comes in a pretty dance tune played by a

tipsy fiddler tapping his booted foot!"

"Amen!"

"And it comes," he shouted, "in the forms of Kentucky racehorses and race meets where men drink whiskey and fight and gamble their wages away and their poor wives and little children go hungry."

"Amen!"

Billy began to squirm. Before Dude could restrain him, Billy stood and raised a halting hand and Quincy ceased speaking. "Reverend," said Billy, "in all due respects, I'd like to say a few words in defense of the horse."

Quincy, overcoming his surprise, nodded for him to proceed.

Billy's chin came up. "The horse, also known as *Equus caballus*, is one of the most beautiful animals the Lord has placed upon this earth for the service of mankind. How man uses this gift is the freedom of choice that the Lord gives us all for better or worse. Each animal was put here for a purpose . . . the racehorse to run, the draft horse to labor all his days, the gaited saddler to carry its master, the trotter and the pacer to pull a sulky — sometimes taking a good doctor through wind and snow and sleet on his errands of mercy. It's been said that 'No gentleman drives a pacer,' because of its side-swaying motion, but many a pacer has saved a life when he sped a mile in two minutes to reach the bedside of a dying child. A fast racehorse may carry a message that may turn the tide of battle. The fate of our nation may ride on his flying feet and within his noble heart." Billy paused and cleared his throat. "It is not the horse that is at fault. It is man. Thank you, Reverend Quincy. I apologize for interrupting your impressive sermon."

The upturned faces on Billy altered slightly, Dude saw, a crack in their stiff piety, and Dude felt relieved when Quincy, giving that painful smile, said, "Thank you, Brother Lockhart. Your remarks are well taken, sir."

Little by little, the reverend returned to the theme of his sermon, "Sin, Everlasting Sin," took after it with verses from Genesis, Numbers, and the second book of Chronicles, gave it a further thumping with quotations from the Psalms and Proverbs, his voice growing more hoarse, whapped it still harder with Isaiah and Jeremiah and Ezekiel, and not sparing the rod, continued the assault with Matthew and Mark, and from Romans 6:1, asked, "Shall we continue in sin?"

By this time the sermon had consumed an hour or more, Dude felt, and the congregation was growing restless again.

Apparently sensing that, Quincy shouted,

"Stomp sin out of your lives!" and went to stomping and waving his arms until great beads of sweat coursed down his face. Suddenly, he appeared to grasp and grapple an invisible foe, struggling, grunting. Dust rose back there. Worshippers leaned forward to watch. At once he seemed to lose his hold as his arms jerked wide and he staggered back. Whereupon, with a mighty shout, he leaped from the pulpit to the aisle in grim pursuit. There he made a desperate grab, tugging, wrestling, stomping, muttering. He took a blow. He fell to the floor, but heaved to his feet. He kicked, he punched, he flailed, shouting, "Take that! – and that!" Now, churchgoers were standing for a better view. Again he seemed to lose his grip and allowed his antagonist to flee. Gathering himself, he ran pounding and shouting down the aisle. At the door, clutching desperately, he caught up again. Then, with all his strength, with a tremendous heaving motion, he threw his rival through the doorway and out of the church. Wiping his hands triumphantly, he strode back, shouting, "Sin is out!"

The Reverend Joe Bob, Dude had to admit, knew exactly how to cap a performance, er – a sermon.

Quietly, soon afterward, following a brief prayer, Quincy dismissed the congregation. He shook hands as each person passed through the doorway.

"Reverend," Dude said, shaking hands, "that's the best rasslin' match I've seen since Professor Jones pinned Plowboy Pete with the Gotch toe-hold in Fort Worth."

"Thank you, Brother McQuinn."

Dude went out, leaving Billy and Coyote to chat further with Quincy, and there was Miss Blossom Price, alone when she should have been surrounded with beaus.

"My, wasn't that a wonderful sermon?" she said enthusiastically.

"Indeed it was, Miss Blossom," said Dude, sweeping off his hat. "The reverend would make a great steer rassler, too." After a moment, when no one came to claim her, he asked, "May I walk you home?"

She hesitated, confused.

He said, "I'll be very nice."

"That would be out of your way," she said, still hesitating. "I don't want to put you out, Mr. McQuinn."

"Be my pleasure, Miss Blossom."

Although she really hadn't consented with words, she allowed him to take her arm lightly and guide her toward the plank sidewalk. As they strolled along, Dude said, "I thought we might drop by the drugstore for an ice cream soda or somethin'. Believe I saw one on Main Street."

"You did. But it will be closed this late."

"Late?" he said, amused. "I've never heard of a town that rolled up the sidewalks on Main this early. It's not long after sundown."

"Reverend Joe Bob says it keeps young people off the streets."

"– And boys into back alleys."

She had no reply to that and they strolled on, Dude fully aware of her lilac-scented nearness and his ears still registering the pleasant tone of her voice, as sweet as a child's. At thirty-two years of age, Dude had been up the long cattle trails to the northern pastures and matched countless horse races with Billy and Coyote and had cottoned to it all. Yet a girl like Miss Blossom made a man think of what he had missed: home and fireside and young ones and settling down, maybe.

"Indian Creek," she said by and by, "has become the citadel of righteousness in this part of Indiana. Last spring a schoolteacher was fired for playing mah-jongg."

"I can't believe it," Dude exclaimed.

"Another was fired for going to a country dance."

"I can't believe that, either, and it's mighty unfair."

She was silent for so long that he feared he had hurt her feelings, until she spoke, slowly and wistfully, "Are girls allowed to go to dances down on . . . the . . . what you call the Salt Fork of the Brazos?"

"You bet! And their folks go, too."

"Even teachers?"

"They're among the first asked. You can bet they don't stay single very long down in Texas."

"How nice. I'd like to be a teacher. I'd like to teach reading, writing, arithmetic, and music. I play the piano and my friends say I have a fairly good voice."

"I'll second that, and it's better than fairly."

"I'm not boastful or anything," she said, quickly. "On Sundays I sing in the choir, and I teach the junior Bible School Class."

"Mighty fine, Miss Blossom. I'd like to be there."

"But I guess I'm afraid."

A powerful desire to defend and please her took possession of him. "Afraid? Why?"

"Because here a teacher has so little freedom. She's caged, like a bird." Suddenly she pressed both hands to her mouth. "Why am I burdening you, a stranger, with my innermost thoughts?"

"I'm glad you didn't say a total stranger, Miss Blossom. I think you should be a teacher.

You'd make a great one. If I'd had a teacher like you when I was a kid, maybe I'd have amounted to somethin', instead of driftin' around the country like a tumbleweed."

"Oh, I think that would be fun, Mr. McQuinn. Matching horse races, seeing new places, meeting new people."

"Call me Dude."

"Thank you, Mr. Dude. You may call me Blossom."

"Dude, without the *mister*," he stressed. "To be a teacher, you'd have to go to college, I reckon. Where might that be?"

"Louisville is nearest. I have an aunt there. She wants me to live with her and go to school."

He looked directly at her. "What's keepin' you here?"

There was a pensive pause, and then she said, "I'm afraid."

"Afraid of what, Miss Blossom?"

"Afraid of life, I suppose. Whatever all that means."

Dude stopped and took her gently by the arm. "Everybody is so held down and pious in this town. There's mighty little fun for you young people. I know Joe Bob is a good man and means well, but he's too tied up with sin and forgets life should be enjoyed. I never figured a body had to go around with a long face to be a Christian. There wasn't one happy face there tonight. Now, let's rope and hogtie this afraid critter and take a close look at it. Let's see what exactly holds you back."

"You've already said it — it's sin. I'm afraid I'll sin if I go to Louisville."

"And just how would that be sinful?"

"Like going to a dance," she said, her laughter pealing out, and he laughed with her.

She directed them on to a little white house enclosed within a picket fence and they drew step at the gate.

"There's one question I've been aimin' to ask you, Miss Blossom," he said, wondering just how to put it. "Guess you know everybody around Indian Creek, or at least have heard of everybody?"

"I've lived here all my life," she said, a curious note of apology in her voice. "Never even been as far away as Louisville. What could I possibly know that would interest you?"

"Well, an oldtimer in Texas asked me to look up an old horseman friend of his if I came to Indian Creek. His old friend's name is Si Eckert. Know him or of 'im?"

"Si Eckert?" she repeated and dwelled on that for a long moment. "All the farmers come to the store, but I know no one by that name and haven't heard it mentioned."

Dude sighed. "Thank you, Miss Blossom. Sometimes old folks get places mixed up."

She held out her hand. "Thank you for walking me home, Mr. Dude, and for listening to me. You have a sympathetic heart."

"Good night, Miss Blossom. And don't be afraid."

He left her not only with regrets at the briefness of enjoying her company, but with heavy disappointment. If Si Eckert wasn't known at the store where the farmers traded, who would know him? It didn't make sense. Si Eckert was said to be here, but he wasn't here. Was the whole thing a hoax, thought up by the Texas cowman, vengeful over losing a once-in-a-lifetime horse? But if a hoax, why had Poge and Elsie Yates known of Eckert?

CHAPTER 8

A Piece of String

Upon returning from town next morning, Dude handed Coyote a pair of new broadcloth pantaloons.

The Comanche was puzzled. "What for, these?"

"For you to wear when you talk to the young people at the church meeting tonight. You can't wear them high-water britches anymore. You look like some hayseed."

Coyote groaned. "Thinking of having devil in belly I am."

"You can't play sick now and back out. You've already given your word."

"I didn't give it. White medicine man took it. What talk about, shall I? Buffalo all gone now. Wild horses, too."

"Tell 'em about growin' up on the reservation. About your father the chief. About the way it was in buffalo days. About how to ride a racehorse."

"Feeling I am, white father, devil in belly coming on for sure."

"You can't do that, Coyote. You might hear somethin' that will help smoke out this Si Eckert fella. You know how kids talk."

"You've been gone long enough to interview everybody in town," Billy said, a bit testy. "I hope it didn't take you that long to buy a pair of britches. Did you pick up anything at all on Eckert?"

"Nothin'. What this town needs is a good saloon where the red essence flows and a fella can visit with his fellow man."

"That didn't help in Petersburg, I recall."

"Miss Blossom did tell me last night they don't know anybody by that name at the grocery store."

"Why didn't you tell us that last night?"

"Because you two were in your bedrolls when I got back to camp."

"Why didn't you tell us this morning?"

"Because I was in a hurry to get Coyote some britches."

Billy threw up his hands. He was, Dude could see, a little crotchety; however, that meant he was back to normal. He hadn't suffered a case of self-pity in a long time now.

Dude left camp after the noon meal and didn't return until past three o'clock. "I want you two to take a gander at this handbill," he said, holding it up for his partners to see. It read:

NOTICE

Dr. William Tecumseh Lockhart, the distinguished Texas horseman, veterinarian extraordinary, breeder, trainer and widely acclaimed author of numerous books from the faithful Morgan to the kingly Thoroughbred, will demonstrate the celebrated Eureka Safety Bridle two o'clock Saturday afternoon at the Indian Creek campground. Following the demonstration, Dr. Lockhart will lecture at length on his favorite subject, "Equine Ills," the alleviation of which he is known as the poet says, "from sea to shining sea."

If you have a horse that is hard to handle, bring the animal to Dr. Lockhart's knowing and gentle hands. The bridle, invented by the late Prof. P. D. Gleason of international fame for the safety of man and horse, will hold any animal under any circumstances when properly applied.

The public is invited.

Billy read with mouth compressed, then

turned away, exasperation glinting in his eyes. "Dude, you've gone and done it again! Just when you promised me you'd cut out this tomfoolery."

"But, Uncle, don't you see? This will draw a crowd, mainly horsemen. It's the only way. We've got to smoke out this Si Eckert."

"Well, I'll tell you, I'm beginning to think this Si Eckert is a figment of somebody's imagination."

"Don't forget what Poge Yates said. That Eckert rode a red roan saddler. That's real." Dude rubbed his hands, exuding satisfaction. "I'm having these distributed all over town, including the livery. Miss Blossom said she'd put one in the front window of the store, besides passin' the word to farmers."

"That's just fine." Billy grimaced with disgust. "They'll bring in every jugheaded horse within miles."

Long after dark, sitting around the cherry-red embers of the supper fire with Billy, Dude heard boots clomping on the road from town. Coyote came in on the slant, aiming for the one unoccupied chair. He slumped into it as Dude said, "We waited up for you. How'd it go?"

"Talk I did to young people. Their medicine man there too was. I told them about growing up as boy in my father's tepee. How hungry we got, with buffalo gone. How my father, the chief, voices heard out of Texas, ghost voices of Comanche braves, crying they were for our Texas lost, and ghosts crying they are in Texas yet. Our Texas gone like buffalo. How in buffalo days when Texas people Comanches saw mad they got their knives they took off Comanches' scalps they took." Coyote paused.

"Go on," Dude said, entertained. "When you talk that sing-song lingo, it reminds me of a riddle."

"Tell them I did," Coyote continued, "buffalo wallows about, but no buffalo. And bones on the prairie white they are, but no buffalo. Tell them I did about buffalo running horses, how fast. Guide them with your knees and they lay back their ears and feel you do the wind around your ears whistling. But no buffalo. Only buffalo horses into the wind running.

"Tell them I did about the time Comanches, my people, tried the Sun Dance, hoping it was powerful medicine, hoping they did it bring back would the buffalo and the white man go back he would the way he came, to the East. But no buffalo and the white man became many more white mans as blades of buffalo grass. And so, being practical people, we Comanches hold not the Sun Dance again.

"Tell them I did about the sky, open it is out

there, and blue and green sometimes like turquoise, which we Comanches buy from the mountain tribes to the West, and about the wind and the buffalo grass and Grandfather Sun and Grandmother Earth. When my talk finish I did, I told the young people to be a good behave and enjoy it a happiness. A strange thing happened then. Up they all jumped and said they wanted to go out West and like Comanches live." He paused, knowing his partners would ask him to go on.

"What did you tell 'em then?" Billy asked.

"I said, 'No — don't go. Too many white mans out there now,' " and raised a hand to his face, unable to hide a sudden, uncontrollable smile.

"Coyote could make a living on the stage, talking that mishmash," Billy said. "Nobody would know he's an honor graduate. He could put on his Indian suit, maybe some war paint, and fold his arms and —"

"Wait!" Coyote interrupted. "Clue I have maybe. One girl told me her grandfather, who lives north of town, buys and trades horses. His name is Ramsey — Foss Ramsey."

"See," said Dude, jumping up, "what did I tell you! It pays to get acquainted."

They started coming early, by ones, by twos,

by threes, then in swarms, entire families, until the campground was bursting with people and horses.

Billy moved to the wagon. Dude heard the stopper on the sour-mash jug go *thung*, and when he saw his old mentor stepping lively on the way back, he knew all was well.

"Now, Dude," Billy said, "you got me into this — so you'll have to help out."

A squealing and kicking erupted. Both men jerked about. Two farmers were leading unruly horses into the campground.

"See what I mean?" Billy gritted.

"I'll help," Dude promised, feeling his first misgivings.

When the crowd had finished gathering, Billy raised a hand for attention and announced, "You have come here today to see Professor Gleason's Eureka Safety Bridle demonstrated. I am Dr. William Tecumseh Lockhart. Assisting me will be my colleague, Mr. Dude McQuinn, and — if needed — Mr. Coyote Walking. . . . Mr. McQuinn, fetch me the bridle from the wagon."

Dude fetched a long piece of cord, a slip noose in one end, which drew gawks from the crowd as he presented it with ceremony to Uncle.

A young, red-faced farmer, gripping the halter rope of a fractious brown horse, already saddled, sang out, belittling, "That's a bridle?"

"It is," Billy replied, "as you will presently see."

Ah, Dude thought, another smart aleck. Every town had at least one. He could almost feel a pity for the young man, once Uncle started working him over. Now, the young farmer said, "Bet it can't hold my Tim Boy here," and Dude, hiding a grin, said to himself, *The show is about to begin.*

"How much would you like to wager, young fella?" Billy asked.

"A dollar."

Billy sniffed. "That's chicken feed down in Texas. I thought you said *bet?*"

The young red face turned a brighter hue. "Then two dollars, Grandpa. I'll bet two dollars that there piece of string won't hold Tim Boy."

Grandpa, Dude knew, was the last form of address the farmer should have used.

"I might consider that," Billy answered, a firmness edging into his voice.

"I'll even raise it to three dollars, Grandpa," the young man said, cocky about it, and Dude shook his head, knowing what was coming.

"I'll take that," Billy said.

From deep in the crowd an older and bantering voice called, "Look out, Waldo. It's deep out there."

"Have you tried a curb bit on Tim Boy?" Billy asked.

"Did. Didn't help much. He's coldjawed and stubborn to boot."

"Have you considered trying patience and kindness?"

Waldo smirked. "Except when I have to get his attention with a club."

"Does he gee and haw?" Billy asked, frowning his displeasure at the last.

"When he takes a notion, Grandpa," Waldo answered, and turned this way and that to the crowd, jiggling his head, enjoying his remark and evoking grins. "Sometimes he pitches with me."

"If he pitches, he isn't broken. How old is Tim Boy?"

"Six."

"Bring Tim Boy over so I can look at his teeth." Waldo led the unruly brown over and Billy spent a minute or more peering into the horse's mouth, while Waldo kept a tight grip on the halter rope. Billy then said, "I regret to inform you, Waldo, that Tim Boy is not six but ten years old."

"Ten! I've had 'im two years. The trader swore he was four."

"A road trader?"

"Yup." Waldo was rapidly losing his aplomb.

Billy folded his arms and gazed off in manifest sorrow. The crowd was chuckling and grinning. With a tired sigh, Billy said, "I'll explain. Tim Boy is ten years old because all four center nippers are getting thicker from the front of the teeth to the inside. You see, Waldo, as a horse gets older his nippers grind down and grow wider. Now, let's see about the bridle." Facing the crowd, he held high the length of cord and assumed his lecturing tone. "This bridle, simple as it is, is the most successful device ever developed for the management of horses made vicious by the inhumanity of man. It is also ideal for the purpose of doctoring the eyes or performing operations."

"I'll just raise my bet to five dollars that string can't make Tim Boy behave," Waldo scoffed, upon which the voice of experience called again, "You're gettin' in over your head, Waldo, boy."

"I'll take that," Billy said. "And this string, as you call it, happens to be ten feet of strong cord, one-eighth of an inch in diameter."

"Who's this 'Fessor Gleason you claim invented the bridle?" Waldo persisted, still dubious.

"Professor P. D. Gleason," Billy said, stressing *professor* and *P. D.*, "now gone to his just reward after devoting his life to correcting what man has done to *Equus caballus*, was the greatest horse tamer this country has ever known."

"Never heard of him."

"You would have if you could read."

Waldo's countenance turned a deeper red again. "I can read real good. I went through the eighth grade and got my certificate."

"Took three times," the jibing voice cut in.

"An' what's this Eck — this Eckus Caboodle?"

"You better go through a fourth time," the teasing voice sounded.

Taking pity, Billy put a hand on Waldo's shoulder and said, "That's just a fancy name for the horse. Let's bridle Tim Boy. Dude, you get a hold on the other side of the halter." While the crowd edged in closer to see, Billy began speaking in a loud and instructive voice. "First, you slip the noose around the neck like this . . . and pass the cord through the mouth over the tongue from the off side. . . . Then through the noose from the near side and pull forward firmly. You see where we are now. . . . Next, pass the cord just behind the ears from the near side . . . and down and under the upper lip, above the upper jaw from the off side . . . then pass through the second cord and fasten firmly in a knot, like this. Thus far we have only one rein . . . so we merely pass the loose end over the neck and tie it, like this, at the off side of the bridle near the jaw and we have closed reins." He turned quickly. "Mount up, Waldo, and take the reins."

Waldo mounted with a smirk and took the reins, but at that instant Tim Boy lowered his head and arched his neck and started pitching.

"Pull up his head!" Billy shouted.

Before Waldo could do so, Tim Boy promptly tossed Waldo forward and he lost his seat and clutched the brown neck with both hands, and horse and rider went round and round, Waldo hanging on, flopping and thumping, both feet still in the stirrups. A comedy of horsemanship that drew a ripple of laughter from the crowd and would have been dangerous were Tim Boy a bronc, sunfishing and pitching right and left, instead of the light workhorse type he was that humped straight and landed with a light jar.

But Dude, deciding this had gone on long enough, grabbed the bridle alongside Tim Boy's jaw and brought him under control.

Waldo, shamefaced, moved to dismount. But Billy said, "Stay put and take the slack out of the reins. We haven't finished the demonstration." Waldo did as instructed and when Dude let go the halter and Tim Boy lowered his head to pitch, Waldo jerked the reins and the brown horse's head came up and he straightened out into a slow trot.

"Now, make him gee and haw," Billy instructed. "Make him behave."

"Gee!" Waldo hollered and reined right and Tim Boy obeyed.

"Now, the other way," Billy told him.

"Haw!" Waldo hollered and reined left and Tim Boy obeyed.

"Now, ride him around in a circle. . . . That's good. Now, make him do a figure eight. Keep a tight rein. . . . That's good. Your horse is under perfect control."

Waldo rode back smiling and dismounted. "Reckon I'd better buy me one of your bridles, Doc. How much are they?"

"I don't know how much they charge for stout cord at the store," Billy said, looking standoffish.

"Mean you ain't peddlin' bridles?" Waldo's surprise said he had expected the usual "catch" when a gullible farmer bought something from a stranger.

"Oh, nooo. The bridle is yours, friend Waldo, and forget the bet. Just be good to Tim Boy and get his attention with patience and firmness. When he learns he can no longer get away with such foolishness as bucking, he'll settle down and behave. All he needs is schooling, and he's not too old to learn, as just demonstrated. But you better let me show you again how to tie the bridle."

Painstakingly, then, Billy went through the wraps and the two ties. "The secret," he pointed out, "is leverage against the lip. So you must keep the bridle tight. By keeping the pressure constant on the lip, you can control the wildest horse."

As Waldo led Tim Boy away, a high voice asked, "Will it work on a Percheron, Doctor?"

"It will work on a bull rhinoceros if you can get it over his head and through his mouth," Billy replied instantly, which set off a burst of guffaws from the crowd. Uncle, Dude knew by that, was back on track and in stride. Suddenly, it was like old times again.

A farmer, white-bearded and frail of build, led forth a massive Percheron of two thousand pounds or more, whose dark hide was dappled.

"What's his trouble?" Billy asked, his tone professional.

"Sampson does all right pullin' straight ahead," the old gentleman said. "Fact, he could pull down a mountain. Only trouble is sometimes he takes a notion not to turn as fast as I want him to, pullin' a wagon, or a plow, when he comes to the end of a row. He keeps movin' right ahead. He's a mite bullheaded, which I reckon comes from his French ancestors."

"Another case of gee and haw," Billy diagnosed. "Fetch me another Eureka from the wagon, Mr. McQuinn." And when he had the cord in hand: "I'd prefer to employ the Eureka on a ridin' horse; however, it will work the same on a draft horse like this fine individual by simply lengthening the reins. First, I'll show you how to attach and tie." That finished: "Would you care to mount Sampson, sir, and put him through his paces?"

"I'm a mite too poorly today."

"Then Mr. McQuinn can oblige us."

"Me?" said Dude, forefinger at his chest, thinking, *Me, a cowboy, ride a draft horse?*

"Yes, Mr. McQuinn, to demonstrate the safety of the Eureka for the good of mankind."

Dude looked upward at the high, glossy back of the Percheron, eighteen hands up there if an inch, too high to fling himself upon it.

Billy, hardly masking an implacable grin, said, "Coyote, give him a leg up."

"High this horse's back is, Grandfather." Coyote was eyeing the Percheron. "All my strength take it will. White father heavy is." With that, he moved in to help.

Just as he gave Dude's leg a powerful heave, the great horse moved and Dude, vainly missing his grab at the mane, tumbled across the broad back and sprawled on the ground and lost his big hat, in his ears an outburst of oohed laughter. Red of face, mouth squinched in embarrassment, Dude rose and dusted himself off and picked up his hat, only to hear Billy's merciless voice. "Let's try again, Mr. McQuinn. The demonstration isn't finished."

Dude got it then. The old codger was getting even for today's promotion. In silence, he circled to the other side of the Percheron and let Coyote give him a leg up. Taking the reins, he heeled the ponderous horse forward.

"Make him gee!" Billy ordered, and Dude reined right and the mountain of horseflesh, after hesitating the barest fraction, turned right.

"Now, haw!" Billy called, and Dude, dutifully, reined left and the great hulk of dappled muscle under him moved left.

That was enough. Dude reined about and rode back, and hearing a round of handclapping, lifted his hat high and flashed his arena smile. He halted the mighty animal and sliding down, drew the reins over the giant's head, curstied to Billy, and ceremoniously passed the reins to the exuberant owner, who burst out, "It works — by grab it works!" He led his horse away to another wave of applause.

"As successful as the Eureka is," Billy said, addressing the crowd, "it was not intended to replace the bit, and couldn't. It's merely a corrective device, effective for schooling and controlling. If it were not for the space of bare gum between the incisor and molar teeth, which provides space for the bit and its operation, man would never have subdued the horse for his use and, I regret, his misuse."

Uncle was in full lecturing swing now, Dude knew, just like the old days.

"Also," Billy continued, without letup, "if the Creator had not endowed the horse with the solid hoof he has, the horse hardly would have been worth domesticating. The hoof protects a most sensitive area, as you horsemen know, from the coronet downward. It enables the horse to travel almost anywhere, through extreme heat and cold. Possibly a strong hackamore alone with special reins would enable man to ride and drive and work the horse, but there is no man-made device that could compensate for the lack of the horny covering of the foot. And I remind you of one rule that never changes: Let the frog alone."

"Amen!" a man followed, and Dude thought he recognized a face he had seen at the church.

"As the farmer said before the mule kicked him," Billy said, "I'd like to say a few more words about friend horse, long subjected to the inhumanity of man, relieved somewhat as you have witnessed here today, thanks to Professor Gleason's Eureka Safety Bridle." He ceased and struck a dramatic pose. "Shall I go on, or am I boring you?"

"Go on," a man shouted. "This beats a medicine show, which we ain't had since Joe Bob took over the town. Go on!"

"Thank you, friend," Billy said, bowing. "I'll make it short and sweet like the old woman's dance, as an up-and-coming fella named Abe Lincoln once said," and he shuffled his booted feet rhythmically, briefly. "This proposition I'm going to tell you about has been gnawing at me for some time. Maybe you have or haven't heard of Mendel's Law?" There was silence, which he smilingly ignored. "Now, Mr. Mendel was the great botanist of his day. He made his reputation by crossing two varieties of peas, tall ones and dwarf ones. When he crossed the tall peas with the dwarfs, he got hybrids. You know what a hybrid is if you know what a mule is, particularly when he tries to kick you into kingdom come after working for you maybe twenty years." That stirred memories with chuckles and headnoddings. "When Mendel crossed the tall hybrid peas, he got tall plants and dwarfs in the proportion of three to one, respectively. He concluded that nature has a tendency to return the breeds to their particular pure state. Are you with me?"

Getting no response, he went doggedly on. "Mendel said certain paired characteristics, one from each parent, don't blend with or alter each other in the offspring. And he said the genes determining such pairs of traits combine in the offspring according to chance. A gene is a hereditary unit. . . ." He broke off. "Maybe I'd better put it this way. I'd admit Mr. Mendel did a lot for plants, but the book scientists who read him have got off the track trying to apply Mendel's law to breeding horses. The horse himself refutes this, since we all know the sire stamps his main characteristics on his fillies, while the dam marks hers on the colts. In effect, what she's doing is passing on the characteristics of her sire." He left off again, then said, "As the farmer put it, after he'd recovered from the mule's kick, 'A horse ain't a pea — shucks no, he ain't.' Thank you, folks, for listening to an old man's rambling and something he's had in his craw about breeding for a long time."

Spontaneous applause followed him as he turned to go. Dude, suddenly remembering, said, "Hold on, Doctor. We forgot something."

"You tell 'em," Billy said wearily, understanding.

"Folks," said Dude, hand raised, "a friend of ours down Texas way asked us to look up an old horseman friend of his, if by chance we happened to drift into Indian Creek. So here we are. The horseman's name is Si Eckert. Any of you folks know him or of him?"

Silence followed. Faces turned in question, but no one spoke and Dude asked, "Are you sure nobody here knows him?"

"Maybe he lives in Indian Hills," a man said. "That's way north of here."

"Thank you, sir, but we were told Indian Creek. That's too bad, too, because just a few days ago we had a letter from our Texas friend and he said Si Eckert's uncle passed away and left him with a mighty sweet inheritance – a great big ol' ranch with thousands of head of fat cattle on it, and hundreds of fine horses and mules, and a big ol' hacienda. The family lawyer is writin' everywhere, tryin' to locate Si Eckert." He shook his head. "Too bad. Too bad. All that waitin' for him down in Texas. We thank you kind folks just the same."

Billy's eyebrows shot up in surprise, but he said nothing. Mutterings and exclamations rose to Dude's ears and the crowd began breaking up. Amid these sounds a man in bib overalls and straw hat, a man of fifty years or so, came over to Billy and said, "Doctor, could you come out to my farm tomorrow? My favorite saddler has the colic and I can't relieve him. I'm afraid he'll get down and can't get up."

At first glance the man looked like just another Indiana farmer until Dude caught the keen eyes in the square-jawed face, the eyebrows like hedges, the dark, close beard, like fur, rimming his face from ear to ear.

Billy, somewhat weary after his stint, seemed to call up a reserve of energy. "Be glad to, sir. How long has he suffered?"

"Two days."

"That's a long time without relief. Has he started lying down and rolling?"

"Afraid so."

Billy pulled out his watch. "It's past three-thirty. So we shouldn't wait till morning, Mr. —?"

"Ramsey — Foss Ramsey."

"Where do you live, Mr. Ramsey?"

"North of town three miles."

Billy turned to Dude and Coyote. "Let's hitch up the wagon. I'll need my medicine chest. Hurry!"

Ramsey said fast, "Thank you, Doctor. My

drivin' horse is nearby. I'll lead you out." He ran.

"Ramsey — Foss Ramsey," Dude repeated in undertone to his partners. "That's the man you heard about at church, Coyote. Makes me wonder. He didn't come forward till I mentioned the inheritance."

"Inheritance!" Billy snorted. "What inheritance? Dude, you've done it again!"

"What if it did have a little molasses on it. Could be we've finally smoked out the real Si Eckert. I'll bet ten to one that colicky saddler is a red roan with an almost perfect three-pointed star and a long, pretty stripe runnin' the length of his face. Come on. Let's hitch up!"

CHAPTER 9

Cure for a Saddler

Foss Ramsey's farm appeared no different from countless others Dude had admired across verdant and fertile Illinois and Indiana. The sturdy fences, the comfortable white houses with the long, cool porches, the towerlike silos, the great barns. Except, Dude noticed, this barn was enormous even for Indiana, and there were more corrals than usual, and more horses than usual: draft horses, riding horses, in the pastures mares with foals at their sides. A little lake over there. At the barn a windmill pumped water into a metal tank the size of a big water hole in Texas, its whirling blades flashing silver in the afternoon sun.

"That bet still on?" Billy asked Dude, spoken with a skeptical look, as they drew up at the main corral.

"Sure thing. When we see that saddler,

he'll be the red roan."

Billy was mocking him. "What then?"

"We'll be face to face with none other than the mysterious Si Eckert."

"What then, since you don't know the rest of the password?"

"I'll think of something, Uncle. Don't worry."

"If I were a riverboat gambler," Billy said, arching one brow, "I'd take some of that ten-to-one money."

"And you'd take a skinnin'," Dude said confidently.

Ramsey was waiting and led them toward the rear of the massive barn, which even with the hayloft had a vaulted look, talking as he went. "I've got Prince out here in a small corral where he can roll and feel more comfortable. Figured that was better than keeping him cooped up here in the barn."

"I agree," Billy said. "A stall is all right so long as he doesn't roll and get cast. Walking does give some relief." He glanced at Dude, who returned him more of his anticipation.

Following Ramsey, they moved through the rear door of the barn, turned right, and then, Ramsey pointing, said, "There's Prince. My favorite saddler. Best I've ever had, or ever expect to have. Kentucky-bred. He's like a member of the family. I think more of him than

I do of most people, I'll tell you."

Dude looked and blinked, his anticipation evaporating, startled to see a chestnut, and swallowed and rubbed his nose. Billy, pretending surprise, said, "I do believe that's a liver chestnut, Mr. Ramsey. You don't see a great many of that particular shade of chestnut." His sidelong glance made Dude look down.

The three entered the corral and Billy stopped to study the chestnut, a gelding, then crossed to the saddler and taking hold of the halter peered into the dark, wide-spaced eyes. "He has the sleepy look of colic," Billy said. "He's fidgety. His breathing is labored, and I see he wants to paw with one foot, trying to relieve his discomfort. What have you given Prince, Mr. Ramsey?"

"The usual home remedy," Ramsey said, apologetic about it. "Two common tablespoonfuls of saleratus, mixed with one and one-half pints of sweet milk, given in one dose."

"How often?"

"Twice yesterday and twice today, with no relief that I can see."

"That is good in mild cases, but as long as Prince has been suffering, I think his case calls for something stronger. I'll be back in a minute."

He left on the double and returned with a

forked stick, a leather strap, and a fruit jar of murky liquid. After instructing Dude to attach the strap to the gelding's upper jaw, he said to Ramsey, "It is cruel to force a horse's head over a beam or pole to administer medicine. Far simpler to take a forked stick or pitchfork and run it through the strap fastened to the jaw. As you know and I know, friend Ramsey – and no one knows better than my colleague, Dude – neither man nor beast can drink unless the lower jaw is free. Now, with you and Dude on either side of the halter, but not jerking on Prince, I shall administer the mixture, while forcing the upper jaw gently up with the forked stick. Are you ready?"

They were, and Billy pushed the stick upward with one hand, thus opening the gelding's mouth, and quickly poured in the contents of the jar with the other. Then he withdrew the stick and sat the jar behind him and stroked the saddler's throat. "There!" Billy said. "He took it all. Now, Mr. Ramsey, lead Prince around the corral. Not fast, but at a steady walk. That will help the medicine to work through."

After a while, Billy directed Dude to relieve Ramsey, and minutes later Billy took over. They followed that order for a long time without results. "I don't like this," Billy said, looking at his watch. "It's been half an hour.

Therefore, I shall repeat the remedy." He hastened away and when he rejoined them, he held the fruit jar full again and a pint of oily-looking stuff.

When both medicines were administered, Ramsey walked Prince around and around. About ten minutes had passed when the saddler, perking up his step, suddenly reared and snorted and broke wind. It happened as Ramsey was leading Prince past Dude, waiting to take his turn at the halter. The gelding expelled a heavy discharge of intestinal gas.

"Get out of the way, Dude!" Billy yelled. "He's about to let go everything! Here it comes!"

Too late, Dude stepped aside and looked down at himself in disgust.

"Keep him moving, Mr. Ramsey," Billy instructed, which Ramsey did, and Billy said, "Ah, it's working, men. He's getting relief. He's going to be all right."

After a time, Ramsey halted the saddler at Billy's signal and asked, "What in the world is that stuff, Doctor? It's surefire, like a charge of dynamite."

Billy smiled. "An old and proven remedy of mine developed over the years. One pint of Kentucky sour-mash whiskey with three level tablespoons of common gunpowder, no more, no less.

On the second dose, I followed up with a pint of linseed oil. Now, no feed this evening, friend Ramsey. Switch him to a clean corral and in the morning give him a little bran and salt. By evening you can give him hay. No grain for three days." He glanced at Dude, scarcely concealing a smile. "Dude, pardner, I believe you'd better go to the tank and wash up a bit."

Ramsey led his horse to an adjacent corral and came back. "Doctor," he said, elated and thankful, "how much do I owe you? I can't tell you how much this means to me, to have Prince well again."

"Not one penny, Mr. Ramsey. Glad to help. Another day or so of this and Prince would have been down."

"Well, I'm not one to forget a favor."

Dude returned, walking slowly, looking sheepish.

"Speaking of whiskey and its benefits, when used properly," said Ramsey, "I keep a jug at the barn for medicinal purpoes. I'd like for you gentlemen to sample it."

In the barn, the farmer went to a pile of hay, rummaged about, and pulled out a brown jug. He blew the straw off, drew the cob stopper, and handed the jug to Billy, who took a trial taste, another, then let the jug gurgle, all the while balancing it on his shoulder. "You're a good judge of good whiskey, Mr. Ramsey," he said, passing back the jug.

"Call me Foss. It's made not far from here by an old gentleman who used to live in Kentucky. Seems there was a little ruckus over some horses that sorta found their way into his barn, so he migrated over here, where it's more peaceful." He handed the jug to Dude, who took a swig and smacked his lips. "Mighty fine. Mix that with some sweet spring water and a man would have tonic."

After Ramsey had a long pull at the jug, they sat on bales of hay in the runway, discussing horses in general, crops, the weather, but always the conversation swung back to horses.

"Doctor," Ramsey said, "I want to say again how much I appreciate this. The nearest good vet is forty miles away."

"Always glad to be of service, friend Foss."

Ramsey passed the jug again and Dude, still searching after his disappointment over not finding the red roan saddler, still suspicious, said, "Mr. Ramsey, I can see that you handle a passel of good horses."

Ramsey grinned lopsidedly. His face had taken on a sociable glow. "Like I told the doctor, call me Foss. Yes, I handle a few head," an oblique grin lifting one corner of his mouth at the understatement.

Dude thought, *No man could handle as many horses of different types as he does and not be a contractor out of state.* He said, "It's plain that you're a great horseman. You sell much stock out of state?"

"Not much."

"I reckon you carry on a considerable breeding program?"

"Not much."

"What's the market around here for workstock?"

"Not much."

"How is it for drivin' horses?"

"About the same."

"And for saddlers?"

"No better."

If the market's not good, Dude reasoned, then why so many horses on his farm?

Billy was beginning to look amused at the one-sided exchange.

Still, Dude kept trying. "Any market for runnin' horses? That is, to be shipped out?"

"The same."

"You think horse racin' will ever come back here again?"

"Not so long as the Reverend Joe Bob is in power."

"How can he control the whole county?"

"He preaches all over the county. Holds

camp meetings. Got everybody buffaloed. Besides that, he's got the womenfolks behind him. That's the main reason."

"I can see there's not much fun around here," Dude said, making a wry face.

"Not much? There ain't any." Ramsey passed the jug around and after he'd taken an extra long pull, he said in a firming tone as if he had come to a sudden decision, "That's why, after what you gentlemen did for my Prince horse, I'm gonna celebrate. Me and the missus. We're gonna have us a dance here Saturday night. Starts at sundown. Gonna clean out the barn and have it here. And you two are invited, you and your Indian friend. Will you come?"

"Will we come?" Dude echoed, thinking immediately of Miss Blossom. "I reckon we will!"

Billy would have stood up to leave, but Dude hung on. "It's a shame that one man can hold sway over so many. Same as it's a shame to think of all the good horses and cattle on that big ol' Texas spread waitin' for Si Eckert. It's another shame that we can't locate him." He paused for Ramsey to supply a lead. When none was forthcoming, Dude said, "Hard as times are, there's nothin' more regretful than a man not knowin' he's got a fine inheritance."

"It is," said Ramsey, as noncommittal as before.

"You'd think somebody around Indian Creek would know Si Eckert," Dude said, getting in a final shot.

"You would," Ramsey said.

Dude rose, seeing that he had reached another dead end. They all shook hands, Ramsey thanked them again and again offered to pay Billy, who refused, and the partners bade him good-bye.

"Well," said Billy as they drove off in the wagon, "we don't know any more about Si Eckert than we did before we got here."

"Foss Ramsey knows something," Dude insisted. "How could a man have all these horses and not have a market for 'em somewhere and not know Si Eckert?"

"Where do we go from here? I'm stumped."

"We stay here till we uncover something."

"If we don't?"

"We will. I can't forget what Elsie Yates told us."

"Let's hope we don't come up with another chestnut saddler."

CHAPTER 10

A Clue or the Runaround?

Dude rolled out of his blankets Monday morning to a feeling of moody restlessness. After breakfast, he moped around camp until Billy asked, "What's the matter, you homesick for Texas?"

Dude didn't answer.

Billy cast him a keen little appraisal. "Wouldn't have the calico fever, would you, pardner?"

"Now, did I say?" Dude mimicked.

"Well, there's only one cure for it."

"What's that?"

"Do something about it, and remember that a buggy behind a good drivin' horse is the coziest conveyance there is to and from a country dance."

Within minutes Dude was riding to the store. He tied up in front, his uncertainty offsetting his anticipation, and found Miss Blossom and a gray-haired man engrossed over a ledger. They glanced up as Dude came in, she, quickly, with recognition.

"Father," she said, "this is Mr. Dude McQuinn. He's with Dr. Lockhart, who demonstrated the Eureka Bridle last Saturday."

"I'm Noah Price," her father said. In his gray eyes, Dude discerned the same gentleness and warmth as in his daughter's, and also, Dude thought, the weariness of a storekeeper tending to girth. "We've been selling a good deal of cord since the demonstration. I must say it's a revolutionary way to control a horse or mule, or a rhinoceros, as one fellow told me." So he had a sense of humor, too.

"It works," Dude said as they shook hands.

"Mr. McQuinn and his friends attended last Wednesday's prayer services," Miss Blossom said, interjecting it, Dude sensed, to place him in proper standing.

"But I failed to make it Sunday," Dude confessed.

"So did I," Noah Price said. "Blossom and her mother made up for my absence, which the Reverend Joe Bob no doubt will consider backsliding. But you know, Mr. McQuinn, that doesn't worry me. If I go to hell for missing church now and then, I'll have a heap of company. Truth is, this town is so strait-laced, people won't move here anymore, and some go out of their way to trade elsewhere. Joe Bob is hurting our town."

"Father!" Miss Blossom said, aghast at his frankness.

"What can we do for you, Mr. McQuinn?" he said, redirecting the conversation.

All Dude could think of was, "A slab of bacon, half a dozen cans of tomatoes."

Price filled the order and Dude paid. Still he lingered, hoping for a private word with Miss Blossom.

"Is there anything else?" her father asked.

"There is something," Dude stalled, "but it's slipped my mind. I'll take a look-see. Maybe I'll think of it." Pacing back and forth, he pretended to scan the shelves, wishing the storekeeper would leave him. Instead, Noah Price stayed obligingly at his heels, while Miss Blossom watched with a kind of bewilderment, close to amusement.

A man entered the store, saying, "Noah, I'd like to talk to you about that set of harness." Price motioned him to the rear of the store to his rolltop desk.

"Miss Blossom," Dude said, holding his voice down, "there's a barn dance Saturday night at Foss Ramsey's. Starts at sundown. He's invited our outfit. Will you go with me? I'll be mighty nice to you."

"Oh . . ." She gasped, and blushed with pleasure. "I'd like to very much, Mr. Dude."

"It's plain Dude, remember?"

"Only . . ."

"Only what?"

"Only — it's out of the question."

"Why?"

"My folks. Father might let me, but Mother . . ."

"I'll promise to have you back whenever you say. We can go in Dr. Lockhart's buggy, and his ol' driving horse, Amos, can cover a mile in two minutes." He rubbed his brow in half-teasing, half-serious concentration. "Let's see. The Ramsey place is three miles north of town. I can have you home from there in six minutes flat."

Her yearning was so evident it filled her face like a glow, and then, all at once, it dulled. "I'd love to, but . . ."

"I know. You've been told it's sinful to dance." He shook his head. "How will you know you can or can't go unless you ask?"

She had no reply for that, her troubled eyes downcast.

"If you'll go, I'll promise not to drink any whiskey and not get in any fights — unless some country boy jumps me because I happen to be dancin' with the prettiest girl there."

Her appealing smile broke through her somberness, like a ray of light across her oval face, then faded. She seemed locked within herself, yearning, yet restrained, devout in the severe piety of Indian Creek, the great blue-green eyes a reflector of her innermost emotions.

Voices intruded. Her father and the farmer were coming back, both talking and gesturing.

"I'll be at the Wednesday night prayer meeting," Dude said. "Will you be there?"

"Yes," she answered in a barely audible voice.

"I'll ask you again."

She said no word, but her eloquent eyes said she would listen.

"Don't be afraid," Dude told her, and taking his purchases left the store.

Dude arrived early at the prayer meeting, hoping to find Miss Blossom alone and sit beside her. He looked all around, but did not see her. The singing had commenced by the time Blossom, her father, and a stout, matronly woman, dignified and militant, wearing a floppy-brimmed white hat, arrived and took the nearest seats toward the front.

The singing drew to a close and the Reverend Quincy advanced to the pulpit and announced, "Friends, the topic of my evening sermon is 'Sin Is Everywhere Amongst Us,' " and without further preliminary he launched into his usual onslaught of quotes from the Scriptures, interspersed with arm wavings. Now and then he would throw a punch and shout as the blow landed. When he scored a particular point, one woman's "Amen, brother!" rose higher than all others.

It was, Dude discovered, Blossom's mother. Also, she would jog her head in affirmation and the brim of her large white hat would flop like beating wings. Noah Price sat quietly through all this. At times he dozed, head drooping, and when he did, his wife would elbow him awake.

The reverend's voice grew hoarse. About an hour had passed, Dude estimated, judging by his own squirmings and of those around him, when Quincy shouted, "Let's stomp out sin!" and he went to stomping and punching until the dust fumed up around him. Dude figured a two-round fight had ensued when, as suddenly, Quincy, sweat beading his face, became rock-still and in a much softer hoarseness announced, "Sin is stomped out tonight," and, in a lifting of both hands, signaled the congregation to stand for closing prayer.

Long minutes later, when the praying ended, Dude was one of the first out the door to shake hands with the reverend, who said in pleased surprise, "Glad to have you with us again, Brother McQuinn. I hope this is lasting."

"Thank you, Reverend. Trouble with horse outfits is they don't stay long in one place. They have to drift on. You got your points over tonight right good. Hardest punches I've seen throwed since One-Round Brown took out Cyclone Callahan in San Antone."

"Thank you, Brother McQuinn."

Dude waited outside.

A long time later, it seemed to Dude, Blossom and her parents emerged from the church. When Dude touched the brim of his hat in greeting, Blossom said at once, "Mother, this is Mr. Dude McQuinn. He's a friend of Dr. Lockhart, who demonstrated the safety bridle I was telling you about, and why we're selling so much cord at the store."

Up close, Mrs. Price looked even more formidable. Although her face was well shaped, her jaw had a stern set and her dark eyes were as uncompromising as a zealot's; in all, she thrust out at him a no-nonsense air, an inflexibility. It was plain to Dude that Blossom was her father's daughter.

"Pleased to meet you, ma'am," he said, sweeping off his hat. "It's been a pleasure to know Mr. Price and Miss Blossom."

She nodded curtly. "I understand you have racehorses?"

"Yes, ma'am. Two nice ones. Judge Blair has never lost a race."

"I see, Mr. McQuinn. Although we in Indian Creek are hospitable to strangers, I do not see that we have anything in common with race-horse people. Good evening, sir."

Upon that, she herded Blossom away as if Dude were the plague. Noah Price hesitated, murmuring to Dude, "Sorry, Mr. McQuinn. Er . . . wife Abigail isn't feeling well this evening," and followed his family.

Blossom glanced back once at Dude, dismay and embarrassment caught in her lovely young face. For an instant her hurting eyes locked with his; then she went obediently on.

Dude didn't move for several moments, still seeing Blossom's face before him. He was breathing hard. Churchgoers moved by him, some staring at him curiously. He took a deep breath and walked out to his horse.

After a restless night, he rode to the store Thursday morning around ten o'clock. Blossom wasn't there, nor her father. Only the handy-man-clerk, Horace. Would Miss Blossom be in later? He didn't know. Likely not. Was Mr. Price about? Mr. Price was out in the country. It was the same situation that afternoon when

Dude returned. Friday morning, however, Mr. Price was in the store, as congenial as if nothing had happened at the prayer meeting.

"What can I do for you, Mr. McQuinn?"

The decision came to Dude in a rush. "Sir," he began, "there's a dance tomorrow night at Foss Ramsey's and I would consider it an honor and a great pleasure to escort Miss Blossom there. I would promise to have her back home whenever you say, and I'm not a man who breaks his word."

Price regarded him through understanding eyes, though not necessarily with approval. "This has been a matter of family discussion, Mr. McQuinn," he said, sighing. "As you probably know by now, the town — led by the Reverend Joe Bob — has banned public dances as an instrument of the devil, as a temptation of sin."

"May I ask, sir, do you think the same?"

"If a dance is properly chaperoned, I do not. However, Mrs. Price has a different view, that of Joe Bob. At the moment, that is where we stand." His tone carried dismissal of the subject.

"I'm sorry if I've caused a family problem," Dude apologized. "That was not my intent. I just wanted to take a pretty girl to a dance and see her safely home."

No more was said. Going out, Dude was aware of a mounting disappointment, which stayed with him the following day. In addition, he worried, the outfit was nearing a decision. If nothing developed on Si Eckert within a few days, and likely nothing would, they would have no choice but to turn tail for the Southwest. Come Saturday morning, he busied himself with chores and moped around camp. He would not go back to the store.

Around four o'clock Dude heard a horseman coming from town. It was Horace, the store handyman, riding a lazy bay mare. He overflowed the saddle, bumping up and down. Without a word, he handed Dude a small envelope and rode away.

With anxious fingers, Dude opened the envelope and found a carefully folded note written in a precise, girlish hand which he drank in at a gulp:

Dear Mr. Dude,
    If you still want to take me to the dance, please call for me at six-thirty. I'll explain everything then.

Sincerely,
Blossom

He uttered a whoop and swung his arms and

charged back and forth, loud of voice. "Uncle, I'll need your buggy and Amos after all."

He scrubbed himself and trimmed his beard with care in the looking glass at the wagon, slapped on some bay rum, shrugged into a gray shirt, fastened a dark red silk cravat, bow-tie fashion, brushed his hat and dress coat and trousers, and blacked and shined his boots.

At precisely six-thirty by his fat Waltham pocket watch, he drove the buggy up to the house, tied the reins to the whip socket, stepped down, opened the wooden gate, and went longstriding to the door and rapped twice.

Blossom opened it immediately, saying, "I would ask you in, but it's better to hurry. I'll explain later."

Taking her arm, he escorted her to the buggy and helped her in, catching again the delightful lilac scent that made his head swim. She wore a fluffy, high-necked, long-sleeved blouse of some kind of cream-colored material that felt like silk when he had taken her arm, and her long, flowing skirt of pale blue swirled when she walked. Her light brown hair was tied at her neck with a blue ribbon. In all, he thought, she was enough to swamp a man's senses.

They were beyond town, Amos going at his ground-eating gait, head thrust forward in that keenly competitive manner that always reminded Dude of a road-running chaparral cock, before Blossom spoke.

"I hurried us off because I was afraid Mother would be coming back from an emergency church-business meeting. Collections are down and Reverend Joe Bob is worried. There's some dissatisfaction in the congregation. Anyway, Father said I could go with you, but Mother said not. Also, today, we had a letter from Aunt Lucinda in Louisville — she's Father's sister — and she invited me again to come stay with her and go to school."

"Are you going?"

"I don't know. Mother is against it. You see, I'm her only child."

"I can savvy that. However, you are also your father's only child. What time do you have to be home?"

"Father said ten-thirty."

"Then ten-thirty it shall be. We'll leave at ten twenty-four."

She laughed softly. "How can you be so certain we'll make it in time?"

"Just as I told you, Amos can go a mile in two minutes. He was on the trotting track back in Missouri until he went blind. Uncle Billy bought him not knowing that he couldn't see and it broke his confidence as a horseman for a while. Now he wouldn't take a good farm for the old hoss."

They drove swiftly on. A bold moon rode the sky. A light wind husked over the rolling land, bringing the sweet smells of grass and growing corn. A disturbing concern for Blossom bothered Dude. He asked, "What will your mother say when she finds you gone?"

"I've never halfway slipped off to a dance before. Nor to any dance, for that matter. Though I can well imagine what she will say to Father."

"I reckon," said Dude, his voice regretful, "I've got you in a peck of trouble, Miss Blossom, while not meanin' to. I'm mighty sorry." He took her hand and held it, a gesture that asked for forgiveness, and she did not withdraw it.

"I wouldn't have gone without Father's permission," she said after a moment, "and I wouldn't have that had you not gone to the store and asked him. That was straightforward of you, Mr. Dude."

"It's still Dude, remember?"

They soon reached the Ramsey farm, the yard already crowded with buggies and wagons, and saddle mounts tied to nearby fences. Dude reined over to a fence, where he tied Amos, and hurrying back gave Blossom a hand down, quite conscious of her delightful nearness.

Music swelled from the lighted barn as they strolled away, a fast-moving fiddle rendition of "Cotton-Eyed Joe." Dude shuffled his boots in time. Blossom, suddenly, drew back. "Oh . . . I don't know. I've never danced . . . and there are so many people. I don't know, Dude. I'm afraid."

"You needn't be. I'll show you." He took her hand and led her onward, feeling once again the wish to reassure her and make her happy.

They were passing tied saddle horses. Dude recognized Judge Blair and Texas Jack.

"What is it?" Blossom asked, when Dude stopped.

"Uncle Billy and Coyote are here. Rode in on these two. This, Miss Blossom, is Texas Jack, our slowpoke but likable runner, and this is Judge Blair, the boss hoss. I won him in a poker game down in Texas."

"In a poker game?" She sounded a trifle skeptical.

"You won't believe this, but I haven't played poker since. I quit a winner." He lost his frivolity and sobered. "I'll let you in on a secret. Judge Blair is a mystery horse. The real reason we're in Indian Creek is to find out his true breeding. Si Eckert is supposed to know, who-ever and wherever he is. He was supposed to be in Petersburg, Illinois, too, but wasn't."

"So he really is a mystery," she said, stroking Judge Blair's blaze. "He's such a pretty horse and so gentle. I thought all racehorses were high-strung. Both horses are gentle," she said, in turn petting Texas Jack. "They look like twins."

"They are close," Dude deadpanned, wondering what she would think of the switch. "Texas Jack is an easy-goin' type. Real nice. He'd make a perfect kid horse. As for the Judge, I'll never have another one like him."

"Why is it so important for you to know his breeding?"

"Miss Blossom," he said earnestly, "wouldn't you want to know who your folks are if you didn't know?"

"Oh, yes, certainly."

"Besides, he's a racehorse, and when you get one that can run a hole in the wind, you want to know what he goes back to on both sides. In another way, we feel we owe it to him, he's such an honest horse."

"Honest?"

"Always does his best. Never quits."

"I wish I could help."

The musicians, led by an energetic accordionist, were playing a lively polka when Dude and Blossom entered the packed barn. She held back, in doubt, and Dude, considerately, said, "We'll wait for a waltz." Seeing Billy and Coyote among the watchers, he waved them over.

"Miss Blossom," he said, "you met Dr. Lockhart at the store." She held out her hand to Billy, who gave her an old-world bow and removed his hat. "This is Coyote Walking, our Comanche jockey." Blossom, impressed, likewise offered her hand to him while smiling up at his coppery face. He held his hat and smiled at her.

"I'm very pleased to meet you both," she told them.

"Miss Blossom," Billy put in, "how can a pretty girl like you run around with such a homely Texan? Why, down on the Salt Fork of the Brazos they'd send Dude out of the house to scare the coyotes away."

"Oh, I don't think he's so bad," she replied, laughing, taking Dude's arm.

"Both of you tumbleweeds should be out there dancing," Dude said.

Coyote shook his head. "How can white mans without drums dance? Strange, it is."

After a short pause, the busy accordionist, accompanied by two spritely elder fiddlers and a spirited boy on a guitar, swung into a slow waltz. At that, Dude said, "This is our dance, Blossom," and took her right hand in his left and placed his right hand lightly around her slender waist.

"I don't know," she faltered.

"Just follow me and everything will work out just fine."

She was light on her feet and easy to lead and soon they were moving briskly, Dude mindful not to step on her toes, whisking here and there on the crowded floor; then they were flouncing.

"Are you sure you've never danced before?" Dude asked, looking down at her.

"Positive."

"I'm just as positive you've already learned to waltz."

Next he led her through the two-step in march time, but she begged off when another polka began. At intermission they drank lemonade. On the warm evening air Dude caught the drift of bourbon fumes as the crowd milled. Two girls near Blossom's age reacted with surprise when they saw her. "Blossom, we can't believe it's you!" one said.

"It is," Blossom said, blushing, "and I'm enjoying every minute of it." She introduced Dude. While the girls chatted, Billy eased over to Dude and said, "Ramsey's got his snoot a little wet. He's plumb maudlin about Prince. Keeps thanking us. He wants you to have a drink with him. I've already made one trip to the jug."

Dude started to refuse, thinking of his promise to Blossom; then a thought surfaced in his mind and intensified, with it his stubborn perseverance, and he remembered the evasiveness the outfit had met whenever Si Eckert was mentioned. He excused himself, leaving Blossom with her chatty friends, and followed Billy through the knots of idle dancers to Ramsey standing near the doorway. He threw Dude a lopsided grin and led them outside and over to a shed. There he reached inside and hefted up a jug.

"Le's all drink t'ol' Prince," he slurred and passed the jug to Dude, who took a nip and handed it back. Ramsey held it out to Billy, who had a pull. Ramsey then had an extra long gurgle. "Le's see. Ah don't want t'ferget your remedy, Doc, ol' friend. One pint o' sour mash, three level tablespoonfuls o' common gunpowder, n'more, n'less." He cackled. "Y'mean some gunpowder is uncommon?"

"Don't forget the linseed oil," Billy said. "A pint after the second dose, if the first one fails to fire."

Ramsey cackled again and his voice broke a little as he said, "Never been a hoss like my ol' Prince. Like one o' th' family. Wish Ah could do somethin' for you fellers in return. Jus' name it an' it's yours, sure as shootin'. Betcha boots, m'friends. Foss Ramsey keeps his word."

"Come to think of it there is something, Mr. Ramsey," Dude said, so bluntly that Ramsey reared back. "You might tell us where Si Eckert is."

"Si Eckert, Si Eckert?" Ramsey chortled. "That fella you asked m'about before. The fella with th' inheritance." He was cackling, as if some hidden meaning amused him. "Well, Ah can tell you this: There ain't no Si Eckert around Indian Creek f'sure."

Disgust twisted Dude's mouth. More of the same old runaround.

"If you know Eckert's not here," he said reasonably, "maybe you can tell us where he is?"

Ramsey was silent for an interval, and when he spoke he sounded almost sober. "Ah'll tell you this an' n'more." A moment passed before he spoke again. "He's over around Lexington somewhere. That's gospel, m'friends."

"About where around Lexington?" Dude hung on, starting to feel a core of excitement, at the same time trying not to push too fast.

"That's all Ah know an' Ah wouldn't be tellin' you that . . . only you're true-blue friends an' you saved my ol' Prince horse. Ah can't never f'get that."

"That's mighty helpful of you, friend Foss," Billy said, all amiability. "Indeed it is. We thank you so Eckert can claim his rightful inheritance, and for another reason. From one horseman to another."

"What's that?" Ramsey cut back, with an awakening suspicion.

Does he think we're Pinkertons? Dude asked himself.

"Eckert," Billy continued, "knows the breeding of our racehorse, Judge Blair. That's all we want to know. No more. Two birds with one stone, you might say."

"Oh — just that," Ramsey breathed, as if relieved. "Now, m'friends, le's all have another little tipple at th' jug an' go back to th' dance. What say, m'friends?"

It was over here, Dude knew. Ramsey would reveal no more, but a surging elation invested Dude. A clue, a hot clue — at last!

Ramsey replaced the jug in its hiding place and set an erratic course for the barn, Billy and Dude lagging behind. "This is it," Dude said, low. "I felt all along our search would lead us back to Kentucky, where the Thoroughbreds run. We can leave tomorrow. You for it, Uncle?"

"We've already come a distance of ground. Let's go on to the finish line."

The musicians were playing "Cotton-Eyed Joe" again, and Dude reclaimed Blossom from her friends and away they whirled in rhythm. The evening seemed to rush by on winged feet. They waltzed, they two-stepped, they even did the polka. Twice Blossom danced with boys from town. With regret, Dude glanced at his Waltham and told her, "It's time to go, Blossom." She made a pretty little face of denial. "I have to keep my word," he said seriously.

It was ten-fifteen when Dude escorted her out to the buggy, behind them the swirling sounds of another polka and fast-moving feet and young laughter and whoops.

Neither spoke as they headed homeward, Amos striding out, Dude wishing the old campaigner wouldn't move quite so fast tonight.

The house was dark when Dude stopped the trotter. "Miss Blossom," he said, "Foss Ramsey told us something tonight. What we've been trying to find out: Si Eckert lives around Lexington. So we're going there."

"You're leaving?"

"Tomorrow. We have to go on. We'll stop in Louisville on the way. Maybe match a race."

"I understand, but . . ."

"I thank you for going with me tonight, Blossom."

"I thank you for taking me, Dude. I do, so much. Such fun."

"My pleasure." He hesitated. "May I write you?"

"Yes – and I'll write you, if you like?"

"*If I like?* You bet! Send it general delivery at Louisville and Lexington."

"I will."

She looked toward the house, so it was time for her to go in, and he helped her out and to the gate. Dude's mind was whirling. Lightning had struck. What right did a tumbleweed horseman like himself have to tell –?

Her voice cut across before he could finish. "This is the most fun I've ever had. It was so nice and you were so good to me." To his astonishment, she kissed him on the cheek, a shy, uncertain kiss, yet so lovely and sweet that he was shaken. She seemed to be waiting. Then he kissed her on the lips with all the tenderness within him and he could feel her responding. Both stood back, stricken mute, staring at each other in wonder.

Finally, he managed, "I won't say good-bye, Blossom, just good night, and don't be afraid anymore," and turning he strode to the buggy and climbed in and drove off in a haze of euphoria.

CHAPTER 11

The Duke of Dexter

Churchill Downs.

The three of them – Billy, Coyote, and Dude – faced the massive grandstand and its spires and gawked like country yokels at the immensity of the sprawling, empty structure, then gazed down the long, killing stretch of the yellow-earth straightaway, where on the greatest of racing days in May a horseman's hopes and dreams could turn to heartbreak as his vaunted three-year-old faltered in final stride to the finish pole.

"Kentucky is the cradle of Thoroughbred racing," Billy said, folding his arms, "and the Kentucky Derby is the hand that rocks it."

"It makes a man feel mighty small," Dude agreed, awed, sensing the stirring history of the Downs.

"Buffalo runner like this track would," said Coyote.

"Aristides, called 'the little red horse,' won the first Derby in 1875," Billy continued, now in a lecturing mood. "He was by Leamington, imported, out of Sarong, she by the noble Lexington, her dam Greek Slave." His voice quickened with excitement. "Volcano took the lead, Verdigris, Aristides, and McCreery up close. They ran like that the first half mile. Aristides moved up to second place along the backstretch, lapping Volcano, then charged to the front. Down the homestretch Volcano came with a rush, but the game little red hoss hung on to win by a length. . . . There were forty-two nominations to the Derby, but only fifteen horses started. The winner took home $2,850, a pile of money in those days. It is interesting to note how they started races then. The horses moved up at the tap of the drum and the starter dropped the flag when they reached the starting pole in an even line."

"Reckon you enjoyed seeing all that," Dude pried, on the sly, fishing into his old mentor's past.

"Now, did I say I saw it?" Billy bristled.

"Wonder who won the second Derby?" Dude asked, to test him further, and when Billy replied, not even pausing, "Vagrant, a brown gelding by Virgil, out of Lazy," Dude pried no more. The old man had an uncanny memory for racehorses and racing history, and was still as tetchy as a riled cougar about his mysterious past. Once in a while a sliver of light would leak through unexpectedly, such as when Poge Yates had let drop about the fast getaway horse, which revealed that Uncle once had running horses in Illinois. Had he ever raced in Kentucky? Maybe so, maybe not. Whatever, he had shown an immediate interest at the prospects of searching for Si Eckert in Kentucky, such as just before they departed Indian Creek, when he had said:

"We've gone to church, Coyote has spoken to the young people, I've demonstrated the Eureka Safety Bridle and doctored horses, and we took in a country dance — and all we've learned is that this invisible Si Eckert is around Lexington somewhere. The same was said for Indian Creek, as I recall. Well, pardners, a change is on the way. Hereafter, we're gonna try it my way. If we find this Eckert fella, I believe it will be around a racetrack, which means we campaign the Judge as the Duke. If you don't see it this way, I'm going back to Kansas."

Dude and Coyote swapped winks: *Good. Heap good. Mighty good. This is like the old Billy we used to know. He is back for certain now.*

"It's all right with me, Uncle," Dude agreed, "and I reckon a man can get too pious. But don't forget that if you hadn't cured Ramsey's saddler of the colic, and if we hadn't gone to the dance, we wouldn't have the Lexington lead." At his mention of the dance Dude thought instantly of Miss Blossom.

"Did I say I'd forgotten that?" Billy snapped. "What do you think, Coyote? If you don't like it, speak up."

"Like that I would, Grandfather. Also, the Duke of Dexter has a poetic alliteration."

"Only don't call me Grandfather." He was crotchety today!

And so it was decided to campaign Judge Blair as the Duke of Dexter, which couldn't have suited the younger partners more.

"Appears to me," Dude observed, gazing suggestively around the Downs again, "this is just the place to see how the Judge, I mean the Duke, would do against these fancy-blooded Kentucky Thoroughbreds before we get to Lexington. Just how would we go about gettin' him a race, Uncle?"

"You go to the Racing Secretary's office," Billy explained, taking the bait as Dude hoped. "If you two don't mind, I'll drift up there and see what I can do. I've got the Duke's papers right here." He patted the breast pocket of his coat.

"This big racetrack stuff is all new to me," Dude kept on. "I'm just a country boy."

"Me no savvy either," Coyote feigned, falling back on his gibberish, and he and Dude nodded as one: *Let's send him by himself. He needs this.*

Billy cut them a keen look and there was a brief but heavy pause before he spoke. "Believe I'm acquainted with a certain Comanche who can spout Shakespeare with any professor, and believe I know a country boy from the Salt Fork of the Brazos who can slick a city slicker out of his last pair of socks."

He was gone so long that Dude feared Billy had run into trouble. When at last he stood before them, he was wearing an expression so indifferent and purposeless that Dude was puzzled.

"You should see the secretary's office," Billy reported, his manner offhand. "Why, there's two clerks besides himself, and pictures on the wall of all the Derby winners, and shiny cuspidors set all around. Mighty impressive. It's —"

"What about our race?" Dude broke in.

"Well, the secretary looked at the papers and said everything was in order. No question there. But he wondered why we were running the Duke here again, after he'd never come close to money before. I explained we'd just come into possession of the Duke and he was sound for the first time in years and we just wanted an out to sharpen him up. That we plan to campaign him in the fall races at Lexington. Then the secretary —"

"What about the race?" Dude insisted, growing louder.

"Oh, the race," Billy echoed vaguely, but before Dude could say more, he broke into a crinkling grin. "A week from Saturday the Duke goes out in the Louisville Handicap, for four-year-olds and up, at six furlongs." He moved into a little shuffling dance and his partners jumped up whooping and slapped him on the back.

"The handicapper should give us a low impost since the Duke has never come close to winning here," Billy said, after they had all quieted down. "The draw will be Friday before the race. The secretary, who also assigned us a stall, expects a twelve-horse field. Winner takes home five hundred dollars. Since we're a late entry, we had to pay fifty dollars to get in."

"Whew!" Dude whistled. "These fancy Thoroughbred races do come high, don't they? How do you figure we should train the Judge for this one?"

"First thing," Billy cautioned, "we've got to

quit calling the Judge the Judge. Next, I don't think there's any danger of somebody trying to slip in and fix our horse, but you never know. One of us should sleep outside his stall every night. Since the Duke thrives on work, we'll gallop him seven furlongs every other day to lengthen him out. Blow him out hard two days before the race, then let him rest." He removed his glasses and pinched the bridge of his nose. "It just comes to me that this will be the first time our horse has ever run between horses, with the exception of a third horse put in a time or two in match races to bump the Judge, I mean the Duke. It can get tight in there with twelve horses. Somebody may try to cut you off, Coyote. Old stuff. In the back of my mind, I guess I'm trying to get us ready for Lexington. I want him to be at his peak then and attract attention. You know what I mean. Now, let's head for the barn. The secretary says we can camp not far from the track."

That afternoon, on impulse, Dude rode to the post office and asked for his mail at the general delivery window. The bored clerk flipped through a stack of letters, paused, and still looking at a letter asked, "You are Mr. Dude McQuinn?"

"You bet I am!" Dude vouched, scarcely believing he could have a letter this soon. He recognized the girlish handwriting at a glance and opened the envelope with impatient fingers. The letter read:

Dear Mr. Dude,

You've been gone but a few days and it seems forever. I wonder if I'll ever see you again. I am still enjoying the memory of the barn dance. Father was pleased that you had me home by ten-thirty. To my surprise, Mother said very little, though I know she was displeased. I don't want to make her unhappy, because I know she loves me and I love her and Father very much. I must decide soon whether to go to school in Louisville or stay here and help in the store. I pray for guidance.

My blessings on you and Dr. Lockhart and Coyote.

Affectionately, Blossom

He purchased envelopes and writing paper at a drugstore and returning to the post office penned this letter in his laborious, cowpuncher scrawl:

Dear Miss Blossom,

Mighty happy to have your letter received today. This morning we went out to

Churchill Downs and I got my tonsils sunburned just looking where the greatest horse race in the world is run. Uncle Billy has us entered in the Louisville Handicap, a six-furlong go, come Sept. 21. Wish you could be here to see our horse run.

My top regards to you and your folks.

Always yours, Dude

P.S. Yes, Blossom, I'll see you again. I promise, and I was brought up to keep my word.

The days passed swiftly as the outfit settled in, each partner taking turns sleeping outside the stall on a cot, Billy insisting that he share the watch. Coyote reported that the "Duke" seemed to like the track. "It's not a hard surface," Billy said. "Maybe it feels like the country tracks he's used to."

On Friday at the drawing for post positions, which the entire outfit attended in the Racing Secretary's office, Billy drew the 5 hole. The trainer of Sandusky, the favorite carrying top weight of 121 pounds, pulled 6, and the owner of Big Duke, the second betting choice and weighted at 118, drew 4. The Duke would carry the lowest impost of 113 pounds.

"We're between the two favorites," Billy said later. "But it's no disadvantage."

"Unless they try to box me in," Coyote said in a worried tone.

"Bide your time if you're boxed in early," Billy instructed. "It's when you turn for home that they separate the runnin' horses from the also-rans."

"What if boxed in I still am there?"

"You'll have to make a decision, Coyote, pardner. Don't worry. You'll know what to do. You always have."

"Wish wise I were like you, Grandfather."

Billy started to retort. Instead, he only smiled reassuringly.

By Saturday morning, when he had not received another letter from Blossom, Dude decided that she had chosen to stay in Indian Creek. Although he could understand why, and what had influenced her, a sad disappointment for her took hold of him. She deserved better. And in his mind recurred the feeling that he had no right to think of her further. He was much older, for one thing. Only out of the sweet goodness of her young heart had she written him, only because, for one evening, she had experienced the rightful joy of a young girl for so long denied music and dancing and fun with mutual friends. Her sweet letter was a thank-you, nothing more. And now he had made a promise which ought not to be carried out.

He was riding along the shedrow, nursing his gloomy thoughts. Early racegoers were strolling past the stalls, viewing the horses, some talking with horsemen. At the Judge's stall two women were chatting with Billy and Coyote. As Dude rode up, the women turned and he saw Blossom and an older woman, a sight that literally froze him to the saddle and sent his chest to pounding. Blossom was wearing a brightly flowered hat and a long-sleeved dress of soft pearl gray. Then, remembering his manners, he dismounted and holding the reins crossed over to them.

Blossom was blushing furiously as she met his eyes and all Dude's doubts vanished. Turning, she said, "Auntie, this is Mr. Dude McQuinn. My Aunt Lucinda Adams."

Dude swept off his hat, seeing a pleasing woman with the same gray eyes as Noah Price, within them the same tolerance and understanding.

She held out a graceful hand. "How do you do, Mr. McQuinn. Blossom told me how nice you've been to her."

Dude almost stammered. "Be no other way. Mighty pleased to meet you, ma'am."

"Auntie is a racing fan," Blossom said. "She's a member of the Louisville Jockey Club and has a box in the grandstand."

"We'd like you to sit with us during the Handicap, if your duties permit?" Auntie said, the gray eyes warmly inviting.

"Thank you, ma'am. But I'll be ponyin' our horse."

"I'll handle that today," Billy spoke up. "Go on with the ladies."

Dude glanced at Coyote, who nodded: *Let Grandfather. Let's keep him going.*

"Whatever you say, Uncle," Dude replied, and to the women, "I'll join you after the horses leave the paddock for the post parade. Ours is the last race."

"Box eighteen in the grandstand, section A, near the finish line," Mrs. Adams said.

Dude's eyes trailed after them, then, "Thanks, Uncle, you and Coyote. You sure it's all right?"

"Think you're the only one who can pony a horse?" the old man snorted. "I could ride the Duke in a showdown."

"Grandfather could," Coyote attested, and drew a rebuking look from the old man for the usual reason.

CHAPTER 12

A Field of Thoroughbreds

The afternoon lengthened into restive boredom. The partners seemed to take turns pacing up and down in front of the stall. They rubbed the Judge down and gave him a sip of water and talked to him. Now and then one would get up and rub on him a little more and say something. At times the dark bay gelding seemed to doze, a deceptive languor that would vanish the moment they saddled him. While they waited, horses were ponied by for the early races, which Dude could see were started by flag alone. No tapping of the drum. The olden times had changed at least some, if not much. He could count the races by the roar and ebb of the screaming, shouting crowd.

Before long Coyote, carrying riding tack, left for the jockeys' quarters on the other side of the track near the stands. The other riders stared when he entered with saddle, bridle, and saddle blanket. He weighed in and the amiable Clerk of Scales, heavyset with a sunburned bald head, said, "You're three pounds under," and inserted lead sheets into a pad under the saddle. Then he pinned a big number 5 on each side of the blanket. "Where are your silks?" he asked, curiously.

"Today I ride naked to the waist," Coyote said. "Just a breechcloth and moccasins. Sometimes I paint my body. Today I did not."

More curiously, "No cap?"

"No cap. Just headband."

"Well, young man, I guess it's proper enough so long as you don't ride naked. Good luck." He was a kind man and Coyote liked him for that.

By this time Coyote had attracted the attention of every rider in the room. He moved to a bench and sat down with his gear, thinking ahead to the Handicap. Never had he ridden against more than two horses, and the put-ins, as Grandfather Billy called them, didn't last long, fading soon after their bumping was done. What he feared most was crowding, horses bearing in on the Judge, making it difficult for him to run.

A pinch-faced man in varicolored silks, years of hard riding engraved across his weathered features, sauntered over, his manner patronizing and inquired, "You an Indian, or some kind of A-rab?"

"Comanche, I am."

"Comanche, huh?" He turned to the others. "Hey, boys, what d'you know, we're up against a wild Indian."

Coyote said no word. *Let the white man talk. Wind does not races win.*

The rider went on. "Where's your whip? You didn't weigh in with one."

"I need no whip."

"No whip? How d'you make your mount go faster?"

"I ride him faster."

They all cracked up laughing. Another jockey sidled up to the questioner. "You're on the Duke of Dexter," the pinch-faced man said, nudging the other. "Couple of years ago here he couldn't outrun a fat man."

"That," said Coyote smiling, "was then. Sound he is now. What is your mount?"

"Sandusky, the favorite, the 6 horse. He's been out five times this year. Won 'em all by daylight. Two stakes. My name is Spider Keeley. I was leading rider in the spring meet here. Maybe you've heard of me?" The last spoken in a tone that implied Coyote should have heard.

"Sorry, I have not. Your fame, great as it is,

has not reached the Plains."

More jockeys drifted over. It was evident to Coyote that they all yielded to Keeley, who now asked, "What's your monicker, Comanche?"

"My name is Coyote Walking."

That produced another burst of laughter, which seemed to encourage Keeley. "Coyote Walking? Why didn't they name you Walking Coyote? Makes more sense." The other riders nodded.

Coyote let his eyes, veiled in amusement, rest on Keeley for a moment or two. "Either way the coyote is walking. That is the thing."

"How come y'don't wear silks? You're supposed to wear silks in a Thoroughbred race."

"My silks are here," Coyote said, indicating his coppery arms and torso.

Keeley was actually sneering, trying to intimidate Coyote. "Or *do* you have Thoroughbreds out there?"

"We have everything, and keep we do not our horses in cramped stalls and small pastures like here. Out there we let our horses run free on the prairie."

"Ease off over there, Spider," the clerk called. "You Handicap riders get ready."

"One more thing," Keeley told Coyote. "Don't crowd me at the break. I wouldn't like that, Injun."

"In turn," said Coyote, looking him in the eyes, "do not grab my saddle when past you I go in the stretch. Do and I will do this." He made a chopping motion.

"Pass me on the Duke of Dexter?" Keeley let out a giant heehaw and held his stomach.

The clerk moved toward them, his voice heavy with annoyance. "I said ease off. Keep this up, Spider, tryin' to buffalo every new boy that comes in here and, by God, you'll go before the stewards!"

They let Coyote alone after that and ten minutes later the clerk called jockeys for the main race and they trooped out to the saddling paddock with their tack.

Dude draped the light saddle blanket over the Judge's short back and carefully smoothed it out, then Billy laid the saddle on, settled it comfortably, and cinched up. Not liking something, a fine point that escaped Dude's notice, Billy uncinched, settled the saddle more firmly, then cinched up again, making certain the latigo strap was securely tied.

The paddock judge, or horse identifier, a lean, intense, methodical man, wearing a white planter's hat, was moving from stall to stall, checking off horses from a list. He came to the outfit's number 5 stall and studied the Judge for a full minute before he spoke. "May I see the registration papers, please, gentlemen?"

That request, Dude knew nervously from watching, had not been made of the owners and trainers of the first four horses.

"Right here," Billy said, composed, taking the papers from his coat pocket.

In between sharp glances at the Judge, the official seemed to be reading line by line. "I'd like to look at his teeth," he said, and Billy, obligingly, was there before him, opening the Judge's mouth. The identifier looked up and down and from side to side. "He's a six, all right," he said, stepping back. "The cups are worn from the two middle teeth and shaded into the next tooth on both sides. As good as this horse looks, I first thought he might be younger."

Just as Dude felt his tension ease, the man, skeptically, was studying the Judge anew. "I remember the Duke of Dexter name more than I do the individual," he said. "That's a high-sounding name, even for a Thoroughbred. The Duke didn't run well here. Seemed sored up. However, I also remember the horse and his markings."

And let's hope, Dude prayed to himself, you don't look at him sideways and see there's no goose rump, sir. We can't hide that. But you might overlook the fact that this horse has that good sloping shoulder and the Duke didn't, if you remember, sir, and let's hope you don't remember the Duke's calf knees. Please, sir.

"He's sound for the first time in several years and is catching up on himself," Billy said. "He's a good keeper and he knows where the finish line is. We got him over in Illinois."

"Do you have the bill of sale, sir?"

Dude relapsed into a cold sweat as Billy answered frankly, "I don't have the bill of sale because there was no bill of sale. This horse was given to me in payment of an old debt. I'll be more than glad to have you verify that by a telegram after the race to Mr. Poge Yates, Petersburg, Illinois, two miles east of town." He regarded the identifier much as he might were they discussing the transaction for a bale of hay. "As you can understand, I wouldn't have the registration papers if Mr. Yates hadn't sold me the horse or given him to me. Nobody would take this horse."

"Well —" said the man, somewhat mollified.

"We'll stay in Louisville as long as necessary to verify ownership," Billy said. "However, we hope there won't be a long delay, since we plan to run the Duke at Lexington, now that he's sound. It's up to you, sir, and the secretary. We'll abide by what you say."

"That won't be necessary, sir. It's my duty,

244

you understand, to check every horse that goes to post at the Downs."

"We do understand, sir, and are heartily in accord with these precautions against any ringers or ill-bred horses being brought in." He gave the appearance of growing taller as he acquired the saintly look of old. "Above all, the integrity of the Downs, where the greatest horse race in the world is run, must be guarded with the utmost surveillance." All the time he was nodding to give impact to his words.

The man, appeased, handed the papers back to Billy. "Sorry about the delay, gentlemen. Good luck."

As the identifier moved on to the next stall, Dude exhaled a long, slow breath and Billy's cherry-red lips formed a very small *O*.

Some of Dude's tension remained even while he watched the paddock official go from stall to stall, checking off the other entries, moving faster now; apparently, he knew these horses and trainers. Soon Dude heard him call, "Riders up," and after that a bugle sounded the clear notes of "Boots and Saddles."

Coyote looked grimly determined. Dude gave him a leg up and Billy, as if he were coaching a boy, said, "Bide your time in the early going, Coyote, and remember your horse can run when you call on him for more. He can go the distance and beyond. Now, good luck, pardner."

Dude slapped Coyote's back; Billy mounted Texas Jack and, taking the lead shank, led horse and rider out to the track for the post parade.

Dude sighed worriedly, watching them, hoping Coyote could avoid trouble, and began picking his way through the clamorous crowd to the grandstand and box eighteen.

He was invited to sit between the two ladies. "You look mighty nice, Miss Blossom," he said, thinking she already appeared more grown-up than at Indian Creek.

She blushed and murmured something indistinct. While they watched the parade to post, she asked him, "What number is your horse, Mr. Dude?"

"Five."

She looked down the program. "But the 5 horse is listed as the Duke of Dexter." Aunt Lucinda also turned to him in question.

Dude hesitated, searching for a plausible explanation. "He has two names. He ran as a quarter horse in Texas as Judge Blair and also back in Illinois. Over here he's the Duke, a Thoroughbred."

"But . . . ?"

"To run on a recognized track like this, he has to use his . . . uh . . . other name, the Duke of Dexter, which is registered."

Blossom wrinkled her brow. Auntie kept silent, but her eyes became wise and secretly amused.

Just then, as Billy ponied the Judge past the stands, the crowd took note of Coyote and started whooping and calling out to him. Coyote waved and made the Judge dance.

"I'll explain more later," Dude said, in haste. "One thing about him, there's never been a more honest horse. He runs with heart. Gives it all he has." To the aunt, he said, "I've told Blossom the reason we left Texas was to find out his breeding. Maybe she mentioned that?"

"Only that you are looking for a man named Si Eckert in that connection."

"We've been told he lives around Lexington and rides a red roan saddler with a three-pointed star and a stripe." He shrugged. "We were also told he was in Petersburg, Illinois, and Indian Creek."

"How do you figure your chances today, Mr. McQuinn?" Out of tact, he sensed, she hadn't used the Judge's name.

"Good — if he can get out where he can run. He's never run between horses before. We blew him out at daybreak Thursday and he went six furlongs in one-eleven and was still full of himself."

Her gray eyes showed an instant interest.

"You said one-eleven?"

"Yes, ma'am."

"Against another good horse?"

"All by his lonesome."

"You-all excuse me," Aunt Lucinda said, rising. "There's the Fat Man down there waving a fistful of greenbacks." She left in a hurry.

Dude looked at Blossom. "Seeing you again makes me believe in miracles."

"I was afraid I couldn't find you in Louisville, even after I got your letter. It's so big."

"But only one Churchill Downs. Glad you got my letter in time so you could come to the race."

"Yes. And you've already kept your promise."

"I just want you to be happy and not afraid. Here, you can go to school and still be close to home."

"I've enrolled at Bryant and Stratton Business School. I thought that would be more practical the first year." She favored him a teasing smile. "You know, the storekeeper's daughter."

He started to take her hand and say much more, when Aunt Lucinda came puffing up the steps, a bettor's glint in her eyes. "I just got forty-to-one odds on the Duke." She winked. "I'd take that on a three-legged mule."

Coyote, going at a slow trot on Judge Blair

alongside Texas Jack and Grandfather, spotted the favored Sandusky and Big Blue just ahead. Sandusky was a powerfully muscled chestnut stud, while the second-choice blue roan had the sleek lines of a speed horse.

"Let 'em all rush up there and sweat out their horses," Billy said. "We'll take our time and relax our horse while we're gettin' there."

By the time they reached the area of the starting pole on the backstretch, the early runners were milling in short circles. Billy released the Judge and yelled a "good luck." When all the horses had arrived, the starter, a Kentucky colonel type – white linen suit, planter's hat, string tie, pointed goatee, and a luxuriant mustache – shouted instructions and waved them to form a line. They jostled and pranced and reared. Assistant starters grabbed the bits of the more nervous horses and led them forward. The confusion cleared and the horses advanced on a fairly straight front. But Sandusky jumped off just before they reached the starting pole, and the starter shouted them back. More turning and milling and persuasion. Once again they formed a line, with the starter shouting at lagging riders to close up. Finally, all heads were about even.

A fraction before the starter dropped his flag, Keeley jumped Sandusky out and the race was on in a chorus of shouts and a rain of clods, the roar of the crowd following in a billow of sound. Keeley had beaten the flag. At the same time Coyote felt the eager Judge Blair stumble and right himself. Thus, they were the last to break, the field sweeping ahead, a bobbing wave of color.

Bide your time early. Grandfather's words drummed through Coyote's head. Patience, yet he fought it. He must settle his horse and begin a gradual move to the leaders. He couldn't make up the lost ground at once. He knew Sandusky had taken the lead.

Grimly, Coyote chirruped to his horse and they took off after the pack. Within a short distance, Judge Blair was taking hold of the track, running smoothly, stretching out. Stride by stride, they began to make up ground. Racing into the turn as he felt the Judge change to his left lead, Coyote suddenly found horses on both sides of him. Too close. Too close. A horse swerved wildly toward Judge Blair. Coyote flinched and shouted simultaneously. At the last moment the other jockey brought his horse back on a straight course.

At the three-eighths pole Judge Blair began passing horses. Ahead, Coyote saw the field thinning. At the quarter pole he could see Sandusky holding the lead, Big Blue driving at him from the outside. On the rail the 1 horse, a bright bay, was coming on to challenge.

Coyote whooped for the first time when the field turned for home at the top of the stretch, and Judge Blair, in full stride, making a flying change back to his right lead, shortened the gap between him and the three front-runners. Of a sudden only a length separated them. Coyote, feeling more power under him as he whooped again, aimed his horse between Sandusky and the bay on the rail.

As if hearing thunder, Keeley jerked and glanced over his left shoulder. He gaped in astonishment. Humping lower, he whipped right-handed and Sandusky, responding powerfully, started bearing to the left, closing Coyote's horse off. A clever move, just enough to block the charging Judge.

They ran in that order to the eighth pole, Coyote unable to drive between the chestnut and the bay, and shut off to the outside where Big Blue ran at Sandusky's right hindquarters. Coyote was boxed in, what he had feared all along in a large field. He kept his horse there, hanging close, waiting, biding.

It was at the sixteenth pole that the race changed. The 1 horse on the rail suddenly lost heart and dropped back, fading. Coyote, seeing the swath of narrow daylight opening, raised a curdling whoop and sent his horse around the bay and cutting to the inside. He was on the rail now, at Sandusky's saddle cloth. Keeley raked Coyote a backward glance, wide-eyed amazement flooding his pinched face. Coyote whooped again and Judge Blair came flying, making up ground. The two horses were running head to head now, Keeley slashing Sandusky without letup.

Dude had raised his hands in pain, stunned to silence, when Judge Blair stumbled at the break. But when Coyote had the Judge moving well into the turn, Dude shouted encouragement and by then Blossom and Aunt Lucinda were adding their voices. They watched, still shouting, while Coyote sent the dark bay between horses in the turn, driving on the leaders.

When Keeley cut Coyote off, Dude groaned, "He's boxed in — cut off!"

"But here he comes!" Blossom yelled moments later as the 1 horse faded along the rail and Coyote shot Judge Blair into the gap. By now both women were screaming and jumping up and down, Aunt Lucinda hollering, "Come on forty-to-one!" and Dude, "Come on, Coyote!"

It was then, above the roaring crowd, that

Dude heard the Comanche's high-pitched whoop, calling on his horse for still more. *Run like buffalo horse. Run, horse, run.* Coyote was so low in the saddle he seemed a mere extension of Judge Blair.

Dude, himself whooping, saw them break the deadlock then, by a nose, by a head, by a neck, by half a length, then drawing away. That margin clearly defined as they flashed past the finish pole, Big Blue driving a length behind the second-place Sandusky. The crowd was strangely hushed.

Dude hugged both women and they hugged him and then as he looked at Blossom, she, blushing, kissed him and he kissed her and they held each other for a moment.

"Let's go down to the winner's circle," he said. The women held back. "It's all right," he assured them. "I own the horse."

"After I see the Fat Man," Aunt Lucinda chortled.

On the happy ground of the winner's circle, a track official placed the victory blanket bearing the Louisville Handicap in large letters over Judge Blair while curious railbirds watched. After the ceremony, Aunt Lucinda said, "This deserves a celebration. You're all invited to my house for supper this evening at six. Can you come?"

"I reckon we can manage." Dude grinned, looking at his partners.

She gave them an address on Oak Street.

On the way that evening, the partners crowded into Billy's single-seated buggy behind Amos, Dude said with a twinge of guilt, "I'd better tell you two that the ladies know about the Judge masqueradin' as the Duke. I showed Miss Blossom the horses that evening at Foss Ramsey's dance. Then today, when she asked me our number and she found the Duke listed on the program, I had to explain something."

Billy shrugged off the disclosure and gave him a tolerant smile. "That's about the first time an Alamo Texan ever got backed into a box canyon and had to talk his way out of it. It's all right, Dude. These ladies won't say anything. Even so, I think we'd better head out for Lexington first thing in the morning."

"Just like old times." Dude made a face. "Take the money and get out of town. Good thing you collected right after the race."

"That's one rule a horseman should always follow."

An exuberant Aunt Lucinda met them at the door. "Gentlemen, that was such an exciting race. A beautiful ride, Mr. Walking. You were up against one of the best jockeys in Kentucky.

By best, I mean he's very aggressive. He's been set down more than once for rough riding. He's also slick about it sometimes."

Coyote nodded. "I know. He cut me off just enough. No bumping."

"If you had claimed a foul, I doubt that the stewards would have dropped Sandusky back to second had he won, it was that close a call."

She was still elated at dinner. "When Mr. McQuinn told me the Judge — rather the Duke — had a six-furlong morning work in one-eleven, I ran down and bet a bunch at forty to one. Afraid I broke the Fat Man. But he's taken plenty off me over the years. Dr. Lockhart, Mr. McQuinn told us you're on a search to trace the Judge's breeding."

"We are," Billy acknowledged, a trifle uncomfortable about the subject.

As if discerning that, she said, "He explained why the Judge was run as the Duke. I understand. It's not the first time a quarter horse has been campaigned under another name as a Thoroughbred. On the other side of the coin, sprinting Thoroughbreds sometimes run in short races."

"Judge Blair could well be a Thoroughbred," Billy said, in a thoughtful vein, "and he has beaten Thoroughbreds in match races. The last one that comes to mind was Royal Road, the fine Missouri Thoroughbred, stolen and taken to Kansas and run as Flying Tom. My wife happened to purchase Royal Road as Flying Tom before we were married, not knowing he was stolen. The horse has since been returned to its rightful owner in Missouri."

"Well, Judge Blair beat a well-bred horse today. Sandusky is by Longfellow and out of a War Dance mare. By the way, Doctor, did you chance to get the time of the race?"

"I timed the Judge — I'd better keep saying the Duke, hadn't I? — in one-o-nine and two-fifths. I might be off a shade."

"In one-o-nine and two-fifths! That should be close to the track record, or maybe a new record. Did anyone tell you?"

"We left soon after I collected the purse money," Billy said, straight of face.

She laughed with abandon, sensing why, and he laughed with her. "The main point about the Judge's breeding is this," he said, growing serious. "Not whether he's a Thoroughbred or a quarter horse, but *who* he is. The Judge was shipped into Texas with a load of workhorses. Dude won him in a poker game. The cowman he won him off of had given the horse the Judge Blair name to make him sound like quality folks and worthy of a wager, unaware that he was a runner. It was later that Dude found out. It's not whether the Judge comes down from kings and queens, though he may well do so, or whether he's just plain country folks, and he may well be that — but just who he is. That's all we want to know, and we feel we owe it to him. It's a crime he was ever gelded. My, what he could pass on: speed, heart, intelligence, conformation, great bone, a calm disposition. A child could handle him."

"You-all just love horses, that's what it comes down to," she said, beaming her liking. "You ought to move to Kentucky, where we appreciate horsemen far more than we do politicians." She glanced at her niece. "I'm doing most of the talking. Blossom hasn't had a chance to get in a word."

"I'd rather listen," Blossom said. "It's all so exciting and interesting. And we shouldn't forget Texas Jack, Judge Blair's stablemate. He's a nice horse, too."

"Yes, indeed," Billy concurred. "He can't outrun a three-year-old turtle, but he can run all day."

"Forgetting you are, Grandfather," Coyote spoke up, "the race he won at Blue Springs."

"I stand corrected," Billy said. "He has won one, and he made us proud."

After dinner, while Blossom was listening to one of Billy's stories, about when the outfit was matchracing in Louisiana against a cagey Cajun horseman, Aunt Lucinda drew Dude aside. "You've been good for Blossom, Mr. McQuinn."

He didn't know how to answer that.

"Something Blossom needed," she went on, not pausing. "To break out of that strait-laced town. The people are so self-righteous and pious, they've become oppressive. I know. I've visited there. I've been to church and I've witnessed the Reverend Joe Bob Quincy staging a pitchfork battle with the devil. I mean that, literally. He brought a pitchfork to the pulpit. And, of course, Joe Bob always wins." As Dude showed a twinkle of amusement, remembering, she said, "It would be good for the town if Joe Bob lost a round or two. . . . My husband, Martin, passed away some years ago and we had no children, so Blossom is like a daughter to me. Therefore, as her aunt and guardian while she's in Louisville, I must ask what your intentions are, Mr. McQuinn?"

"Honorable," he said, feigning a formal bow. Sobering, he followed with an inconclusive shake of his head, and his voice was unaffected and earnest when he spoke. "I'm not sure, Mrs. Adams, that I'd be good for Blossom in the long run."

"How do you mean?"

"She's just a girl and I'm thirty-two years old."

"Nonsense. Martin was sixteen years older than I and we loved each other dearly. I lost him five years ago. I never wanted anyone else and I still don't, and I don't consider myself an old woman by any means." Her eyes flashed. "As for Blossom, she may be only nineteen, but she has a mind of her own."

"Besides," Dude said, "I live in Texas and we travel about the country matchin' races. We're sorta like wanderers."

"You'll settle down someday. When you do, you might try Kentucky. Next to God we love horse people and horses." Her blitheness waned as her eyes searched his face. "Do you really love Blossom, Mr. McQuinn?"

"I do. Very much."

"Have you told her?"

"No, ma'am. Not yet. Somehow I don't feel I have that right yet. I —"

Blossom called at that moment, her voice teasing. "Auntie, you're monopolizing Mr. Dude. Please bring him over here."

The evening slipped away before Dude quite realized. Now the partners were paying their respects to their hostess and Miss Blossom. Dude, delaying with Blossom on the porch while Billy and Coyote drifted on to the buggy, said, "I'm glad you're here with Aunt Lucinda. I wasn't sure you'd make the move. Not that coming here means you give up your family — you don't."

"I'm going to live my life, thanks to you, Dude."

A sense of guilt touched him and he felt an instant responsibility for her. "I believe you would have, whether I'd come along or not."

"Certainly not so soon. I've been pondering this for a long time. Like I told you back in Indian Creek, I was afraid."

"Well, you're not afraid anymore."

"Maybe just a little uncertain. Dr. Lockhart says you're leaving tomorrow for Lexington."

"Yes. The search goes on. We have to finish it."

"It seems you're always leaving." She looked down and up. A silence gripped them both. After a moment, she asked, "Will you be back?"

Now I'm the one who's afraid, his mind raced.

"You don't have to promise," she said, her voice trailing off when he didn't answer.

"I'll be back," he said at last, his affection for her almost more than he could stand. "That's a promise just like the first one." He ached to tell her more, but somehow he couldn't. "Good night, Blossom." She was waiting again, the half light revealing her sweet young face turned sad by his leaving. At once he bent and kissed her and walked quickly out to the buggy, wondering whether he had been right to promise.

CHAPTER 13

A Pale Horse Stands

They were in the heart of the Bluegrass now, not far from Lexington. The land rolled away like a vast park of wooded, rounded hills and undulating sweeps of fine pasture, a bluish tint to the grass, enclosed within white plank fences. Here and there Dude saw mares with leggy foals and an occasional lordly stallion in the domain of his own extensive paddock.

"We'll never see prettier horse country," Billy said, gazing as they rode along. "Think you might like to settle here?" His voice was bantering. "Or say around Louisville?"

"Aw, I'd miss that Texas dust like buckshot against my face on a windy morning, one day hot enough to melt a saddle horn, the next a blue norther with nothin' between it and the North Pole but a bobwire fence. That grows

262

on a man, you know."

"You Alamo Texans! You also sound like some fella that's just swore off of women."

Dude let that pass.

"I knew a fella like that once," Billy reflected. "Few weeks later he was in double harness and geeing and hawing without complaint."

Up ahead a buggy had stopped on the road, and a woman was standing beside her head-down brown horse, her concern evident as she stroked his face and looked helplessly about.

The outfit, Dude and Billy in the lead, Coyote following in the wagon, pulled rein, and Dude asked, "Ma'am, can we help you?"

She turned, a swift gratitude rising to her face. There was a catch in her voice. "Thank you, young man. But I doubt there's anything you can do unless one of you happens to be a veterinarian."

"It just happens one of us is."

Billy was already getting down from the buggy. He touched his hat brim to the woman and asked, "What seems to be wrong with your horse?"

"He keeps stopping and when I give him a little flick with the whip, he resents it and still won't go on. It's been a hot day and we've come a long way. I fear it's time to retire Skipper. He was twenty-three last spring."

"Let's see what we can do for this fine old gentleman."

Billy studied the horse's eyes, reflected a moment on what he perceived therein, and moving on placed his hand on the animal's left flank, which Dude saw was beating violently. Coming back, scowling, Billy listened to the brown's breathing, felt of the ears, and found the pulse under the lower jaw, drew his watch, and presently, turning to the woman, said, "I'm sorry, lady, but your Skipper has the thumps. The principal symptom is the rapid throbbing of the flanks. His pulse, which normally should beat no higher than forty-six times a minute, is eighty."

She was distraught, but practical. "You mean he has heart trouble?"

"Yes, I'm sorry to say. But there is something we can do for him. First, let's unharness him. He shouldn't be pulling the buggy."

"But how will I get him and the buggy home?"

She was probably near Billy's undetermined age, Dude guessed, a perky little lady with lively black eyes behind spectacles, her features small and delicate, her gray hair peeking out from beneath a flowered hat. She had a clear voice, which matched her erect posture.

"We'll put one of our horses in the traces and

tie Skipper behind our wagon. Before we do anything, let's give Skipper something to relieve his stress and put some go in his get-along. Dude, bring the forked stick and the strap, while I mix up a little medicine." In a few moments Billy stood ready, holding a pint jar of an amber-colored mixture. "Now, Coyote, you remove Skipper's bit and fasten the strap around the upper jaw. . . . That's good. Now, Dude, carefully insert the fork under the strap and slowly raise Skipper's head. We don't want to scare him."

Dude had no more than accomplished that when Billy poured the jar's contents down Skipper's throat, hardly a drop wasted.

"Medicine?" the woman protested, sniffing. "Why, that smells distinctly of whiskey"

"Merely whiskey and water," Billy explained. "What you give any old-timer who needs a bracer. I'll write you out a prescription for him later. I'd say the time has come for Skipper to rest on his laurels as a pensioner. Coyote, you and Dude unharness Skipper and bring the Ju – I mean the Duke – up."

"The Duke?" the woman asked, interested.

"Yes. His full name is the Duke of Dexter."

"A horse by that name, a long shot, won the Louisville Handicap last week."

"That's right," Billy said, "and there he is," as

Coyote led Judge Blair out from behind the wagon. "He can pull a wagon or a buggy and you can ride him like a saddler, though I can't claim he's gaited. Few running horses are. Sometimes one has a running walk."

When the horses were exchanged and Skipper haltered behind the wagon, the woman, hesitating, said, "He's a racehorse. He might run off with me."

"Not if you use the reins," Billy said. "Dude will ride alongside the Duke as a precaution." He moved to assist her into the buggy, a courtesy which she declined. She took the reins, clucked at Judge Blair, and away they went at a trot.

"Slow down," Billy called. "That's too fast for Skipper."

Before long they were traveling under a cool canopy of oak trees. Now and then the white fences gave way to rock fences, left over from an earlier day, Dude thought. After some distance they passed a closed wooden gate, flanked by stone pillars and bearing the lettering: OLD DOMINION STUD. Beyond, more white fences enclosed paddocks of abundant pasture. A narrow, tree-lined road wound to a columned white house of antebellum elegance.

Some spread, Dude thought, impressed.

After about a mile, the woman turned up a

lane leading to a small stone house which sat on the gentle slope of a wooded hill, rolling pastures on both sides of the house. She drove around it to a barn and a corral.

"I would keep Skipper up for a while," Billy told her as the old horse was led around to the barn. "See that he gets plenty of salt and rest. Go light on grain. Give him mostly hay and mashes once a day. If that fails to bring improvement after three or four days, give this prescription three times daily in his feed."

She frowned as she read aloud, "One ounce, spirits of camphor, one ounce, muriate of ammonia, one ounce, sweet spirits of niter, one pint of water. Mix and give as a drench." Her face softened and she smiled her appreciation. "Thank you, Doctor . . ."

"William Tecumseh Lockhart," Billy said, hat in hand.

"I'm Daisy Corum. The Widow Corum, I'm called hereabouts."

Billy then presented his partners. By now the afternoon was wearing away. Dude eyed the sun and was looking at Billy, hurrying him, when she asked, "Were you gentlemen going on to Lexington? If not, you are welcome to camp here. I have a large yard, plenty of pasture, as you can see, good water, and you can help yourself to the wood. You're most welcome after all you've done for Skipper."

Dude didn't hesitate long. "Thank you very much, ma'am. We'd like to while we get the Duke in a race or two at Lexington. Meantime, we'll do your chores."

"And I'll be glad to look after Skipper for you," Billy offered.

She radiated appreciation. "That's very kind of you all. We Kentuckians think of our horses as family. My late husband, Isaac, bought Skipper for me as a yearling. My other horse, Peter, my saddler, also is getting along in years. He's eighteen. I don't ride him much. With Skipper retired, I'll have to look around for another buggy horse."

"We'll be glad to help you find a successor, too," Billy said. "Meantime, you are welcome to hitch up one of our sorrels whenever you want to go to town."

Dude nodded to that, thinking he had never seen his old mentor so obliging and full of vigor. Leaving his rocking chair on the hotel porch and traveling and matching wits with other cagey horsemen had started his recovery. But coming to horse country was the real cure. His heart was here. An old question rose. Had Uncle campaigned horses in Kentucky? Dude could only speculate. He'd probably never know.

"Now I'll be indebted to you more than ever," Daisy Corum was saying. "Times haven't been easy for most folks these past years. I raise a little tobacco and lease some pasture. I should tell you that besides being called the Widow Corum, I'm sometimes referred to as that blue-bellied Yankee, old lady Corum. Isaac and I believed the Union should not be split asunder by hotheaded slave owners. Kentuckians were drawn to the South through slavery and family and social connections. On the other hand, Kentucky had business ties with the North and a national sentiment that went back to Henry Clay. When the war came, Isaac stayed with the Union and fought at the Battle of Perryville. He was wounded and invalided out for the rest of the war. It was brother against brother around here, even after Kentucky formally declared its allegiance to the Union."

"We understand," said Billy, shaking his head.

"My grandfather McQuinn fought in General Hood's army at the Battle of Franklin down in Tennessee," Dude followed up. "He was always bitter about the terrible loss of life there. Said the many charges Hood ordered against the Yankee works were senseless. He said it was rightly called the Gettysburg of the West. Hood's men charged time after time. It was two miles across. Pickett's charge covered about a mile. Well, enough about that."

They all shared a long silence, as if each were remembering, Dude wondering if Billy had served in the war, and knowing that if he had it was with the North. Anybody who whistled "The Battle Hymn of the Republic" and called the War Between the States the Great Rebellion couldn't have been a Johnny Reb.

"Coming in," Billy said, breaking the quiet, "I noticed the Old Dominion Farm." (No gentleman would say "stud" when speaking to a lady.) "That name has a Virginia connotation."

"Indeed it does," Daisy Corum said. "It's owned by Colonel Horatio P. Buxton. He served with Stonewall Jackson, and he's still fighting the war. He tips his hat to me as a woman, but even though we are neighbors, I have yet to have a conversation with him."

"I'd venture he has some good horses."

"His Sir Roderick is the top handicap horse in Kentucky."

"He wasn't in the Louisville Handicap."

"They say he's been priming Sir Roderick for the Jockey Club Handicap here. That's the big race for older horses." A touch of pride entered her voice. "Except for the Derby, folks around here think it's the most important race in Kentucky."

"When is it?"

"Early October. I'm not certain about the date. I haven't heard about the field. Not every horseman wants to go up against the Buxton horse. He's coursed the mile in one-thirty-five and four-fifths and six furlongs in one-o-nine and two-fifths."

"Hmmnn. I can see why. That's the same time the Duke ran six furlongs at Louisville."

They camped in a little grove of oaks near the house, watered the horses at the trough by the well, and turned all of them into a large paddock behind the house that Dude insisted on calling a pasture. After supper, as late evening shadows purpled the rolling hills and Billy and Coyote took to their bedrolls under the wagon, Dude sat by the lowering campfire a while longer, his mind fixed on Miss Blossom. He seemed to think of her every few minutes. There might be a letter from her in town. That anticipation inspired him to effusive phrases, but when he had pencil stub in hand, his verbosity deserted him and he found only simple words:

Dear Miss Blossom,

We're camped tonight on the outskirts of Lexington on the farm of Mrs. Daisy Corum, a real lady and a true Kentuckian. We're told folks here are still fighting the Civil War. Not with guns, but with attitudes and cold manners. All the time I thought the war was over.

Tomorrow Uncle Billy goes to the track to see about getting our horse in a race. Maybe we'll scare up Si Eckert. Billy thinks if Eckert exists, he'll show up around the track.

We all send our top regards and thanks to you and Aunt Lucinda. That was a fine dinner and evening. Enjoy your school. Next time I see you, you'll be so smart this ol' cowboy won't even be able to carry on a confab with you. No, I didn't go through the eighth grade three times. I never got that far. I don't claim to be long on savvy, like a feller back home they said was as full of information as a mail-order catalog. No, I can't claim that. But I do know where the sun comes up and where it goes down and I know how to forefoot a horse, and who I am and where I'm from and who my friends are. Best of all, I know for sure there's a mighty fine young lady named

Blossom just arrived in Louisville.

He hesitated over how to sign the letter. Should he say "love," if he wasn't sure he could make it good? After much deliberation, he wrote, Love, Dude, because that was what he truly felt.

Following an early breakfast, Billy said he would drive to town for veterinary supplies and visit the Racing Secretary's office.

"Appreciate it if you'd mail this for me," Dude said, giving him the letter, "and ask if there's anything for me at general delivery."

"Who'd be writing you?" Billy deviled him. He drove off, snapping the whip at Amos, without having invited either partner.

"Grandfather up to something is," Coyote said, dark eyes reflective.

"It's his show," Dude said. "I figure he's been in Kentucky before as a trainer or something, but think he'd admit it?" Dude threw up his hands. "We'll never know."

"Maybe so Grandfather in white man's War Between the States was?" Coyote conjectured, looking wise.

"You mean the Great Rebellion, don't you?" Dude snickered, and they both laughed, and Coyote said, "We Comanches never had just one war. We fought all the time."

Billy was so late coming in that Dude and Coyote were pacing the camp when he drove up.

"About time," Dude scolded him. "How many toddies did you have?"

"Not one."

"Any mail for me?"

"Sorry, Dude. Not a thing."

"Grandfather, worried about you we did," Coyote said.

"Don't know how I'll ever break you of calling me that," Billy sighed, "and since when did you two get the idea I can't take care of myself?" He patted the breast of his coat and Dude saw the bulge of his handgun. So he had started packing that again.

"Any sign of the mysterious Si Eckert?" Dude needled him.

"A fox won't come out of his hole until there's something to catch or something that entertains his fancy." He dismissed the subject with a gesture. "I did find out they still call it the Kentucky Association track."

Dude caught that instantly. It was a slip, a rare peek into Uncle's hidden past. "Just like it was years ago when you sent out horses here?" Dude pried.

"Now, did I say?" the old man parried the question and began unharnessing Amos.

The door was shut as usual, Dude knew, and switched the talk. "Are we in a race or not?"

"We're in," Billy said, excitement in his eyes. "We go in the Jockey Club Handicap ten days from today. This time the ante went up — a hundred bucks for a late entry."

"A hundred bucks?" Dude groaned.

"For a chance to win a thousand."

"How far?"

"A mile."

"A mile!" Dude objected. "We've never run a mile. How can we get him ready in ten days?"

"He's in good condition. If he can go six furlongs and have plenty left, he can go a mile. We'll have to lengthen him out, sure. We'll jog him more. Jogging is a neglected conditioner because it looks slow. It gives a horse bottom because he uses all the muscles. Galloping is good, but a horse can loaf while galloping. Two or three breezes, with the last one two days before the race, and he'll be ready. A sharp work close to a race is better than a long, hard work. It sharpens him."

Dude gave a rejecting jerk of his head, but said no more, and Coyote looked troubled.

"We'll work him on the road," Billy said. "Then stall him at the track the day before. That's enough to give him the feel of it."

"Why not stall him earlier?" Dude questioned.

"Safer here. Word's already around the barns that the Duke won at Louisville and beat Sandusky. You never know who might try to fix your horse."

The days drifted by like tranquil clouds, each a pleasant routine of working the Judge in the early morning, each afternoon spent in the shaded grove of the camp. The early October nights were cooler now. Twice within the week Dude rode to town to inquire about mail. There was none. His doubts took root. Had he misread her feelings? He knew he had not his own. He would not write again until he heard from her. Maybe she had met someone else, a young man near her own age? Well, he wished her happiness. She deserved that.

A yearling sale drew the outfit to barns in the vicinity of the track. Prospective buyers strolled the area — gentlemen and their fashionable ladies, mostly in white and all fancying large hats, some with veils.

Grooms were parading yearlings, coats brushed gleaming. Bright ribbons adorned the manes of spirited fillies. Dude's eyes lit up at sight of the fancy horseflesh. Over there a portly, mustachioed, goateed gentleman of apparent means —

planter's hat, linen suit, dark cravat — was speaking to a rather round-faced man, a merchant type, Dude judged, new to the game and likely easy pickin's in a horse deal.

As the outfit stopped to listen, the man in the planter's hat spoke, his voice like melted butter. "Mr. Vogel, trot out our Derby prospect for this gentleman to see."

The man addressed as Vogel was long-jawed and lean. Experienced eyes squinted above a thick, brown beard. Slumped against the wall of the barn, he showed a gap-toothed grin, spat a stream of amber tobacco juice, and asked, "Which Derby prospect you mean, Colonel? The bay or the black?"

Not till then did Dude notice the sign over the barn's entrance:

OLD DOMINION STUD
Col. Horatio P. Buxton

"The bay, Mr. Vogel, the bay."

Vogel, gone but a moment, led forth a stringy-looking bay colt that toed out in front and had a straight shoulder and was over at the knee. Dude noticed these defects, conspicuous to a horseman, at first glance.

Looking gratified, the Colonel said, "He'll do. Guess he can run a little, eh?"

Vogel's jaws worked again. "Can he run, Colonel? Don't you remember? When he was foaled he hit the straw on the run – ran right out the door. I don't mean he ran far, but I had to run 'im down."

"I always remember a foal that shows early run," said the Colonel. "This colt," he said, looking at the round-faced individual, "is by none other than the great Glengarry, imported, and out of one of my best mares, Kentucky Babe, she by King Alfonso. This colt is bred to run short or long, the track heavy or fast."

"I see," the man said, his interest beginning to build.

"I always try to be reasonable when a gentleman like yourself is starting a stable," the Colonel said, his manner expansive. "Be glad to treaty with you at around two thousand or so."

Dude first sensed impending trouble when out of the tail of his eye he caught Billy edging forward, elbows flapping, both signs of confrontation. Before Dude could pull him back, Billy blurted out, "I wouldn't give fifty dollars for a yearling that's short in the shoulder, over at the knee, and toes out in front."

Both men whirled, the Colonel, sputtering, demanded, "Who are you, sir, to intrude into our conversation?"

"And who are you to hornswoggle this gentleman into purchasing a yearling with these conformation defects?"

"I've never misrepresented a horse in my life, sir," Buxton swore, straightening, face reddening. "Had you not intruded, sir, I was going to point out this colt's conformation. No horse is perfect. Breeding is what counts and this colt was bred in the purple." Ignoring Billy, he turned to the prospective buyer, his face changing to amiability. "Now, sir, as I was saying —"

"Never mind, Colonel. Defects!" The man strode off.

Buxton turned flinty eyes upon Billy and walked away, motioning Vogel to take the colt back to its stall.

Dude, embarrassed, drew Billy quickly on, saying when they were out of earshot, "You shouldn't have done that, Uncle. Maybe cost the Colonel a sale. That colt may not look like a runner, but he could have the heart to make up for it."

"If there's one thing I can't stand," said Billy, still keyed up, "is a breeder trying to bamboozle some greenhorn into buying an inferior horse so he can get into the racing game."

"Seems I remember a time or two when one William Tecumseh Lockhart doctored a horse for the heaves before tradin' it off."

"That's different. Catch-as-catch-can among horse traders."

No more was said. They made the rounds of

the other sale barns and late in the afternoon returned to the little farm where Daisy Corum had invited them to supper.

She served a gracious meal, replete with Kentucky ham, and afterward Dude told her of the skirmish between Billy and Colonel Buxton. "I'm afraid Billy nixed a sale for the Colonel."

"Don't worry about the Colonel," she said. "He probably sold that colt to the next novice that came along. He keeps his best Glengarry yearlings in the barn on the farm. Likes to campaign his best ones, sell the others. He does have fast horses. Sir Roderick is also by Glengarry. Roderick had cannon problems as a three-year-old. Didn't run in the Derby. Came to hand later than others. Been a champion at four. The Duke will have to be both a sprinter and a stayer to beat him."

"Who is the man called Vogel?" Dude asked curiously. "I expected a black man to handle the yearlings. Neither did Vogel talk like a southerner."

"Rube Vogel showed up around here five years ago. Needed work, they say. The Colonel hired him as a groom. Before long he became the farm manager. When the Colonel goes anywhere to race a horse, Vogel goes with him. He's the Colonel's shadow, they say. He stays pretty much to himself I understand. No family here. That's about all I know."

A light, wind-hurried rain was falling, which pleased the hostess, who commented on the dry early fall, and with dinner over they all moved to the doorway to appreciate the needed moisture even more. A gray horse grazed in the east paddock, wraithlike against the failing light of evening. The wind brought the sweet scent of rain and grass.

They were standing in the doorway, Daisy Corum gesturing toward the horse. "There's my old saddler, Peter. He's getting on in years like Skipper. His coat is faded out. Sometimes when I stand here in my doorway and gaze out at him, he looks so pale I think of a ghost horse."

Something clicked in Dude's mind, like a bolt of light. All at once he clamped a hand to his forehead and started jumping up and down, yelling, "I've got it! I've got it!"

"Got what?" Billy asked, startled.

"Yes — are you ill?" Daisy asked, concerned for him.

"The password," Dude gasped, facing Billy and Coyote. "It just came to me. It's . . . it's, 'At my door . . . at my door . . . the pale horse stands.'" Then faster, conclusively, " 'At my door the pale horse stands.' That's it!"

CHAPTER 14

A Side Bet, Sir?

On the morning of the drawing for post positions, Colonel Buxton and Rube Vogel were waiting in the Racing Secretary's outer office among owners and trainers and track officials and a seedy-looking individual in a bowler hat, armed with notebook and pencil, whom Dude took for a reporter. Buxton glared at Billy, who glanced in the Colonel's direction without change of expression.

Dude caught an air of tension. A hard rain had fallen that morning and the track was heavy. What did that portend tomorrow? What horses were mudders, if any? If no more rain fell today, and a light rain came in the morning and the track was dragged before post time, the footing would be fast, rather than heavy. Dude heard these murmurings while the horsemen waited.

The Racing Secretary, a composed and gentlemanly oldster very much in command of himself and aware of his official duties, emerged from an inner office, followed by a young woman, who carried a small box. He held a small glass jar. Looking at the secretary, Dude thought of a family portrait: the proud, bony face, the white hair and mustache, the immaculate dark suit, white shirt and string tie. The secretary jogged his head at the crowd and announced, "In here," tapping the jar, "are marbles numbered one to ten. I'll shake out one at a time and it will be matched to a name drawn from the box by the young lady. Any questions?"

No one spoke.

The secretary shook out a marble into the palm of his left hand and called, "Number four," held it up for all to see, and the young woman shook the box vigorously and from it drew a slip of paper and read, "General Hill."

A man whooped. "Anything but the one hole on a muddy track."

The outfit had gone over the field before the drawing, evaluating on the basis of backstretch gossip, what Billy had picked up additionally around the track offices, and what the Kentucky *Gazette* carried. General Hill was a speed horse.

Next, the secretary called, "Number ten," and the woman clerk read, "Uncle Jim," which evoked a happy shout. This horse, Dude remembered, was rated a late closer.

In quick succession, Gallant Rebel drew the 5 hole, Mr. Drake the 3, Ole John the 2, Envoy, another speed horse, the 6, and Blarney, which ran off the pace, the 9.

Dude's uneasiness grew. There were three positions left: 1, 8 and 7. Nobody wanted the 1 hole next to the rail, which was the heaviest after a downpour, because the track drained to the inside.

Now the secretary rolled out a marble and holding it high called, "Number eight," and the clerk read, "Dixie Dan." A man dressed like a farmer nodded his liking for the outside position.

Dude's forehead wrinkled. Dixie Dan, the backstretch tattlers said, was actually owned by Colonel Buxton and ran today as a "rabbit," put in as a sprinter to draw the top horses out early and wear them down, while Sir Roderick, lying off the pace, made his bid when the tiring front-runners turned for home.

Now, with the dreaded 1 hole still not taken, Billy's only perceptible reaction was to tug once at his shirt collar. Dude chewed on his lower lip, waiting.

The secretary, quite deliberately, rattled the jar and poured out a marble and holding it aloft called, "Number one." The clerk, somewhat nervously, as if feeling the tension, shook the box and pulled out a slip and announced, "The Duke of Dexter," which left the favorable 7 position to Sir Roderick.

Dude groaned to himself. But that's racing, he told himself. A horseman generally had more bad luck than good. You had to overcome the bad. At that, despite the many shenanigans the outfit had run up against in match racing, a man had better count his blessings when he had a sound horse with speed and heart like the Judge and a top jockey like Coyote.

Buxton, obviously pleased with the draw, moved over to the secretary and, his smile ingratiating, said, "Mr. Lane, we all appreciate the way you write the races. However, if I may say so, sir, I believe you have my horse weighted a little high at 126 pounds this time."

The secretary could be just as ingratiatory. "Colonel, Sir Roderick is topweighted because he is the top handicap horse in Kentucky. As you know, I adjust the weights for the purpose of equalizing all horses' chances."

"I understand that, sir. I do. But you also have the Duke of Dexter, which recently won the Louisville Handicap, at 120 pounds."

"Because that is the only race of stature that the Duke of Dexter has won in Kentucky this year. He still has much to prove, Colonel. Your horse far outranks him."

Stubbornly, Buxton went on, yet without a show of anger, his voice at the same bland and persuasive level. "That's still giving six pounds over the long haul. And General Hill and Uncle Jim, both veteran campaigners, come in at 118, Blarney at 116, and Envoy as light as 115."

"Equalizing, Colonel, equalizing. To give every horse a fair chance." Lane centered an obscure look on Buxton, as if perhaps he knew something but withheld it. "Dixie Dan is also at 116. A pure sprinter over his distance, sir." His eyes lifted from Buxton to the other horsemen, he said, "Good luck to all of you gentlemen," and walked back into the inner office.

The Colonel, a remembering in his keen brown eyes, and Vogel looming tall at his shoulder, made his way through the departing crowd over to Billy. "Sir, for your information, the Glengarry colt you ran down before my prospective buyer, I sold later that day to an Alabama cotton man for fifteen hundred dollars, cash in hand."

Billy, calmly, with a touch of malice, inquired, "Was the man's eyesight impaired?"

"He was a true gentleman, sir, which you are not, who served gallantly throughout the War Between the States."

Billy replied loftily, "I believe, sir, you are referring incorrectly to the late Great Rebellion."

"I mean exactly what I said, sir, the War Between the States, and so shall it ever be." By now the Colonel was fuming and Billy's voice had risen to a dangerous edge. Dude put his arm on Billy's shoulder to placate him, but Billy seemed unaware of it.

"Such inaccurate historical references will be corrected as time marches on," Billy stated, standing very erect.

Buxton, equally erect, advanced a step. Now the two adversaries stood face to face, their bodies almost rubbing. The Colonel was round-bodied and ruddy of face, Billy lean, his whiskery jaw thrust out. In another moment they would be fighting.

Dude stepped between them. "Now, gentlemen . . ."

Vogel, behind Buxton, said, "Stay out of this," his voice like a rasp.

Dude, caught off guard, shot back, "You stay out." Vogel was making a big show of backing his boss.

The Colonel, muttering, cheeks puffing,

waved his man aside and confronted Billy again. "Would you dare make a side bet, sir?"

Billy took it up at once. "Just how?"

"That my horse, whether he wins or not, will finish ahead of yours."

"How much?"

"Say, a hundred dollars."

Pure disdain filled Billy's face. "We throw that to the chickens in the Southwest."

"Then two hundred."

"If you want to bet, Colonel, let's get down to some real countin' money. Say, five hundred."

The Colonel blinked, but replied at once. "It's agreed, sir." He held out his hand. They shook briefly, each as if the touch of the other was repugnant.

Buxton flung away, Vogel in step beside him, the farm manager casting Dude his retained hostility.

Dude, eyeing them, thought, This won't end with the race. This is just the beginning. It's an instant, mutual dislike. Such as he'd seen happen in his early teens on the long trail drives up from Texas to the Kansas railheads, when two men clashed the first time they met. Not much said, not much need be said. They just rubbed each other wrong. Something deep, hard to explain. Something more felt than seen. But it was there, like now.

They were outside before Dude spoke. "Uncle, that was a heap of money to bet with us in the one hole on a muddy track."

"I realize it was, Dude. If we lose, it'll come out of my pocket."

Dude slipped an arm around the thin shoulders. "We're still pardners, win or lose, remember?"

All three partners slept on cots outside the Judge's stall that night and awakened to dark skies and the growl of thunder in the west. One by one they went to breakfast at a small restaurant near the track. A downpour greeted them at ten o'clock and continued for an hour. When it cleared, Billy said, "Let's take the Duke to the farrier and shoe him with mud caulks."

"Wait a minute," Dude said, holding back, glancing around before he spoke. "We blacked out his white-sock forelegs to look like the Duke's. If it rains before we get back, the paint will run."

"We'll put brown wraps on his forelegs now," Billy said.

"And smear mud on the wraps before to the saddling paddocks take him," Coyote suggested.

"It's gonna be real sticky out there," Dude said moodily. "By the time they run those six races ahead of ours, the track will be fetlock deep, even if the sun comes out."

He still didn't like the mile.

The sun did not return. After the fourth race, Dude rode with Coyote over to the jockeys' quarters and brought the other horse back. When the call came to take the horses to the paddock for the Handicap, a light rain was falling and the whipping wind carried a chill.

Hunched against the rain in their slickers, they mounted and Dude ponied the Judge on Blue Grass and Billy rode Texas Jack. The track was like grease under their horses.

The identifier was waiting, a restless, hawk-nosed man in a yellow slicker and a dripping hat. He glanced at a notebook held close. "So this is the Duke of Dexter," he said, viewing Judge Blair, "winner of the Louisville Handicap? I don't recall that he's ever raced here before."

Then he won't know the Duke's many defects, Dude decided, relieved.

"Registration papers, please."

That, Dude hadn't figured on here.

Billy produced them and hesitated because of the rain and the official came in under the stall's roof. He read rapidly, glancing back and forth at the horse as he did. Slowly, he handed the papers back to Billy, his gaze split between him and Judge Blair. Without another word, the identifier opened the Judge's mouth and peered at length. Stepping back, he put his glance on the Judge again, back and forth. "I see you've wrapped his front legs."

"He's been sore in his cannons," Billy said succinctly.

For a hanging moment Dude feared another question was coming. Then the man, humping against the chill, said a hurried "Good luck" and went to Ole John's stall.

"Thank the Lord for a cold rain," Billy breathed, and in low reply to the question in Dude's eyes, "They always give a new horse an extra once-over." He put on his saintly look. "Always on the lookout for ringers."

Coyote came out of the jockeys' quarters wearing a blue shirt, breechcloth, plain moccasins and a red headband.

Billy wrapped an arm around the Comanche's shoulders, his tone fatherly. "Don't run with the early speed horses. I want you to have something left when you make the last turn. I expect Dixie Dan will break running, if it's true he was put in as a rabbit for Sir Roderick. Don't go with him. Don't worry about the lead going into the first turn. Bide your time. . . . Maybe your horse won't like mud in his face. If he resents it and slows down, you'll have to find a way outside on the backstretch. I want you away from the rail, anyway. Main thing is, when you turn for home, be on the outside where the footing is firmer. Coming in, I heard a man say outside horses won the last three races. That tells us something. I expect this Sir Roderick, the seven horse, to be out there. . . . Now, just take care of yourself and your horse."

"Yes, Grandfather."

"Riders up," the identifier called.

Dude gave Coyote a leg to the saddle, mounted Blue Grass and taking the lead rope rode out to the track to the notes of "Boots and Saddles" for the post parade. The rain had let up slightly. The shower had left the track sloppy, which was better to Dude's mind than drying mud with the sun out. The size of the crowd surprised him. The stands were full and an array of multicolored spectators lined the fence below the stands.

The rider leading the parade jogged past the finish line, where the race also would start, turned and retraced his course past the stands, turned again and there he left the horses. No long warm-up gallops today on a slippery track.

It was then that Dude got his first clear sighting and assessment of Sir Roderick. What he saw only fueled his misgivings. The favorite was a dark brown stallion of extraordinary size and balanced conformation.

This would be a barrier start, Dude saw. Something new for Judge Blair. The starter stood on an elevated platform just outside the inside rail. Three slickered finish-line judges stood at the pole. The starter was lowering the barrier now, a tape stretched across the track and fastened at either end to a metal arm. When the horses were in line, he would release the arms, which would throw the tape slightly forward and upward, out of the horses' way. Dude had only heard of such a modern apparatus. Better than the old flag when starting a large field.

The starter was calling for the jockeys to line up.

Dude untied the lead rope from the Judge's bridle, said, "Good luck" to Coyote and rode back to the paddock, where he would watch the race on horseback. As usual, Billy would be at the finish line.

Watching, his concern deepening anew over the distance that the Judge had never run, Dude saw the horses form an irregular front and approach the barrier, like a dim streak above the track in the misty light. They were nearly there when the 8 horse, Dixie Dan, jumped ahead and broke the barrier. His rider brought him under control about thirty yards down the track and an assistant starter ran out and took Dixie Dan's bridle and led him around and into the line of milling horses. Another assistant repaired the broken tape by merely tying the loose ends together.

Judge Blair, ears pricked, was moving alertly with the others. It looked like a start. But in the last steps before the barrier, the 4 horse, General Hill, surged ahead and broke the tape.

Dude could hear the frustrated starter yelling at the riders above the chattering crowd. Again the assistant starter repaired the tape and again the horses came together. All heads straight.

Then Dude saw the barrier fly upward like a writhing snake and heard shouts and saw the hail of mud as the horses broke. Just then the rain started peppering down again.

Dude winced in pain as the 2 horse, Ole John, sliding at the break, bored in and bumped Judge Blair. For a terrible split second Dude thought his horse, knocked off stride, was going to be slammed into the inside rail. In another heartbeat he saw Coyote right Judge Blair and Ole John's rider came out a bit and the two horses were away, now strides behind the field.

Sure enough, Dixie Dan was already coursing out into the lead from the 8 hole. Envoy and General Hill took after him like hounds on a fox hunt. Into the first turn, mud flying, they raced, lengths of daylight between the three speed horses and the rest of the field. Sir Roderick settling comfortably into fourth place off the pace, Judge Blair and Ole John laboring at the rear.

Entering the backstretch, Coyote took Judge Blair past Ole John and began working outside for the flying leaders. To Dude's eye, the Judge seemed to be running relaxed, important at this early stage. Midway down the backside, General Hill put Envoy away with a burst of speed and sailed on to challenge Dixie Dan. The field was stringing out. Gallant Rebel and Mr. Drake, already fading, Ole John still in the ruck near the rail. Always there on the outside, striding easily, raced the favored Sir Roderick in fourth, behind him Blarney and Uncle Jim, the other late closers, likewise biding time. When the field headed for home, they would make their runs. Beaten, Envoy appeared to lose heart all at once, dropping back wearily, soon trailing the three come-from-behind horses.

Where was Judge Blair? Dude sighted him farther back as the Judge, seeming to find himself in the mud, drove past Gallant Rebel and Mr. Drake and now the spent Envoy.

As the horses tore into the far turn, Dude

glimpsed a gap along the rail. Nobody wanted it today. But that avoidance was making a jam on the outside. Dude, worrying, next saw Coyote, on the turn, slip past Blarney in tight quarters and gaining clearance, go head to head with Uncle Jim, both horses running harder now. Still, Coyote hadn't whooped. It was too early. Dude could see the Judge changing leads as he came off the turn.

Dixie Dan was charging out on the stretch by this time, with General Hill only a trailing length in determined pursuit. The two dueling sprinters maintaining open daylight on the Buxton horse. Dude saw the lead change then as Dixie Dan weakened abruptly. He'd run his race as planned, finished, just beyond the top of the stretch. He lagged toward the inside, out of all contention.

Behind Dixie Dan and General Hill, Dude could see Sir Roderick picking up the pace, coming on powerfully. Part of the strategy. But there was something wrong. Dixie Dan was through, but General Hill wasn't. The bold sprinter had heart to go with his speed and enough class to steal the race if unchallenged.

Coyote must have sensed that as well, because Dude heard him whoop once, no more than a distant screech against the wind and rain, and the Judge broke past Uncle Jim, while Blarney ran gamely two lengths behind. A three-horse race now, unless Uncle Jim gathered himself, and Dude soon saw that he couldn't.

From there Dude seemed to view the race as if through a grayish screen in the slanting rain. General Hill flying down the middle of the track, the Buxton stud coming to him, liking the off track, and Judge Blair firing, coming to the favorite, though not yet lapped on him.

At the eighth pole the General held a length's lead. About fifty yards beyond, Dude saw his head come up and some of the drive went out of his charge. Sir Roderick ran him down, a killer's instinct, though the General tried to fight back under whipping. For a flash Dude lost sight of his horse. Then he saw why. Coyote and the Judge, running inside the Buxton horse, had been hidden momentarily by the big, long-striding horse. Suddenly the two front runners were lapped.

At the sixteenth pole, Dude saw Sir Roderick's rider begin whipping lefthanded, calling for more run, and the big chestnut moved up. Coyote whooped and Judge Blair moved up. Now the horses ran as a team. Neither would give. The shouting crowd raised a great din, urging the Buxton horse on.

As Dude watched the runners charge past

the paddock, Sir Roderick's jockey, still whipping lefthanded, slashed Judge Blair twice across the right shoulder. Judge Blair's head jerked, but nothing changed. Coyote's whooping was continuous and Judge Blair was still coming on, coming on, the horses somewhat unreal, as phantoms fleeting through the gray drizzle.

They tore past the finish pole.

Dude couldn't tell for certain. Did his horse get up in the last few strides? It was hard to tell from this angle. He clapped heels to Blue Grass and galloped for the finish pole, his mind alternating between hope and dread. Looking for Billy, he found him crossing the track at a fast walk to the finish-line judges, who were still conferring.

"Well, gentlemen," Billy half shouted, "I had the one horse by a head or half a neck." He waited, on edge, glaring at them, as if daring them to disagree.

The judges didn't answer immediately. Then one turned. "We all caught the one horse by a head," he said, and the other two nodded.

Billy gave a little hop and smashed his hands together and Dude, whooping, swung down from the saddle and clapped Billy on the back, seeing in his face the light of pure joy. The old man, suddenly, had to remove his spectacles and wipe his eyes. He kept shaking his head, overjoyed.

There was a rush of people onto the track as the rain eased off again, among them Colonel Buxton and the ubiquitous Rube Vogel.

"Did I hear you say the one horse by a head?" Buxton asked, confronting the judges.

"That's right, Colonel," the spokesman said. "It was very close. A great race. We also clocked it in one-thirty-eight, two-fifths, remarkable on this heavy track."

Buxton, in disappointment, looked away and then, taking hold of himself, reached for his wallet and from it drew five one-hundred dollar greenbacks, which he handed to Billy, who inclined his head in thanks.

Buxton said, "I'd like a rematch at the same distance."

"You mean a match race?"

"A match race on a dry track. This was a fluke win today."

"Fluke, hell," Dude broke in, "when your boy struck our horse twice across the chest with his whip, coming down the stretch? I saw it from the paddock. Was he instructed to foul if challenged?"

The Colonel drew himself up in that way he had when offended. "Sir, I have never instructed any boy riding for me to foul. I did not see the infraction you claim because people were jumping up and down in front of me, but I assure you the young man will hear from me."

"Also, Colonel, both horses were running on the same bad track." Dude had to rub that in.

Buxton confronted Billy. "The match race, sir?"

"You have it, Colonel. When, depends on how our horse comes out of this. If he's sound, we run."

"Since I am the challenger, sir, I should call on you to discuss when and other details. May I ask where you are quartered?"

"We're camped at the Widow Corum's."

The Colonel's face changed. Then his southern manners took over and he said, "I'll ride over some morning soon."

Billy threw him a horse-trader's smile, thin and gauging. "We forgot one little item, Colonel. How much would you like to wager?"

"A thousand dollars."

"A thousand it is, Colonel. We'll be looking for you."

"Good day, sir," said Buxton and went to await Sir Roderick. Vogel cut Dude a look and followed.

"Don't believe the farm manager cottons to me," Dude said, "and I can't say I'm particularly fond of him." He smiled from the teeth. "I don't understand why, unless he's jealous of my good looks."

Then Coyote was trotting back on Judge Blair, and Dude and Billy hurried to meet them.

CHAPTER 15

The Red Roan Saddler

Dude brought in an armload of wood and carefully dumped it into the kitchen woodbox. The aroma of baking bread overspread the room and made his mouth juices run.

"My," Daisy Corum said, "you-all keep doing all the chores. You've cut enough wood to get me through the winter and next spring. You've stacked the hay in the barn. You've cut all the weeds around the house, and straightened up the fences and repaired them. You've got Skipper feeling perky, though I'll never drive him again, and you-all helped me find another good buggy horse. I can't tell you how obliged I am."

"Why, ma'am," said Dude, giving her arm a little pat, "we're the ones that should feel obliged, and you bet we do. We camp on your property and water our horses and turn 'em out into your blue-grass paddocks. All this has agreed with the Duke, the way he ran."

Her rich black eyes, quite youthful this morning, conveyed an extra liveliness. "I'm going to tell you something," she said, her voice on the brink of apology. "I have a cousin who bets on horses and drinks whiskey, which I don't approve. He's better at that than he is at raising tobacco. Well, for the first time in my life I took some money over to him and asked him to bet it for me. On the Duke, I said. On the nose, I believe is the term. When he came over that evening with my winnings, I couldn't hold it all, it was so much. I said to him I said, 'J.C., you take some of this money and buy yourself a jug of the best Kentucky whiskey,' and he said, 'I believe I will, Cousin Daisy, for my cough. Thank you.'" A confessional dampened her voice. "That's the only time I've ever bought whiskey."

"That's all right," said Dude, all proper and forgiving, "and I'm glad you won some money on our horse. I'm sorry you didn't get to see him run."

She handed him a loaf of fresh-smelling bread wrapped in a towel. "Have this for your supper tonight."

He thanked her profusely, again and again, adding, "Now I know how Cousin J.C. felt when you bought him that jug of good whiskey." A thought arrested him as he started out the back door. "The other evening I said I'd remembered a password and passed it off as a joke between Billy and Coyote and me. There's more to it than that and I hope I can tell you the whole story sometime. Before I can I need to know the whereabouts of a man called Si Eckert. Ever hear of him around Lexington?"

"Si Eckert? Lawyer, doctor, farmer, horse-man?"

"A horseman."

"A newcomer."

"Some years back. Not far, not near."

"I don't recall the name. An old friend of yours, perhaps?"

"Just somebody we's told to look up before we left Texas. An old friend of an old friend."

"I see. Perhaps he got into trouble with the law around here and is out of circulation? Perhaps he rode off on the wrong horse?"

Dude chuckled. "Sometimes down in Texas a good horse has been known to follow the wrong fella home, if you know what I mean. Cows, too. That happen much here?"

"More than you might think, as careful as people are about their horses. Horse thievery is a very serious offense in Kentucky. That and stealing hams."

"What if a man shoots another man?"

"In the early days of Kentucky, there were many killings over land claims. They say cloudy land titles was one reason why Abe Lincoln's father kept moving until finally he took the family across the Ohio over into Indiana." She sniffed. "Indiana also brags it gets more corn to the acre than we do. So often claims overlapped, or a settler would find a squatter on his land. Then they'd shoot it out. Based on that tradition in Kentucky, a man can get a few years for murder, but life for robbing somebody with a gun. In Ohio, for example, it's the other way around — life for murder and a short term for armed robbery. In Kentucky, sentiment is generally with the defendant in a murder, if there was good reason for the killing and the victim deserved what he got. Especially, if he impugned the virtue of a good woman. On the other hand, men have been hanged for stealing horses."

"Been much of that around Lexington?"

"Now and then you hear about it. As long as there are good horses, there'll be thieves. A stolen horse taken far away and sold, no questions asked, is like money in the bank."

"Has Colonel Buxton lost any horses?"

"Not lately that I've heard, but years past he has."

He cocked a teasing eye at her. "About how

serious is stealing hams?"

"That, Mr. McQuinn, depends on how many hams the person took and whose hams were taken."

Laughing quietly to himself, he left on that new understanding of Kentucky justice. Once outside he took stock of the outfit's situation. They were no closer to finding Si Eckert than they had been in Illinois and Indiana. Daisy, who should know, had never heard of the man. After the match race, they would head back west. The thought of leaving fetched Miss Blossom to the forefront of his mind, along with unresolved reflections.

That afternoon he rode to the Lexington post office and asked for his mail. None today, he was told. Riding glumly back to camp, he unsaddled Blue Grass and sat mooning in a shaded chair. Coyote was reading and Billy was shifting bottles about in his medicine chest.

Dude drowsed, stirring when he heard hoof-beats on the road, the regular cadence of a gaited horse. He glanced up, slack and listless. A horseman was coming from town, his mount saddling along in a running walk, that rocking-chair gait. Dude was about to settle back in the chair. Instead, he sat bolt-upright, startled. The man was riding a head-noddin' red roan, which was going easy, picking up its feet just so. Yes, his waking senses told him, a red roan saddler. Meaning jarred through him, bringing him instantly awake. Horse and rider passed at that moment, lost in the shadows along the tree-fringed road.

He jumped up to call his partners, but some warning sense made him lower his urgent voice, "Billy — Coyote. Come here! Quick!"

Coyote put down his book and came over. Billy answered from the wagon. "What is it? I'm busy."

"A red roan saddler just passed on the road coming from town."

"So what? That's not a rare color."

"Listen. I hope you haven't forgotten what Poge Yates's wife told us about the three-pointed star and a stripe runnin' down its face?"

Billy came out then. "Did you catch the white markings?"

"Just a glimpse of the horse. Couldn't tell from here." Dude was in motion as he spoke. "I sure aim to find out." He ran to his horse.

By the time he had saddled and covered the one hundred yards or more to the road at a gallop, the horseman was no longer in sight. There was, Dude saw, a bend some distance beyond. He heeled the gelding into a hard gallop and reined through the shadowed bend, but saw no one when he dashed out of it. At the most, he figured, he couldn't be more than two minutes behind. Galloping on, he looked for side roads leading off to farms, but saw none. Then he remembered that Colonel Buxton's extensive holdings bordered the road for a long way. The road bent and straightened, an avenue under the cool arcade, and still he sighted no movement.

There, at last, stood the proud stone pillars of the Old Dominion Stud. His impulse was to go on, thinking he had lost his quarry, which puzzled him because he'd passed no side roads and no paddock gates. He halted and looking beyond the closed gate, up the tree-lined road winding toward the great white-columned house, he discovered the red roan, traveling in that smooth, ground-eating walk. No wonder Poge Yates had wanted the saddler.

Dude hesitated, hearing his horse blowing, his mind tightening. He must not rush in there. This must look casual and unhurried. Only an interest in the saddler, until he could check the roan's markings. He'd seen the saddler go by and noticed its easy running walk. Was the horse for sale?

On that, he came down from the saddle, unlatched the gate and pushed it open, led his horse through and closed the gate, relatched, mounted and swung Blue Grass into a running walk down the winding road.

He passed the lofty house, elegant in its grace and refinement, drawn on to the vast barn, where in the runway a slab-bodied man was unsaddling the red roan. The rider stared at Dude as he rode up and dismounted. The rider was Rube Vogel.

"Good afternoon," Dude opened. "I didn't recognize you when you rode by the Corum place, Vogel. I am interested in your fine saddler. Is he for sale?"

Vogel shook his head, his eyes cool and distant.

"Can you tell me his breeding?"

Dude was moving toward the runway as he spoke, leading Blue Grass. The roan's head was still turning away from Dude. At the sound of another horse, the saddler turned its head and Dude, with an inward start, saw the three-pointed star, out of which ran the stripe like spilled milk the length of the face to between the nostrils, the white markings well defined on the face, which was darker than the roan body.

Dude checked his step. A cold quiver clutched him.

"What's his breed matter if he ain't for sale?" Vogel replied, jaws working. He spat and wiped his chin with the back of his left hand.

A certainty pounding through him, Dude said as casually as he could. "Believe it's time we got acquainted, Si Eckert. 'At my door the pale horse stands.' " He waited, his pulse jumping.

The squinting eyes changed not one whit. "What kind of talk is that? You a poet or somethin'?"

Dude grinned. "You ought to know the password. Figured maybe we could do a little business."

Vogel stared, his face inscrutable. A cool one, Dude sensed.

"I'm from Texas," Dude said, hoping he sounded confidential. "We can always use more good horses, runnin' horses or saddlers, even some workhorses, if the prices are right."

Vogel's angular face was like so much stone.

"Well," Dude carried on, "I wouldn't expect you to meet me with open arms. A man needs credentials. Credentials like Poge Yates, in Petersburg, Illinois, and Foss Ramsey, Indian Creek, Indiana."

"I never heard tell of either man," Vogel said, straight out. "Now, mister, I got chores to do." He led the red roan away.

Dude's voice followed him. "I'll still be camped at the Widow Corum's if you want to do business."

Vogel walked on.

"It's the red roan with the white markings, all right," Dude reported back at camp, "and the rider was Rube Vogel. I called him Si Eckert and gave the rest of the password, but he didn't bite."

"Expect him to pull the cork under the first time?" Billy reasoned. "He'll have to check you out first. Could be he thinks you're a Pinkerton."

Colonel Buxton arrived not long after breakfast the following morning, riding a high-stepping chestnut saddler.

Billy invited him to campfire coffee, which the Colonel declined, saying, "I forgot all about catch weights, Doctor. Is that agreeable with you?"

"It is, Colonel."

"For the starter, I know we can get Mr. Smedly, the regular starter at the track. Also, the same finish-line judges."

"Fine. I liked the way Mr. Smedly started the field in the rain and mud. Every horse seemed to break well, none left standing, and the judges impressed me as veteran horsemen."

"Very well. Then I'll see about that. Now

about when would you want to run this race, Doctor?"

Billy studied on that. "I don't like to bring a horse back too early after a hard race, even though the Duke came out of it sound. Just a little weary. Would a week from Saturday at two o'clock meet your approval, Colonel? I say Saturday, knowing you don't run on Sunday."

"We do observe the Sabbath hereabouts, Doctor, but I can't vouch for the rest of the week." His eyes were twinkling, which cast him in a revealing light to Dude. The Colonel wasn't all high southern pride and humorless, after all. "Sir Roderick is sound and ready to run. It's his Glengarry blood, sir. In fact, behind him now, I have two fine Glengarry yearling colts in the barn. At this stage they look more promising than he did at that age."

Billy cocked a cynical eye at him. "You mean you didn't offer them at the sale?"

The Colonel, as if not to be outdone, fixed on him a look as cagey as any traveling horse trader's. "Would you have, Doctor?"

"I'd much prefer to sell off the culls at a fancy price to some gullible newcomer and race the cream of the crop."

For a moment their eyes met, exchanging knowing looks, like two conspirators finding a common ground. The Colonel coughed and found his formality again. "A week from Saturday, then, Doctor."

Billy, bobbing his head, asked, "Do you insist on forfeit money, Colonel? I've never liked the idea."

"Nor have I. The race is the thing. Not forfeit money."

Dude's amusement stirred. Why the sudden change, the civility between the two? Only a few days ago they were firing bitter salvos over the war. Today, Billy was sickening nice, the Colonel nicey-nice. If they kept this up, they'd be bowing and scraping.

"The inside post position may pose some advantage on a dry track," Buxton was saying. "Would you like to flip for post position just before the race, Doctor?"

"That's suitable with me."

"Is that all, Doctor?"

"I believe it is, Colonel."

I'm gonna throw up if they go on like this, Dude said to himself.

"I do have a request of you, Doctor," Buxton said. "I'd like to see your horse."

"Coyote, bring out the Duke for the Colonel to see."

Buxton noted Judge Blair's fine points aloud as he circled the gelding. "Great heart girth. . . . Good head. . . . Long shoulder. . . .

Great bone. . . . Straight legs. . . . Exceptional muscle. . . . Compact. Must weigh eleven-fifty."

"Twelve hundred," Billy said, with obvious pride.

"His only fault as a Thoroughbred, I'd say, is his height. He lacks a bit."

"Fifteen hands," Billy said. "Neither was the great Janus tall."

"Janus — Janus," the Colonel enthused. "Imported into Virginia from England in 1752. By Old Janus, a son of the Godolphin Arabian, his dam by Fox. Janus stood fourteen and a half hands."

"Beg pardon, Colonel. Janus stood fourteen and three-quarters."

Buxton's face reddened. "Fourteen and a half hands, sir."

"Fourteen and —" Billy seemed to retrieve himself all in one breath, and the Colonel, ready to retort, likewise pulled back, each appearing a little foolish, saying, "Whatever his height, Janus was an outstanding speed sire, much of which he passed on to quarter horses. South and west of the James River he truly made his mark as a sire."

"He did," Billy agreed.

The Colonel regarded Billy questioningly. "You didn't tell me his breeding, Doctor."

"So I didn't. He's by the Duke of Highlands, out of Trixie M."

"I've heard of the Duke of Highlands, but not Trixie M. Her breeding?"

Billy couldn't hide a faint sheepishness. "That's all I know. This horse was given to me in payment of an old debt."

"It must have been a good-sized debt," said the other, his voice quizzical.

"It was," Billy said, " – his life," and left it there. "We all respect good breeding and conformation. But there is another element that's often overlooked. As yet there is no way to judge the heart of a horse, which is what makes him run."

"I have to agree with you, Doctor."

Off and on, Dude noticed, Uncle had been glancing at the chestnut saddler. Now he said, "Colonel, I don't want to alarm you, but I believe your horse is hurting in his right foreleg. He lifts it now and then as if it hurts him."

In concern, Buxton turned to the horse, while Billy, not waiting, crossed over and raised the saddler's foreleg by the fetlock. "Here it is," he said, after a pause. "A quarter crack in the hoof."

Buxton made a gesture of loss. "Just when he is reaching his peak. Now I'll have to turn him out for three months or longer."

"Maybe not. I have something in my medicine chest I'd like to try, with your permission."

"Go ahead."

"I won't promise a miracle."

Billy was quickly back, in his hands a small brush and a whiskey bottle containing a grayish mass and another whiskey bottle containing whiskey. While the Colonel held the saddler, he soaked a white rag with whiskey and cleaned the crack and poured some in the crack. Next he brushed the grayish matter into the crack and along the sides. He did this repeatedly.

"What is this er . . . medicine?" Buxton asked skeptically, when the old man had finished. "Looks like paste."

"I got it from a vet in Juarez, Mexico (when Judge Blair beat the great Mexican mare, Yolanda, Dude remembered) and he didn't know exactly. Said it came out of the Mexican jungles. Said it heals and holds. Said it would clog up a canal. It's used at the Juarez track. After it dries, presently, I'll put a tight wrap around the hoof. If he quits favoring the foot in a few days, you'll know it works. While we're waiting, Colonel, I believe it would be proper to offer you a drink at the wagon."

"Thank you, sir. And I appreciate your attention to my horse."

Dude, who seldom joined Billy and a visitor

or trader socially at the jug, knowing the old man wanted to make his own deal or make his own spiel, heard the stopper on the jug go *thung*. A pause followed, then an undertone of voices. Billy's, the first distinct voice.

"This whiskey's probably not what you're accustomed to, Colonel. It was made in Indiana."

"I do detect a difference, Doctor, between it and our Kentucky Bourbons."

"What is that, Colonel?"

"A faint bite, Doctor, maybe caused by too much rye or lack of aging in a charred keg."

The voices were becoming more and more formal, Dude could tell, tending toward edginess, as if they were getting back on true terms.

"I taste no bite, Colonel."

"Maybe that's because you're used to it by now. I'd say it has a definite whang, Doctor."

"A whang! I still say —"

Silence. Dude could imagine Uncle roping in his tetchiness, because next to horses, he prided himself on his judgment of whiskey, good or bad. And apparently he did as Dude heard him say in a tactful voice, "Be that as it may, Colonel, and compensating for our different likes, would you care for another drink?"

"Thank you, Doctor. I believe I will have another morning phlegm cutter. I seemed to have picked up a scratchy throat." The Colonel's voice likewise coming down. More silence as they partook of the jug again. And again the Colonel's voice. "Doctor, I do believe the whang is getting less and less all the time!"

Listening, Dude could only shake his head. Was all this back-and-forth, nicey-nice, colonel-and-doctor talk just two cagey old codgers angling to get the advantage of the other on race day?

CHAPTER 16

Horses Don't Lie

Dude and Coyote had never seen Billy set so strict a training schedule. They would work Judge Blair on alternate mornings, he said, trotting and galloping, and take him to the Kentucky Association track every other work. On rest days the Judge would graze in the west paddock until noon, where he was always in sight of the camp. Peter, Daisy Corum's old gray saddler, occupied the east paddock.

"Since the Judge thrives on work," Billy said, "we'll give him a sharp half mile, say around forty-eight seconds, the day before the race. That should put him on edge."

Dude did not sight Vogel again until Tuesday afternoon before the race, when the farm manager rode past the Corum farm on the red roan. That set Dude to sorting out matters again. Whenever he gave up on the Si Eckert lead, his logic would swing him back to Poge Yates and Foss Ramsey. If it was phony, why had they passed on the name? Given reluctantly at that, as if they should not. Or was it fear? All along Dude had figured that Judge Blair was stolen as a young horse, not sold. He showed too much race breeding, character and conformation. Somewhere along the line somebody had made a workhorse of him, or tried, hence the collar and chain markings. Although he drove well with another horse pulling a wagon, he wasn't big enough for heavy farm work.

Clarity came to his mind while he watched Vogel saddle down the road to Lexington. Why not continue pretending to want a deal on stolen horses such as Dude had hinted at when he caught Vogel at the barn? The deal had to come first. Only then would Dude learn the Judge's true breeding. By now it was plain that Vogel wasn't coming to him. Dude would have to go after him. Be a gadfly.

The resolution gathered momentum while he saddled Blue Grass and made for the road.

Following at a trot, keeping Vogel in sight, Dude entered the outskirts of Lexington before long. Vogel did not glance back, Dude passed houses with white picket fences and reached the outer business district and its red brick buildings. Vogel tied up at a store and went inside. Dude dismounted and waited by the red roan. When Vogel emerged, a new halter in his hand, he glanced in surprise at Dude, who said, "Don't believe we finished our little visit the other day."

"What we got to visit about?"

Dude pulled on the lobe of his left ear and gazed off, speaking softly, "Wasn't time to tell you that my outfit does more than match races as we travel about. We buy good horses to sell, if the price is right."

"What's that got to do with me?"

Dude let a suggestive grin curl his mouth. "That's why your fine red roan saddler caught my eye. Another horse like that would fetch good money anywhere."

"I told you he's not for sale." Vogel untied the roan and rose to the saddle.

"I can see he's your personal saddler. I mean horses of his class. Any good horse that can travel will sell. We're also in the market for yearlin' runnin' horses, if you catch what I mean?"

Vogel stared at Dude, the squinting eyes devoid of response, the long jaws working. Reining about, he headed out of town, leaving Dude feeling unwise and rash. But what other course had he? Horses didn't lie. The red roan with the white markings was the link. Preoccupied, he rode slowly back to camp. The Old Dominion Stud wasn't the place to talk business. He would resume his vigil and keep after Vogel, meanwhile hoping Vogel would let prospects of a deal simmer in his mind.

Wednesday afternoon Vogel rode by again on the red roan. Dude followed at a leisurely trot. This time Vogel rode farther into town and for no other workaday purpose than to stop at a feed store. Dude, in his projections, had pictured the farm manager rendezvousing with a confederate at some out-of-the-way place, up some lonely country road or at an abandoned farm house.

Dude was waiting when Vogel left the store. "You again," he said, irritation sliding across his face.

"Guess I didn't make myself clear about buyin' good horses?"

"Plenty horse traders around." Vogel spat as he finished. At times he drawled, sounding like a Texan. He had drawled just then.

"I'm interested only in first-class horses. No plugs. I'm not the first man that noticed the class of your saddler, for example. He caught Poge Yates's eye in Petersburg. Yates tried to buy him, didn't he?"

Vogel, his face impassive, took out a plug of tobacco, cut off a chunk and wallowed it around in his mouth as a schoolboy would a piece of hard candy. He spat, then said, "There are other red roans."

"I've never seen another one with his exact markings — that almost perfect three-pointed star and the stripe dripping out where the fourth point would be. That's the same description folks remember in Petersburg. They say a man who called himself Si Eckert rode the roan."

"I don't have nothin' to say to you, mister."

"You're a hard man to deal with. I'm just tryin' to tell you I'm in the market for some good horse deals."

Vogel drawled, "You know, mister, I could get you in bad real quick with the law. All I got to say is that you tried to bribe me so I'd fix Sir Roderick before the match race. Savvy? Don't follow me again." Mounting, he clapped heels to the roan and struck out the way he had come.

But you won't go to the law, Dude said back silently, because you're on the other side of the law yourself. Just how, I don't know yet, but I sure as hell feel it.

Without much hope, Dude stopped at the post office on the way back and inquired about his mail. The clerk nodded in recognition and flipped through a stack of letters.

"Still nothing for you, Mr. McQuinn. Sorry. Maybe tomorrow."

Was it over? Dude had never felt so heavy of heart, so filled with gloom.

He begged off from going to the track with Billy and Coyote early Thursday morning for Judge Blair's blowout sharpener for Saturday's race, saying Vogel might ride by and he wanted one final stab at a talk with him. Maybe sight of some money would grease his tongue.

The early hours passed without change.

"Forty-eight flat," Billy announced, satisfied, when they rode in later, "We'll give him his usual breakfast Saturday morning, with only a handful of hay. After that, just a few sips of water at noon. I want him lean and ready and a little hungry at post time. All day tomorrow he can frolic in the paddock with the birds and the bees."

"Well, Vogel hasn't showed up. You know what, Uncle? I think he's a Texan. I can tell by the way he drawls. I've talked just enough with him."

"And what does that tell us?"

Dude's expression was dry. "Just that he's a Texan."

Vogel did not show up the entire day.

By Friday afternoon Dude was ready to admit

defeat. After the race, the outfit might as well break camp for the return trip west. Still, he watched the road.

A short time after three o'clock he heard a horse coming hard from the direction of the Old Dominion Stud. It was Vogel, the red horse at a hard gallop.

Dude, his earlier doubts dissolving, mounted and followed. In town other riders were about and he hung back among them when he saw Vogel slow his horse to the running walk. Vogel passed the stores where he had previously stopped. He seemed in a hurry. He rode through the main part of town and turned off into a section new to Dude. An occasional store of unpainted plank siding, blocks of shabby houses and cluttered yards with loose dogs which barked at the roan. Now Vogel's horse was out of the smooth running walk into the gallop again. A plank building with a broad overhang, which Dude saw was another store, materialized ahead.

Dude reined back to a walk as Vogel tied up at the crowded hitching rack of the building next to the store and entered. The dogs raced back to bark at Blue Grass. Riding on, Dude found an empty place at the end of the rail for his horse. Glancing up, he saw the sign: BUCK-HORN SALOON. Idlers hung around the doorway.

Next door loomed a large brick warehouse. Painted across its broad front Dude read the faded letters: FAR WEST STORAGE CO. A sign in the fly-specked office window read: CLOSED. There was a narrow passageway between the buildings. Dude moved past the loafers and through the swinging doors of the saloon.

Dude looked all around. Vogel wasn't in sight. At the far end of the bar a bartender motioned and the saloon swamper hurried out the back door. Dude squeezed through the customers to where a second barkeep stood at station and ordered whiskey. The drink was slow coming. One taste of it made him flinch. He put the glass down and watched the rear door.

At that moment the swamper and a short, lumpish man came in. His movements were jerky and he had worried eyes in a harassed-looking face that twitched spasmodically on the right side. His brownish whiskers were unkempt and his lips moved loosely when he spoke to the bartender, a thickset man in a dirty white apron.

They talked briefly, then turned toward a room near the rear door. The little man kept rubbing his jaw as they entered.

"What's the matter, friend, don't you like your whiskey? You're drinkin' like a hummin' bird." It was the second bartender speaking, gazing accusingly at Dude's unfinished drink.

Dude loosened a suffering smile. "I've tasted worse, but I don't know where. Why don't you pour me one outa that bottle marked Old Green River?"

"You get what you pay for around here. That'll be double what the house brand is," the man said, pouring the Old Green River.

Dude laid a dollar on the bar and sipped, watching the back room.

A little later the bartender and the short man came out. They were gesturing, arguing. The bartender said something that appeared to quiet the short man. His face twitching, he gave an assenting jerk of his head and went out the rear door.

Where was Vogel?

Dude returned to his drink. The bartender, who was holding a bottle for Dude to see, said, "If you wondered about our house brand, here it is, bottled for us: *Battle Buckhorn, A Fight Every Ten Minutes*. We're proud of that label. Gets a lot of laughs."

"I'll bet it works in five minutes," Dude said, grinning.

He did not know where Vogel had come from, but when Dude strayed his eyes over the crowd again, Vogel was heading for the front.

Dude followed and caught up with him at the hitching rack.

Vogel wheeled, anger sharp across his face. "What the hell! You again."

"Just being sociable," Dude said. "I'm still ready to deal."

"Deal – what deal?" Suspicion swelled in Vogel's voice and eyes. And then an insight struck Dude: *Billy's right. He thinks I'm a Pinkerton.*

"I'm still in the market for good horses, if the price is right."

"You're talkin' to the wrong man." He was drawling again.

Dude saw it then, the deadend. He was thinking fast. There would be no working up to a deal. The man was too cautious, or maybe he didn't need a deal. It was time to gamble. "All right," Dude said, holding his voice down, "forget the horse deal. Just answer one question for me. That's all I want. You've seen our horse, the Duke of Dexter. Are his markings familiar to you? Did you ever see the horse before? Do you remember him as a yearling, maybe, or a two-year-old? Think back. There's money in it for you if you can place him and know his breeding. That's all I want to know."

"How would I know, as many horses as I

see?" The suspicion hadn't ebbed; it was grow-ing.

"More reason you should know. You're a horseman and he's an exceptional runner to beat Sir Roderick."

Vogel's lips flattened into a thin line. "Still doggin' me, still tryin' to drag me into some-thing, ain't you? I warned you once. Now I'll make it plainer. Keep this up, somebody's gonna get hurt. Includes that cagey old gent, your trainer."

Dude went stiff. "You try to harm one little hair on that old man's head and you'll be face up to this blue Kentucky sky — only you won't be seein' it."

Vogel, instinctively, made a motion inside his coat, then hesitated and bit by bit let his hand drop. Damn his slippery hide, he's packed a gun all the time, Dude thought, and mine's back in the wagon.

"I meant what I said," Vogel grunted and swung to the saddle.

"Don't try me," Dude said.

Standing there, watching the man ride off, Dude was conscious of a heavy sensation of defeat. He had run the string out. It was over now and he guessed he hadn't handled it well. There was a wrongness about today. About Vogel's riding here, about whatever had gone on inside, about Vogel's instant suspicion over a deal, about his wariness. And horses didn't lie.

Obeying a sudden urge, he stepped back into the saloon and ordered another Green River. "I see this building next door is closed," said Dude, conversationally. "Wonder if it's for sale?"

The bartender shrugged.

"That little fella who was in here talkin' to the other bartender. Reckon he'd know?"

Another shrug.

"Believe I'll ask him." He worked his way through the crowd to the rear door and outside. Amid the scattered trash of an alley, mainly boxes and whiskey barrels, he looked both ways and then at the warehouse, seeing the heavy padlock on the broad rear door, windows higher than a man's head on each side of the door, wondering where the short man had come from when summoned by the swamper. That was when he saw the cubbyhole office in the near corner of the warehouse. The door was open and glancing inside he saw an inner door that led into the warehouse, a cookstove, a coal oil lamp on a wooden box, a cot with rumpled blankets, a wooden water bucket on the floor, and beside it a hay hook. Before he could knock or call out, a jerky voice behind him asked, "Lookin' for somebody?"

It was the lumpish little man who had argued with the bartender. To Dude's chagrin, the man had followed him unnoticed out of the crowded saloon. "For you," Dude told him. "I saw the closed sign on the office window. Is the building for sale?"

"Nope."

"Reason I asked I'm looking for a business opportunity. Who owns it?"

"There's several owners, I understand. I'm just the caretaker."

"I'd like to take a look at it. Mind showing me around?" The request surprised even him, springing out of instinct alone.

"No can do." The man's face was twitching. "Not to strangers."

"Who are the owners?"

"I'm paid from an office in town. Man's paid regular, he don't ask questions." He was rubbing his jaw.

"If I buy it," Dude insisted, "I'd have to see it first."

"Not to strangers." He spread his hands fanwise. "I just work here and draw my pay, such as it is."

It wasn't right, Dude knew. Nothing here was right, and he walked back through the saloon to his horse.

At the post office he asked for his mail,

expecting none, and felt his pulse quicken when the friendly clerk said, "There is something for you, Mr. McQuinn."

Taking the letter, Dude drank the feminine handwriting with his eyes and turning away carefully opened the envelope and read:

Dear Mr. Dude,

I haven't written you because my mother was taken ill and I went home to help my father care for her. She is fine now. Father thinks my leaving home made her ill, but she is beginning to accept my growing up.

Aunt Lucinda tells me your Duke (I'd never tell his real name!) won the big handicap race in Lexington. We're so proud. He's such a beautiful horse. My, how I wish I could have seen him run again.

I cherish your letter and am sorry I'm late answering. I'm also behind in school and must make up. Speaking of schooling, you are not fair to yourself. You are educated in many ways that cannot be learned in school, only in life. You are true to your friends and your beliefs, generous and thoughtful of others.

Whether you find Si Eckert or not, I sincerely hope you'll come back this way soon. But do not feel obligated by your promise. I don't want you to feel that you have to. Don't unless you want to. Be honest with yourself. In turn, I shall be honest. I want you to because I know in my heart that I love you dearly.

Sincerely,
With love, Blossom

Dude uttered a whoop that startled the post office patrons and immediately penned this reply:

Dear Miss Blossom,

You made this cowpoke kick up his heels ready to rassel a pack of grizzlies when he got your letter. I'm sorry your mother was sick and glad she's better. You bet I am.

Tomorrow we run a match race against Sir Roderick, the top horse we beat in the handicap on a muddy track. We've located the red roan saddler with the white markings I told you about, but the rider won't talk. There's something wrong. I hope we get to the truth before I see you.

Blossom, I've loved you all along. I started loving you that day in the store. Later I was the one who was afraid. I was afraid my way of life as a horseman wouldn't be best for you and I was afraid I couldn't provide you with a good home. Now I know I can.

See you soon. I promise, like always.

Love, Dude

Billy and Coyote were fixing supper by the time Dude reached camp. Eagerly, he told them what had happened, ending with, "I'm goin' back there tonight."

"That sounds like a tough part of town," Billy cautioned. "We'd all better go."

"Not after Vogel's threat. You'd both better watch yourselves — and the horses."

"I don't like your idea, Dude. Why go back there at all?"

"I want a look inside that warehouse. There's something wrong."

"What makes you think so?"

"More hunch than anything. Why did Vogel ride hard to the saloon?"

"Going to a saloon is not unusual." Billy smiled. "You know that."

"But Vogel rides the red roan saddler. We've got the right horse and horses don't lie. Vogel's our man. He's Si Eckert."

"He won't talk, but what can you do about it?"

"Keep searching. There's a key to this somewhere."

It was an hour past nightfall when Dude left camp, his old six-shooter on a gunbelt strapped around his middle under his coat. With the brown saddler traveling in that easy, four-beat running walk along darkened streets, past dimly lighted houses, he came to the center of town. There he turned down a tree-bordered street which gradually took him into the rundown section of town. The dogs ran out barking; they followed in a yapping chorus to the noisy Buckhorn, and as if that were the line of demarcation, there they quit. He could hear loud voices and an off-tune piano. Free of the dogs, he rode a block past the saloon and circled back. The warehouse loomed like a dark cliff under the crescent moon playing hide-and-seek with drifting clouds. There was a contradiction here that wouldn't go away, which again was only instinct. He started to enter the passageway between the saloon and the warehouse, when he remembered the caretaker's office at the end of the building. Warned, he pulled back and moved along the front to the other end of the warehouse. As he did, a horseman galloped up, dismounted and went clumping into the Buckhorn.

Reaching the alley, Dude saw that the care-taker's office was dark. The alley's only light was a sliver from the saloon. He held up, weighing the hard decision of whether to heft an empty whiskey barrel to a rear window of the warehouse. The thought had no more than crossed his mind when a shaft of light broke from the opened back door of the saloon and a man called hoarsely, "Sug — come out."

Dude stared hard as he hugged the wall. The man was the main bartender, the big man.

There was no response.

As if impatient, the bartender took the few steps to the office and pounded on the door. A man's sleepy voice answered, "Who is it?"

"It's me — Tank. Get up. We got to talk."

"What about?"

"About tomorrow. Get up, damn it."

A low light glowed in the office. After a wait the caretaker opened the door. "All right, what about tomorrow?"

"Some new details. We'll talk about 'em in the saloon."

"You can tell me here."

Tank muttered something too indistinct for Dude to catch. Then they were drifting toward the saloon, the tone of Sug's voice complaining, Tank's appeasing. They entered the saloon.

The moment they did, Dude slipped up the

alley and inside the office, his mind fixed on the inner door he'd seen that afternoon that led into the warehouse. He opened the door, and closing it stepped into almost total darkness, blinded. He smelled hay. As his eyes adjusted and he went tentatively on, arms feeling ahead, he made out that he was in a storeroom. At the same time he stumbled over a bale of hay and fell to his knees with a thump; his mind flashing back explained the hay hook he'd noticed on the office floor by the water bucket. A crack of light showed beneath a door. He opened it and came out into the general warehouse.

He could see much clearer now, with light filtering in from three murky windows high on the opposite wall. Simultaneously, he smelled horses and heard hooves stamping softly beneath the windows. He moved closer, chest pounding, seeing, quickly, the vague shapes of haltered horses: three rangy animals and a yearling-size horse. Warehouse, hell!

He'd seen enough. Horses didn't lie.

Turning back, moving faster, he came to the open storeroom door. Closing it and going on, his boots brushing the bale of hay he'd tumbled over, he reached the office door. The rise of grating voices reached him from the alley as he let himself in and glanced out the doorway.

Tank and Sug stood in the saloon's out-thrown light. Sug made a slow turn toward the office and Dude froze, then drew the handgun. He heard Tank's heavy voice say, "I said I'd make it right, didn't I?"

"I've heard that before," the little man whined, still on a drift for the office. Dude stood rigid. Sweat started out on his forehead.

"You'll get all of it after tomorrow."

"No, by God," Sug said over his shoulder, slowing step. "I take the chances, you handle the money. I want half my share tonight, on the barrelhead. No more puttin' off like before."

There was a pause before Tank spoke again, in a giving-in voice. "All right. But I'll have to get it from the safe. Come on."

Not till then did Sug halt. He swung about, his movements jerky, and followed Tank inside the saloon.

A surge of relief coursed through Dude and he ran outside and down the alley and around the building, not slowing until he saw his horse.

CHAPTER 17

The Glengarry Colts

Race day.

The outfit rose early, walking and feeding Judge Blair and then brushing and currying and rubbing him until he shone. Billy had taken him to a farrier on Thursday after his half-mile sharpener to be reshod with light shoes.

"Just look at him," the old man praised, walking around the gelding. "He's as relaxed as a kitten in a sewing basket. I don't know anything more we can do to get him ready." Billy couldn't keep the sense of loss out of his voice. "I've said it before and I'll say it again. What a shame he was ever gelded. My, what he could pass on to his sons and daughters: intelligence and a calm disposition, balance, muscle, speed and, above all, the will to run, which you can detect in a horse's eyes. That look of eagles.

This horse has it." His voice faltered. "And we'll never know his breeding. All we've found out is that Vogel is afraid to talk and somebody is hiding horses in the warehouse. We'll have to tip the sheriff off after the race before we leave town."

By midmorning the road to Lexington had become a flood tide of buggies, wagons and riders. Families, dressed as if for a holiday and picnic, waved when they saw the blaze-faced dark bay, undoubtedly a racehorse, haltered to the wagon.

Daisy Corum, coming over to the camp about then, likewise was dressed for the occasion: jaunty green hat with a little tuft of artificial flowers and a long-sleeved dress of green and white.

"Everybody from miles around seems to be coming in," she said, eyes bright. "The Kentucky *Gazette* says this is the biggest match race in years. Sir Roderick is favored because it's a dry track, but I don't see it that way. The *Gazette* also called the Duke a country mudder." She placed hands on hips. "That made me mad. There's nothing wrong with being from the country, and if a horse can run in the mud, that's all that matters."

"No horseman knows what makes a mudder," Billy said. "My experience has been that some horses don't get untracked in mud for fear of slipping — that's natural. Some horses don't like mud thrown in their faces, so they back off. We had mud caulks on our horse and Coyote stayed wide where we figured the track was firmer. But I'd say the Duke, like any horse, prefers a dry track that's not too hard. Some cushion to it. A sore-footed horse will prefer one that's a bit soft."

"The main reason I came over," she said, "besides wishing you good luck, is to tell you what I heard. My Cousin Amelia, whose husband runs the feed store where Colonel Buxton trades sometimes, says the grapevine is that the Colonel is planning new strategy this time."

"And what could that be?" Billy asked.

"I asked the same question and she said that's all she'd heard," Daisy said, with a wry smile. "So be on the lookout. I'm leaving early to catch Cousin J.C. before he goes to the track and have him place a little bet for me. I'll be there, too. If the Duke wins, I'll give ten per cent to the church, same as I did the last time."

"That should keep you in the clear," Billy said, bowing, old school. "Good luck."

"Good luck to you-all!"

At eleven o'clock the outfit came out on the still-crowded road to go to the track, Billy driving the buggy, Coyote beside him with his

341

tack, Dude on Blue Grass, ponying Judge Blair. They stalled the Judge at the track and sat around for the long wait, watching across the infield at the crowd filing into the stands. The day was cool and bright, the track fast, Dude reported, after walking the backstretch part way.

Shortly before two o'clock a man rode up and said, "Mr. Smedly suggests that the horses be saddled over here and you meet at the entrance to the paddock for the post parade. The flip for post position will be at the barrier."

"Where is Colonel Buxton's horse stalled?" Dude asked.

"At the end of the shedrow."

"We'll meet him at the paddock."

"Very good, sir. Good luck."

"Coyote," Billy began, his face thoughtful, "we know that Sir Roderick is a late closer. Likes to come from off the pace. If he hangs back early, you go to the front. If he goes to the front, you stay with him. If the other rider tries to lure you into a slow pace, move out and take the lead. Save ground on the turns. You can do that today. When you make the turn for home, let the Judge out. We know he can go a mile or more. Just ride your race. You know what your horse can do and when to call on him for more run. Now, good luck, pardner."

They carefully saddled Judge Blair and Coyote mounted, stripped to the waist. Once, when the outfit had matched a race against a shady banker in western Kansas, Coyote had painted the Judge like a war horse and himself as well. Dude kind of wished he wore paint today. By not, he was giving in to mannered Kentucky.

Saying he would see Dude at the barrier for the post position flip, Billy struck out afoot across the track for the infield.

Dude, feeling the pre-race tension he always did, ponied horse and rider around to the paddock entrance and waited, hearing the rising chatter of the restless crowd. Not only were the stands full, but from the stands to the railing. Vendors' shrill voices hawked their treats. Waiting, Dude was aware of the conflict within his mind. A dejection that all the partners felt. *All this goodness,* he thought. *We've come to this. Another big race. A fine truck. Horse-loving people. The wooded, grassy Kentucky country rolling away like a horseman's dream. All this, and yet our search has failed.*

Soon, the Colonel trotted up on his saddler, ponying Sir Roderick. A glance told Dude of at least one change in strategy. A wizened crab of a man, his face like crinkled leather, rode the big chestnut stud, hunched in the saddle. Eyes like steel marbles. A brought-in rider, Dude knew at once. A veteran rider, the imprint of hundreds of races stamped upon his campaigner's face. Likely from the Chicago or New York tracks. Maybe Maryland.

The Colonel waved courteously and Dude, acknowledging the salute, led Judge Blair out to commence the post parade. Buxton took the lead. Starting past the gaping, eager crowd, Coyote kept faced ahead. But when someone clapped and the applause swelled, Coyote turned and waved. For the fun of it, he nudged the Judge's flank and the dark bay pranced and tossed his head and arched his neck. Up ahead, the Colonel's jockey seemed oblivious of the noise and the crowd. At the barrier Billy and the starter waited.

"Who will call it in the air?" Smedly asked.

"I will," Buxton replied, and when Smedly flipped a silver dollar, the Colonel called, "Tails."

The spinning coin struck the loose earth, bounced and lay still. "Tails it is, Colonel. You have your choice of position."

"The inside, of course," Buxton said, not hiding his elation.

"Now, gentlemen," Smedly instructed, "circle your horses back and walk up for the start."

Hearing that, Dude reined back to a rail-gate opening into the infield. Buxton was close behind him. Leaning down, Dude swung the gate open, and when Buxton was through, closed the gate and rode over to where Billy stood with the three judges inside the rail near the finish pole. Dude dismounted to stand beside Billy, who now held his stopwatch.

The racehorses were now making their final turn in front of the hushed stands.

Dude figured Buxton's rider would attempt to beat the barrier. Instead, as the horses moved up, head to head, he sat perfectly still in that crablike posture. But as the barrier flew up and away, he raised a great shout and Sir Roderick broke running, sprinting for the lead, the Judge half a length behind on the outside.

Into the first turn, hugging the rail, dirt flying, Sir Roderick ate up the distance. Coyote, saving ground, ran at the chestnut's hindquarters, going no wider.

Dude got the other part of the Colonel's strategy now: No lying back early in the race. Wear the other horse down, knowing your horse could go a distance of ground, draw the Indian into a duel. A country mudder couldn't sprint a mile on a dry track. *The hell he can't, Colonel!*

Dude jerked when Billy called out, "The first quarter in twenty-two and a fifth!"

Stretching out on the track's long backside,

the horses kept those positions, Coyote staying with the chestnut, the Judge, to Dude's gauging eye, settling down more and reaching the full rhythm of his long stride.

At the half-mile pole, Billy called, "The half in forty-four and four-fifths. They're flying, Dude!"

Sprinting into the far turn, Coyote tightened up the margin and moved his horse to the chestnut's girth, both crouching riders very still.

At six furlongs, Billy shouted the time: "One-o-nine and a fifth, Dude! Isn't it beautiful?"

"Can they keep it up?"

"Coyote hasn't used up all his horse yet!"

Rounding to the quarter pole, Coyote gained ground. Warned, the chestnut's rider glanced back and opened up a length's lead. Dude was biting his lips. Was the Judge fading after that early burning pace?

As the horses drove into the stretch, Dude saw Judge Blair change back to the right lead and come up, gaining narrowly on the switch. On that, Coyote went after Sir Roderick, ranging up to the chestnut stud's girth again. Then, running as if the heel flies were after him, Judge Blair ran to the Buxton horse's saddle cloth, now to the shoulder, now to the bobbing neck. At the eighth pole they ran head to head.

Now, Coyote whooped for the first time and the Judge broke in front by a head. At once, Sir Roderick, under righthanded whipping, rushed up and again the two battled head to head.

At the eighth pole, Coyote's whooping rising to a curdling screech, the Judge stuck his blazed head in front, then a neck. The crowd, as if sensing a blanket finish, was roaring and screaming.

The horses seemed locked in flight as they charged by the sixteenth pole, Sir Roderick gamely making up ground to Judge Blair's throatlatch, trying to run the leader down with his killer's instinct, the Judge, ears flattened, just as determined to hold him off.

They appeared to burst past the finish pole.

Dude whooped and jumped up and down, waving his arms. Billy glancing at his stopwatch, shouted, "The mile in one-thirty-four and four-fifths! Not bad for a country mudder!" Suddenly, he seemed to sag, his thin shoulders drooping. Tears slid down his whiskery face like huge raindrops.

The roaring of the crowd ebbed and died like a passing storm, in its wake a settling stillness, a greater stillness around the finish pole. The judges were huddling, heads together; they exchanged comments and presently one called out, "The Duke of Dexter by a head. A great race, gentleman."

Colonel Buxton, who had watched the race from his saddler, dismounted and coming over, visibly disappointed, said, "You have my congratulations, Dr. Lockhart," and held out his hand.

Billy, understanding, shook hands and said, "I know how you feel, Colonel. You take the loss like a true horseman and gentleman."

"I won't be a true horseman-gentleman unless I pay off my wager," Buxton said, all wryness, taking greenbacks from his wallet and handing them over.

Billy thanked him. "I've never seen two horses show more heart. Neither horse deserved to lose. The race was run in record time, but who will know? It wasn't a recognized race by the state association. Just a match race."

"Kentuckians will know, sir. The word will be passed. They won't forget."

By now Rube Vogel was at the Colonel's shoulder, deferring as usual, glowering at the victors. "Colonel," he said, "I thought the bay came in on Sir Roderick on the home turn. Interfered."

Buxton's eyes flicked sharply to the farm manager. "I had a clear view from horseback and saw no infraction, Mr. Vogel. Besides, Sir

Roddy was in the lead. The other horse could not have impeded him."

Vogel's claim left a weight of uncomfortable silence. Buxton, inclining his head in leaving, turned away with obvious displeasure and was preparing to mount when a commotion in the infield distracted him.

An elderly black man rushed up on a lathered mule, riding bareback. "Colonel, suh! Colonel Buxton!"

Buxton grabbed the mule's bridle. "What is it, Sam?"

"Your two Glengarry colts, suh — they're gone!" Sam had to stop for breath.

"Gone? What do you mean?"

"Stole, Colonel! I been feelin' poorly as you know. Ever'body else was at the race. I heard a noise down at the barns an' looked out an' there was a white man on a big horse leadin' 'em out to the road."

"Took 'em out to the country?"

"No, suh. Took 'em towards town."

Facing Vogel, Buxton said, "Have a groom take Sir Roddy home, then come back here." He turned to the black man. "To town, to town? I don't understand it. Doesn't make sense."

A door began to swing open in Dude's mind, slowly at first, then faster, and he heard himself saying, "Colonel, we may be able to help you. Maybe. It's a long shot." And he plunged into what he had found at the warehouse, telling it concisely.

The Colonel listened with mounting intensity. Vogel came back moments after Dude had finished. "We're riding to town, Mr. Vogel," Buxton said.

"Town, Colonel? Be hard to race the colts there by now. I suggest that we notify the sheriff."

Impatience hardened Buxton's face. "I can't wait for the sheriff. Come on, Sam, you'd better come along too in case you're needed to identify the thief."

Vogel said no more, but held a look on Dude.

"Coyote's bringing the Ju — the Duke back now," Billy hastily told Dude. "Hold up till I tell him where we're going."

Afterward, as they set out for town, Billy following the horsemen in his buggy, Dude took the lead and they rode at a hard gallop. Sam trailed on the mule.

They reached the main part of town. When Dude turned into the tree-bordered street that would lead into the rundown section, Vogel became visibly uneasy and dropped behind Dude and the Colonel, who rode grimly erect. The orderly blocks of gracious white homes fell away to unpainted houses and cluttered yards. Mongrel dogs swarmed out, barking; again they gave up the chase at the Buckhorn.

Motioning to go around, Dude reined off the street and cut in behind the warehouse to the alley, not halting until he pulled up before the office. At the horse clatter Sug came to the door.

"Open up," Dude told him. "We want to look at your horses."

"Horses?" Sug tried to shrug it off. "No horses here."

"There were horses in there last night. Open up or we'll do it for you."

"Sug Hines," Buxton said, glaring. "You were barred from the track here years ago for fixing horses."

There was movement at the rear door of the saloon and the man who had called himself Tank stood there. He stepped into the alley. His voice shot out. "What is it?"

"Sir, we request that you open the warehouse at once for our inspection," Buxton demanded. "I am Colonel H.P. Buxton. I'm missing two fine colts."

"That will require a court order, Colonel. This is private property."

Buxton looked at Dude. "I don't think we can force entry into private property, though I'm tempted."

An oncoming hoof clatter in the alley broke across the last of Buxton's words, and Dude saw Sam coming at a run on the lagging mule. Jerking at his mount, his eyes seeking, the black man pointed at Sug, his voice high with accusation. "That's him, Colonel! The one that took your Glengarry colts!"

A sudden motion. Vogel was wheeling his horse and facing them. As if in a dream of frustration where everything is futile, Dude found Vogel covering them with his handgun. His voice came in a burst. "You're goin' to see the warehouse, all right, but not the way you think."

A low but distinctly firm voice intruded. "Raise your hands, Vogel, unless you want me to bore you a set of new buttonholes."

It was Billy, on foot, standing behind the farm manager, covering him with a six-shooter that looked oversized in his small, deft hands.

Slowly, Vogel raised both hands.

"Take his shooting iron, Dude."

Dude did so, quickly, wondering how Uncle could have left the buggy, yards down the alley, and worked in so fast behind Vogel. But he had.

"Now," Billy ordered, talking to the bartender, "you and Sug open the warehouse door. We're going to look at those horses, private property or not."

Tank didn't stir. Billy's hand blurred, quicker than the eye, and the six-shooter exploded and dust spurted at Tank's feet.

"Move!"

Tank crossed to the warehouse door, his eyes sending Vogel a killing look every step of the way. Sug followed. Tank opened the padlock with a key and swung back the door.

And in there, in the murky dimness of the light from the dusty windows, stood two haltered chestnut yearlings, placidly switching flies and munching hay.

"My Glengarry colts!" Colonel Buxton yelled and rushed inside, Sam at his heels on the mule.

They untied the yearlings and as they led them out into the alley, the man called Sug, his face twitching, looking appealingly right and left, his voice choking, broke out with, "He's the one!" pointing at Vogel. "He started it when he came here – then Tank got in. I took the chances, they handled the money." He waved his arms, his voice rising hysterically. "But what could I do, I couldn't ride anymore? I was banned. But I love horses. Look how good I took care of 'em. Look at 'em back there!" Something akin to raw hate stood out in his eyes and choppy movements as he looked at

Vogel. "His name's not Vogel. He's got a bunch of names. Sometimes he's called Si Eckert over in Indiana and out in Illinois and down in Texas."

Vogel literally spat his words. "Shut up, Sug, you snivelin' rat!"

"I won't. By God, I won't! In Texas you're wanted as Nate Thompson — wanted for murder an' bank robbery an' horse stealin'. You been hidin' out at the Old Dominion Stud for five years."

He seemed to crumble, weeping, and covered his face with his hands.

It's over for him, Dude thought, somehow feeling sympathy for the little man, because, as he said, he did love horses. Yet, it was over for all of them, and the search for the breed also was over and still without resolution.

Next morning while the outfit was cleaning up preparatory to breaking camp, having said good-bys to damp-eyed Daisy Corum, Colonel Buxton trotted up on his saddler. "Thought I'd better come over early after Dr. Lockhart said you'd likely be leaving today."

"Step down, Colonel, and have some coffee," Billy invited.

"I believe I will, Doctor. Thank you, sir."

"There are some loose ends the sheriff tied

up for me which I feel you-all should know," Buxton said, sipping at the tin cup which Billy handed him. "Sug Hines talked on and on. He actually seemed relieved. If he were not a plain horse thief, I'd feel sorry for him. Yet, maybe I do, because Vogel and the man at the saloon used him. . . . Seems Vogel was the master-mind of a stolen-horse ring that began here — to my regret, while he was employed by me. A ring with relay stations along the route in Indiana and Illinois, where they stalled the horses. Mainly racehorses and saddlers. Some-times they'd mix draft horses with blooded horses as a cover, such as a contractor would ship. Generally, the horses would be shipped carload from Illinois, down into Missouri and Kansas and Texas. Most of the stock went into Texas."

Dude listened intently. That much con-nected, at least that.

"Several times Vogel would ask for time to go see sick relatives, he said, over in Indiana and Illinois, and he would ride the red roan saddler, which is the best travelin', head-noddin' road horse in this part of Kentucky. Covers a lot of ground. I guess he was contacting his relay stations."

And Dude thought of Poge Yates and Foss Ramsey. Would Vogel implicate them? *Well, they're grown men. They should know better.*

"In my opinion," said Colonel Buxton, "there is nothing lower than a horse thief, and not only can I thank you gentlemen for getting my Glengarry yearlings back, but also for breaking up the ring. The sheriff thinks he knows where the other horses in the barn were stolen." He put his tin cup down on a barrel. "There is one more matter before I get to the final matter and that is, Doctor, to thank you for healing that quarter crack my saddler had. Whatever that stuff is, it works."

"I'll write my friend in Juarez and see if he can send you some," Billy said, pleased.

"And now," Buxton said, "I'd like to look at your racehorse one more time, if you don't mind."

Coyote led Judge Blair out on halter and Buxton, as before, circled the gelding judgingly, then stopped to look at his face. "Four and a half years ago," he said, "I had a coming two-year-old, dark bay colt that everybody on the farm knew was a runner. He was by Stonewall, my stud, since gone, a son of the celebrated Lexington, out of my best mare, Verona, which I still have, a daughter of the very fast imported Glencoe. Stonewall was named in honor of General Stonewall Jackson, under whom I served in the War Between the States."

Dude set himself for Billy to take up the issue, but for the only time in Dude's memory the old man said nothing, and the colonel went on.

"This colt looked so much like his sire that we registered him as Sonny Stonewall. We hadn't trained him much. I don't believe in rushing young horses — their legs won't take it. Even so, he showed outstanding speed and heart. Loved to run and learned fast. Made very few mistakes. Easy to handle. Well, Sonny Stonewall was stolen under circumstances identical to yesterday's. I had a three-year-old in a Lexington stakes race and Vogel was with me, like yesterday, and when we returned home after the race, Sonny was missing. I felt as if I'd lost a member of my family. We never saw him again. No trace whatever. I even hired Pinkertons. Sent 'em all over the East and South. . . . I hadn't the faintest suspicion of Vogel. And I lost no more horses, although some of my neighbors did."

He looked down, his ruddy features somber, reliving the loss, and strolled around Judge Blair again. "Like many horsemen, I have an almost infallible memory for markings and conformation. Maybe I'm like the old fellow who said, 'I may forget my own name, but I never forget a face." In my judgment, gentlemen, this gelding fits Sonny Stonewall's description exactly."

Dude tensed. *Now we are about to know and maybe we don't want to know, if we have to give the Judge up.* Billy and Coyote had become quite still.

"Except," Colonel Buxton said, shaking his head, "this fine racehorse has white socks only on his hind feet, while Sonny had socks front and back. Otherwise, the markings and conformation are remarkably the same."

Dude's spirits sank even further.

"However," Buxton said, "if Sonny Stonewall were found today and he'd been gelded, I don't think I'd want him back, so long as he was well cared for. I'm a breeder and I'm afraid I couldn't stand the thought of all that fine Lexington and Glencoe blood gone to waste because of some fool's hand with a knife. Lexington was the greatest distance horse of his time and Glencoe carried both distance and burning speed." He fell silent, as if considering many things, then seemed to dismiss the past with a wave of his hand. "Since a horseman is destined to have more bad luck than good, he has to be an optimist. Therefore, I have great hopes for my two Glengarry colts, even more than I had for Sir Roddy as a yearling. I can thank you gentlemen for making that possible."

He shook hands all around and went to his saddler.

"We thank you, Colonel," said Billy, earnestly, and Dude and Coyote added theirs.

With another wave, Colonel Buxton mounted and as he rode away, Dude met his partners' eyes. Their glances held, filled with a misty fulfillment. At last they knew.

About the Author

Fred Grove has written extensively in the Western field, both in fiction and nonfiction. He has received the Western Writers of America Spur Award five times – for his novels *Comanche Captives* (which also won the Oklahoma Writing Award and the Levi Strauss Golden Saddleman Award), *The Great Horse Race* and *Match Race,* and for his short stories, "Comanche Woman" and "When the Caballos Came." His novel *The Buffalo Runners* was awarded the Western Heritage Award by the National Cowboy Hall of Fame, as was the short story "Comanche Son." Mr. Grove also has contributed short stories to many anthologies, among them *Spurs West* and *They Opened the West.* This is his eighteenth novel.

For a number of years, Mr. Grove worked on various newspapers in Oklahoma. It was while interviewing Oklahoma pioneers that he became interested in Western fiction. He now resides in Silver City, N.M.

THORNDIKE PRESS HOPES you have enjoyed this Large Print book. All our Large Print titles are designed for the easiest reading, and all our books are made to last. Other Thorndike Press Large Print books are available at your library, through selected bookstores, or directly from the publisher. For more information about current and upcoming titles, please call us, toll free, at 1-800-223-6121, or mail your name and address to:

THORNDIKE PRESS
P. O. BOX 159
THORNDIKE, MAINE 04986

There is no obligation, of course.